THANKS

to Bill, my partner in crime, who encouraged me to write this book and helped me to finish it...

to Lynne, whose skill with a paintbrush is equalled only by her mastery of life...

to Kathy, Anne, Hank, Chip, Juliana and all my friends and family who assisted in countless secret ways...

and to George Orwell for writing *Animal Farm*, which continues to inspire us all.

ANARCHIST FARM

by Jane Doe

III Publishing
P.O. Box 1581
Gualala, CA 95445

1st Printing: August 1996

Cover painting and map by Lynne Margulies

ISBN 1-886625-01-8

1

Margaret is still very sick," the golden retriever announced to the concerned gathering of animals outside the kitchen door. Despair and frustration rippled through the crowd. None of them knew of a time before Margaret. She had always been there, feeding them, caring for them when they were hurt, milking them, organizing them, putting them to bed at night. They trusted Margaret and more, they depended on her.

"Who will feed us?" asked the chickens.

"I need to be milked." Rosy was right; her udders looked ready to explode.

"The barn is a mess. It needs cleaning out." The mule had gotten used to clean straw in his stall.

"When will Margaret be well again, Goldie?"

The retriever sighed and shook her head. "Margaret is very old. No one knows how old, and she doesn't seem to be getting better. I don't know what we can do." She sat down on the back stoop to wait. All the other animals stood or sat or lay around the yard under the empty clothesline and waited, too.

There had been a time, a few remembered, when Margaret's husband had been alive and the farm had been a busier place. Ed had made big plans for the future, always planting some new exotic crop and trying out the newest theory on pest control. He had brought Juanita and Carlos all the way from a far off land.

The llamas were still at the farm, but Ed had been dead for years. Margaret ran the place herself after that, putting her whole heart into it. The plans were of a more modest scale, now, but the wonderful orchard had matured, the meadows reseeded themselves for summertime grazing and she had planted a large garden by the kitchen door. The animals could see the garden looked desperate for water in the summer sun.

"The plants will die if someone doesn't water them," said a young sow named Susie, "and then what will we eat?"

"I'm really hungry," complained a kid.

"Do you like milk? asked Rosy.

"Yes, I do!" answered the kid, and Rosy beckoned him to her bulging udder.

"I don't think that's proper, do you, Goldie?" an indignant goose asked the dog.

"Why ask Goldie? It's my udder and unless you have a better idea it seems proper enough to me." The kid was doing his best to nurse from the cow's teat, although he had been weaned for some time.

"Whatever works," Goldie said. "These are desperate times."

"We're hungry too," the chicks were chirping, "but we don't like milk."

"I know," said the hen, "but we must wait for Margaret to get well and feed us."

Goldie looked at the hungry chicks and she knew waiting for Margaret was not a good plan. "I don't think we can wait for Margaret anymore. She is too sick. We can help her by doing some of her chores for her. She will be happy if we do. It will be a burden off her mind. We all know where our food is kept, I think we should feed ourselves."

It was a radical idea, but one they were just hungry enough to try. The hen took her chicks to the hen house and slowly opened the bin of cracked corn. Her whole life she had known of its existence, but had never dared to look inside. It was almost full and the plate Margaret always used to scoop out breakfast for her lay on top. Penny took the plate in her wing and dug it deep into the grain. The other animals gathered around and watched Penny do the unthinkable. The hen carried the plate of corn into the yard and sprinkled it out in front of her chicks. They fought to gobble it up. With a smile on her beak and the plate waving in the air she turned to the others and squawked, "We can do it!"

All the animals raced to where their food was kept. Oats and hay and corn: everyone ate their fill and it tasted extra sweet that day. Everyone was careful to put everything back just the way

Margaret always kept it. "I hope she isn't mad at us for feeding ourselves," said Rosy, feeling much better after being milked and fed.

"Of course, she won't be mad," assured Goldie, who knew Margaret best, since she was allowed in the house. "She will be glad you did this for her, to help run the farm."

Susie, the sow, having finished her mash, looked again at the thirsty garden. "I'll water the garden for Margaret," she announced.

"I don't know, Susie," said the goose. "Margaret doesn't let us into the garden." It was true, the garden was fenced to keep the animals out.

"Margaret doesn't want the garden to die, she would be happy if I watered it. Don't you think so Goldie?" Susie turned to the dog, now the Margaret expert.

Goldie thought it over. Margaret didn't let the animals in the garden but there would soon be no garden if they did not water it. "Susie, Margaret would be happy for you to water the garden." The dog had spoken.

Soon everyone thought of something to do for Margaret. The mule swept the barn for Margaret. The pigs picked the apples for Margaret. The ducks even ate the worms for Margaret. All the animals spread themselves around the farm to perform chores, some necessary, some not so necessary, to help poor old Margaret.

Days and weeks passed as Margaret lay in bed getting sicker and sicker. Goldie brought her food from the garden and orchard. Margaret smiled and patted her golden fur. As Margaret got weaker, the farm got stronger. The animals found they knew the farm routines and even improved on them. Together they brought in the harvest and stored it away for winter for Margaret. They planted the garden with winter vegetables and even pruned the roses for Margaret.

Through the winter the animals made plans for spring, what they would plant in the meadows, what the kitchen garden would be like, maybe they could build an addition to the barn, to help Margaret, of course.

With spring almost there and the sun warming the land again, Margaret died. For Goldie the loss was a personal one. She had been at Margaret's bedside at her last moments and had nursed her all these past months. Margaret had been her friend. But for the others, Margaret's passing was abstract. They had never known her as Goldie had and yet Margaret's death loomed over the farm like a vulture. Margaret's illness had been a rallying point. It had driven all the animals to try and do things they never thought they could. The farm was alive as never before and now Margaret was dead. How could they help Margaret now?

Margaret was buried on the north side of the house, next to Ed, under the oak tree. The animals paraded slowly around the graves, weeping for their beloved Margaret. Tales were told of Margaret's kindness and love for all animals. Goldie told them Margaret would always be with them in spirit since she lay buried right there on the farm. They could continue to do things for Margaret because it would help her dream of a wonderful farm be a reality. The animals loved Margaret even more now that she was dead. They begged Goldie to tell them more about Margaret and the dog felt truly moved.

"I will tell you what I heard Margaret say many times, it was her guiding rule." Goldie closed her eyes and repeated from memory. "Always treat others as you would wish to be treated." The animals soaked it in. Goldie's rule became the motto of the Circle H farm.

2

Much later, on a different farm, far across the forest...

is brain raced as fast as his heart; if only his legs would catch up! He hit the ground running with all the energy of terror, the dogs inches behind him as he tore across the muddy pasture. Clots of mud flew from his feet into their slobbery mouths. "What should I do? The farm is fenced. I'm trapped," he thought.

Suddenly in a puddle he slid on his side through the mud, slamming into the wooden fencepost. A bit stunned, he scrambled to his feet and took off down the side of the pasture, tracing the fence line.

"Boy, that was close! I can't believe they didn't catch me." He glanced quickly behind.

The dobermans seemed to have backed off a bit, but were still barking and snarling as loudly as before. He came to the corner, took a ninety-degree turn along the hedgerow, and then suddenly remembered: "There's a hole in the hedge. I was going to assign a work crew tomorrow. I hope I can find it."

He slowed down his pace to search for the hole. Strangely, the dogs slowed also. "There it is, I hope I can make it through." The hole, probably made by a small animal, perhaps a rabbit, would be a tight fit. Squeezing his front half into the hole, his bottom half got stuck. The dogs skidded to a halt and stood facing the plugged hole in the hedge. They chuckled sarcastically as one gave the curly white tale a sharp bite, which proved to be just the inspiration the pig needed to shoot through the hedgerow.

Popping through the hole, the renewed adrenalin from the dog bite sent the pig flying through the neighbor's cornfield and deep into the woods beyond. Only a stumble on a tree root brought him to a halt. Hiding behind a bush he peered out to see he was not being followed.

He sat beneath a pine tree to catch his breath and examine his bitten tail. It hurt, but was not too bad.

"That dog could easily have bitten it off." He felt lucky, but why? Then it came to him. "The dogs were following orders. They were to chase me off but not kill me. Of course, how could they kill me in front of all the other animals. They love me, I'm their leader. Even now they are probably searching for me to bring me home." But no one appeared within view. Then the pig had a turn of thought. Things had changed on the farm. In the beginning he had felt love and support from the other animals, but now? He spent less time with sheep and cows and chickens. He was always with the other pigs. "And now the pigs have turned on me, and the other animals don't care enough to stop them. After all I've done on their behalf."

He leaned back against the rough bark, a tear rolling down his cheek, as he remembered the old times. The revolution, ah, that had been glorious. He had been a hero, with a medal to prove it. Running that greedy farmer off the land and turning the farm over to the animals to run for the benefit of all, now that had been a wonderful achievement. The pig smiled as he thought of the parades he had led and of the stirring speeches he had made to the grateful animals, in the early days after the revolution.

As a pig he had been more naturally inclined to leadership than, say, sheep or ducks. Was it his fault that it turned out that not all pigs were kind and just? His eyes narrowed as he thought of the pig who had trained the doberman pups into the vicious killers who just minutes ago had run him off his own farm. The farm where he had been born and lived his whole life. In fact, the farm was his whole life; making plans for the farm, organizing the animals, inspiring everyone through tough times... "And this is the thanks I get," he moped as he rubbed his sore tail.

The memory of his former power and unforseen fall from grace caused an empty ache in the pit of his stomach. Or perhaps he was just hungry.

The pig looked around. Trees. Never in his life had he set foot off the farm. Now he had no food, no friends, no place to sleep and no plan. The last was the most frightening of all. He always had a plan. But now it was getting dark in an unfamiliar wood and he sat all alone with no plan.

He picked up a stick and set to work. From the bushes a dozen eyes watched a muddy white pig with a stick scratching strange lines in the dirt:

Plan for Survival in the Woods.
1. Find Food.
   A. Apples or other fruit if possible.
   B. Good fresh water source.
2. Find place to sleep.
   A. Must be safe.
   B. Warm and soft.

The eyes moved closer and tried to decipher the scratches.
3. Find

The pig bent over even closer to the ground to see his list in the failing light. After thinking for a minute about #3 he decided to scratch it out. "Yes, 1 & 2 are the true essence of the plan," he announced suddenly as he stood back to admire his work.

The eyes jumped back to the bushes in something less than silence.

His back stiffened and his sore tail twitched as he realized he was not alone.

Mind racing, eyes open wide to peer through the darkness, he croaked out hopefully: "Comrades?"

There was a moment of silence, then sounds of a scuffle and a muffled giggle.

Every pig has an acute sense of smell. Even a pig as distant from his true nature as this one could tell many things by his nose. He could tell who this was not: pig, cow, sheep, man, or dog. In fact, it smelled like no animal he had smelled before. Since the scent was strong and unknown to him, his mind began to spin out possibilities.

"What lives in the forest? Bears! Wolves! Tigers? No, not here. Well, also deer and rabbits." Aloud he said: "Are you rabbits?" The reply: more giggling. "Don't be afraid, comrade rabbits, I won't hurt you."

This seemed to really hit a funny bone. The laughter grew more menacing as six adolescent raccoons tumbled out of the bushes, surrounding the pig.

The raccoons moved more quietly now, circling slowly around the pig. Getting a grip on himself, the pig tried a friendly tact. "Well, I guess I was wrong, I beg your pardon, you're not rabbits but squirrels."

"Squirrels!" One of the largest raccoons jumped at him and at that range even in this dim light he could see his mistake. "Who are you calling squirrels?"

The pig sniffed the animal in front of him and still couldn't identify him. "You're not bears, are you?" All farm animals had heard of bears, but few had ever seen one. Still, the stories of their fierceness and strength were told at night in the barn to entertain and frighten young piglets who might consider venturing outside the farm boundaries.

"Well, no, not exactly bears," admitted one raccoon. "Where are you from, anyway?"

"I'm from a farm over there, or ... maybe there." He moved his pig leg around in an arch as he realized he had no idea where he had come from. It is a wonderful farm run completely by animals and I was their beloved leader, until today when I was run off by a pack of vicious dobermans."

"Dobermans!" A shudder ran through the raccoon pack. "We really hate dobermans. I'm called Riff Raff and we are Raccoons." He spoke slowly so the pig would not mistake them again. "This is Bandit, Rascal, Mischief, Rags and Ripper. What's your name?"

The pig began to answer "S..." before he caught himself. He was a rebel fugitive now, hiding, on the run. It would never do to give his real name. Besides, he had always hated it. It had no dignity, no romance. And it was no name for a rebel. He needed a name that would inspire legend and command respect. He knew just the name. He had always seen himself as ...

"Pancho," he said, "the name is Pancho," and then smacked the uplifted paw of Riff Raff with his foot. "Pleased to meet you all."

Pancho was not at all sure he was pleased to meet them, for raccoons had a bad reputation among farm animals. But since he had never actually met any raccoons he decided to keep an open mind.

"We were watching you scratch with the stick," said Mischief.

"Ah, yes," said Pancho. "I was making a plan." It was quite dark now and the lines in the dirt were nearly invisible to his eyes, but the raccoons seemed to have no trouble seeing them. "Shall I read it to you?" He was always pleased when he had a plan to explain.

The raccoons huddled around the plan and stared at the dirt, so close that they blocked the view even if there had been enough light to see. No matter, Pancho knew it by heart. "At the top it says 'Plan for Survival in the Woods.'" There was a murmur, the raccoons were impressed. "Then it says, '#1. Find food, #2. Find place to sleep,'" he announced.

A moment of silence followed, then Riff Raff asked, "Is that all?"

"Well, I left out some A's and B's, but yes, that's pretty much it." Pancho was the quiet one now, thinking perhaps he had left out some important survival points. A #3 jumped to mind: Avoid Raccoons.

Finally Rags, after sniffing the entire plan and smearing most of it, stated "I don't get it."

"You don't get it? What part are you having trouble understanding?" said the pig in his patronizing voice. He had spent much time explaining complex plans to animals of lesser intellect. Surely raccoons would fall into this category.

Rags did not care for Pancho's tone. "I don't get," he said emphatically, "why you would waste your time scratching 'Find Food' in the dirt. If you want to find food, why don't you find food!" and with that he did a little raccoon shuffle-step all over the plan. The other raccoons found this quite amusing. Amid laughter and playful shoves Bandit said, "Let's get out of here."

"Wait," cried Pancho, "where are you going?"

The raccoons all turned to face the pig. With a glance at each other for timing they yelled "To Find Food" and they were gone. It took only a heartbeat for Pancho to know what to do. In the dark his eyes were almost useless, but the smell of six raccoons was hard to miss. Plus, the laughing and shouting made their trail easy to follow even for a farm pig. They were young and moving fast.

Pancho stumbled, crashed into a tree, ran through a blackberry bramble picking up quite a few stickers, and slipped into a brook while attempting to imitate the raccoons' hopping from stone to stone. This was more exercise than he was used to getting in a year. What a day! What a night! Suddenly, he heard no more laughter, no more joking or sounds of any kind. The raccoons were moving slowly and silently as they approached an old wooden fence. As they came out from the cover of the trees the moonlight allowed shapes to form in front of Pancho's eyes. "It's a farm!" he spurted out.

"Sh-h-h-h," six heads turned to scold him. "If you're coming, keep quiet."

He nodded his head and they all slipped under the fence.

Riff Raff signaled him to keep his distance and Pancho obliged. He hung back and watched the six small figures glide through the pasture. As he moved near to the barn his nose picked up a friendly odor: pigs. While sniffing out the pig pen he caught sight of the raccoons circling what appeared to be a large hen house. So the rumors he had heard at the farm were true.

At the pig pen Pancho saw several sows and piglets sleeping in one corner. He sneaked under the gate and tip-toed to the trough. Hurrah! Corn, and they had not eaten it all. Pancho began to pig-out as only a true pig could. He was trying to eat quietly and also to eat fast, not an easy combination, especially for a pig. He supposed this was stealing, technically, and so it was wrong. But these sister pigs had eaten their fill and had left this corn to help him in his rebel cause. "If they were awake," he thought, "I'm sure they would be glad to share with me, they would be proud to do it," and yet he was careful not to waken them. The raccoons were not so careful.

At the hen house feathers were flying. The hens, trapped by six hungry raccoons, screamed for help. The terror in their voices made Pancho's blood chill. A collie ran to the rescue, barking loud enough to wake the whole farm. Lights went on in the farm house and the half-dressed farmer raced out screaming and firing buckshot from his shotgun. Pancho sank down in the soft mud of the pig pen. Maybe he could stay here. He could fit in with these pigs and start a new rebellion on this farm eventually.

The raccoons took off, chased by the dog and farmer, with barking and gunshots ringing through the meadow.

"Yes," he thought, "I'll stay right here." As he turned around to look at his new home, for the first time, he noticed a huge boar leaning against the barn. Awakened by the ruckus, he had just noticed Pancho.

"New plan," was all Pancho had time to think as he ducked under the gate and took off running towards the woods but away from the raccoons.

Reaching the cover of trees, he slowed down. It was too dark to run in the woods and he felt very tired. "I must get deep enough into the woods to be safe," he thought. "But how deep would that be and would that be safer?" While he was thinking it out, he crawled into the blackberry thicket. He fell asleep mumbling, "Got to make a plan."

3

It was late morning before he opened his eyes. Inside the thicket, under the pines, the light barely glowed. Pancho awoke from a long and troubled sleep, dreaming of the dogs chasing him and the horrible massacre at the hen house. Now his little pink eyes squinted at the blackberry thorns in front of them and he knew it had not been a dream.

He groaned as he struggled to his feet. Every muscle ached and each step sang of yesterday. Crawling from the thicket to get his bearings, Pancho realized he had no idea how he had arrived at this spot. He circled the bushes looking for clues and sniffed at the nearby trees. "I don't know how I got here, I don't know where I am and I don't know where I'm going, so ... perhaps it doesn't matter. This was an amazing thought process for him. "Right now what matters is that I'm hungry."

With his priorities surprisingly clear, Pancho closed his eyes and sniffed the air. There were many unfamiliar smells in the woods and no clear smell of corn or apples or carrots, but he did smell something. It was dampness, maybe water. Rather proud of his clever deduction, he headed north, or was it east? At any rate toward the water smell.

The woods seemed much less threatening by day, and, as no one was chasing him, he rather enjoyed this morning stroll. He stopped every few minutes to check his direction with a sniff at the air. Even with sore muscles he made good time. "Finding water would be an important thing," he mused. "It was in my original plan, I believe. Perhaps there will be plants along the banks of this stream or pond that would make a good breakfast."

To the left in some brush he heard a large twig snap. Suddenly alert, Pancho faced the sound and sniffed. No mistaking that smell.

"Raccoons," he sighed. "I'll go to the right to avoid them." Just a few steps later he heard giggling behind a tree on the right. He thought of going back and making a large arc to avoid the pack, only to see two raccoons dive beneath a log behind him. If Pancho wanted to avoid a confrontation there seemed to be only one way to go: ahead. He could smell his escorts and sometimes hear them, but they stayed out of sight for the most part. Still, whenever he turned to the right, towards the water smell, he found his way blocked.

"Are the raccoons protecting the water, I wonder, keeping it for themselves?" Slowly but surely Pancho found himself climbing uphill in the opposite direction of the low-lying water. Soon he was on a narrow path through a grassy meadow. "Many animals have passed this way," he thought. Being on an established path made Pancho feel less lost and soon he forgot that he wanted to go toward the water. The raccoons no longer flanked his sides but followed behind at a polite distance. As the terrain got steeper the path narrowed and began to climb. One side of the path hugged the mountain, the other side dropped steeply, so Pancho was obliged to go forward unless he wanted to deal with the raccoons. Besides, it was lovely up here and obviously went somewhere, although he had no idea where.

The path took several sharp switchbacks and grew steeper. The pig's stomach began to growl and his stiff legs complained as well. For a moment Pancho sat down to rest, but then he noticed the raccoons only one switchback behind. "Where are we going?" he huffed as he turned another corner and answered his own question. The path ended and the opening of a large, dark cave stood before him.

"Great!" he squealed. "I'm trapped!" He took a cautious step into the mouth of stone. His eyes could see nothing yet, but his nose told all. What a smell! "I have no idea what is in there, but I'd rather deal with raccoons," he thought, turning and starting away from the cave.

Then he heard a familiar hiss: "Hey, it's me!"

Pancho could see two yellow eyes and then dimly the shape of a black cat in the black cave. "Sabo?" he whispered. It was the cat from his old farm.

"It's okay," she purred. "Follow me."

Pancho glanced behind him and saw the raccoons entering the mouth of the cave. He hurried to catch up with the cat who had no trouble negotiating the dark of the cave. "The cat can see in the dark, the raccoons can see in the dark. Only me — I can't see in the dark," he mumbled, then tripped on a stone. The stench in the cave was intense; so many overlapping scents that his nose overloaded. The cat walked ahead of him, the raccoons right behind. "Where are we going, Sabo?" Pancho asked, trying to seem nonchalant. Was this a trap set by his enemies from the farm?

"I want you to meet some friends," said the cat.

"Well, why didn't you come to get me yourself?" asked the pig suspiciously.

"The raccoons volunteered," shrugged the cat.

There was giggling from the rear, but as Pancho turned to glare at them they smiled sweetly.

"Here we are" announced the cat. They turned a corner and entered the belly of the cave. A shaft of sun from a natural skylight cut across the space and brought in blessed oxygen. Animals crowded the floor space, raccoons of course and squirrels and deer. Then Pancho saw in the back of the circle five huge shapes so magnificent and terrifying that, although he had never seen one, he knew: Bears!

He stumbled backwards till his body pressed against the cool stone wall. His eyes shot daggers at the cat as she sauntered over and curled up at the feet of a smaller bear sitting near the center.

"Welcome," said the small bear.

Pancho felt weak, his knees collapsed and he went quite pale. (This was especially impressive on an already white animal.) Almost instantly a silvery squirrel appeared at his side with a wooden bowl.

"Would you like some water?" he asked the pig. Pancho nodded and lapped up the water. "It's okay, you're with friends," the squirrel whispered, then scurried off with the empty bowl.

All eyes were on the white pig. He felt his dignity required him to display a certain amount of bravery. He forced his shaky legs to center stage. "Thank you very much for the water," he explained. "I was so thirsty I almost fainted!"

Whether believed or not, the story served its purpose.

"You're probably hungry, too. We'll all have lunch soon. My name is Judi," said the bear.

"I'm..." his mouth was still not used to the name. "I'm Pancho," said the pig and shot a glance at Sabo Cat, who rolled her eyes but said nothing.

In fact no one spoke, so to break the ice Pancho decided to ask what was for lunch, hoping the answer was not pork.

Sabo spoke. "I told them what happened at the farm yesterday. We thought maybe you would want to join us."

Us? Pancho thought Sabo was a farm cat, but apparently she led a double life.

A giant scruffy brown bear with a basso voice that made Pancho feel like clearing his throat growled "Sabo says that you can read. What else can you do?"

"Well," stammered Pancho, "I can also write and do some adding. I make plans and supervise and organize other animals."

Whispering among the bears was not as quiet as it should have been and Pancho detected disappointment.

The basso bear asked, "Can you stop a clearcut?"

Riff Raff Raccoon asked, "Can you find food in the woods?"

And a new animal in the crowd bounded forward. He scampered over to Pancho and put his funny face right in the pig's snout. "Can you build anything?"

The pig breathed in the scent of this amazing creature. Lithe and agile, the tiny animal did a backflip and scampered up to sit on the shoulder of the big bear.

"I can't really build things," said Pancho, "but I'm very good at supervising others while they build things."

"Well, aren't we all!" chattered the strange animal and started a roar of laughter that travelled like a wildfire through the raccoons.

Sabo leaned over to Pancho and said, "That's Bonkers. He's a monkey. Escaped!"

Judi Bear started talking and the laughter died down. "If you can't do something, how can you supervise others to do it? And if they can do something, why do they need you to supervise them?"

Pancho was stumped. Tired of being laughed at, he turned the tables. "What exactly is it that you do? Do you have a farm?" It was a good question. This was an odd collection of animals.

"No farm," said Judi. "We live in the forest and we work to protect the forest."

"And you live and work together?"

"We live near each other and sometimes work together, sometimes not," she said.

"Are you the leader?" His question was honest and he meant no offense by it, but the groan that rose from the animals told him he had committed a faux-pas.

"We have no leaders!" snapped Bonkers. "No leaders, no followers."

The awkward moment was relieved by the chirpy voice of a squirrel: "Let's eat." Then all the animals raced to the mouth of the cave.

Judi moved slower than the rest. She had been recently injured by a trap set by humans and was still recovering. "Don't worry, there's plenty," said Judi. Sabo and Pancho slowed their pace and accompanied her.

The food was served outside under the trees, a little way from the cave. Many more animals came to eat than had been at the cave meeting. The squirrels had prepared an acorn stew and although not fancy it was filling and tasted good to a hungry pig. Over the food flew a flag reading Nuts-To-Everybody. That was the name of the squirrels who had the awesome courage to undertake feeding such a large and motley assembly.

Pancho sat down between Sabo and Judi. "I've heard about your farm from Sabo," Judi said. "It seems like it started off well with a successful rebellion. It's too bad some of the animals became just as bad as the humans." Pancho's jaw dropped. Was this how Sabo had seen the efforts and struggles of the farm? Come to think of it, he thought, eyeing the cat, where was she when there was work to be done on the farm? Here no doubt. Pancho said nothing; Judi continued, "I always wondered, once you were free, why did you stay on the farm and continue working like slaves? Why not run off to the woods and be truly free?"

It had never occurred to him, or to any of them as far as he knew. Pancho shook his head and said simply, "I don't know." And he didn't.

The pig looked up and noticed a couple of last night's raccoons, Mischief and maybe Rascal, getting back in the food line for seconds. "I saw those raccoons raid a hen house last night," Pancho tattled. "It was a horrible experience, but I told myself they were probably very hungry. Now I see they could have eaten here, probably did, and were just out causing trouble."

Judi and Sabo chuckled. Sabo purred under her breath to make sure the squirrel cooks couldn't hear: "Sick of acorns."

"That's hardly an excuse," thought Pancho, but he noticed that although his plate was empty, his companions had hardly touched theirs.

Sabo pushed her wooden bowl toward Pancho. "Be my guest, I'm not as hungry as I thought," the cat said, relieved to be free of the acorn stew.

"Thanks," Pancho snorted as he started on the bowl.

"You're right Pancho," said the bear. "This is perfectly healthy food and the squirrels worked hard to fix it," and she began to eat, but not with the gusto of the pig.

Pancho finished quickly. His stomach now full, his mind could turn to other matters. "You said you work to protect the forest. Who do you work for?" he asked the bear.

"We work for the forest," she answered, "and the forest pays us back by feeding and sheltering us." Pancho sat silent for a few minutes, so Judi continued. "Humans are cutting too much forest too fast and in the process destroying many forest homes. Animals must band together to save themselves and the trees and streams." She was on her favorite subject now and had a new, fascinated listener. Judi talked in close personal terms of the environmental disasters and opened Pancho's mind to the global consequences.

Pancho was moved to tears. He felt the importance of this cause. "I will help however I can," he promised, "but I have no plan."

"That's fine," Judi told him. "Plenty of others have plans." Pancho smiled and looked around himself at his new friends. He hoped it wasn't Bonkers or the raccoons who had these plans.

In the next few days Pancho got to know this wild bunch. They were not interested much in plans or organization, but many were very intelligent and well-informed. The pig wondered how he would fit in and what he had to offer. "At least I'm enthusiastic," he thought as he tried to learn the trick of making a camp fire.

Pancho always liked to be doing something and the lazy days at the Cave Camp had begun to bore him. Many of the other animals had enjoyed the leisure, napping in the sun, playing games and talking environmental revolution, but doing little, just showing up for meals and playing their drums at the evening meetings. After a few days of unwinding, Pancho had volunteered to help Nuts-To-Everybody. The squirrels had moved like speed freaks through the woods gathering everything edible they could find, especially acorns, and Pancho had been unable to keep up. So, next he had tried his hand at cooking. The Nuts-To-Everybody recipe remained constant: take everything you gathered that day and throw it into one big pot. Cook for a couple of hours, make up a new name for the dish, and serve.

This was fun for the pig, since he loved to play with food, but it did not seem mentally stimulating. He had, however, developed a deep awe and admiration for the squirrel group. Pancho hadn't really met any squirrels until then. He had assumed they were less capable than most of the farm animals he knew. But never had he seen such dedication, energy, cleverness and selflessness, all without supervision. They were the quiet heartbeat which kept this group of creatures going.

Pancho listened more than talked at the occasional meeting, but cornered Judi later for more detailed explanations.

"Corporations," the pig wondered. "Are they the new enemy, or is it just another word for humans?"

"It's the same old enemy in a new disguise," Judi told him. "Very tricky and hard to fight."

"Why don't we just tear off the disguise?" the pig asked simply.

"That's just what we're trying to do," the bear said, shaking her head, "but it's harder than it seems."

Judi took a deep breath, then started to explain. "The corporations say, and it's true, that the only reason they exist is to earn money for their shareholders, in other words themselves."

Pancho nodded, adding, "I knew that. It's no surprise that they don't care about the animals that produce their profits for them, or about the environment."

Judi raised her paw for emphasis. "But why are they corporations? I mean instead of businesses?"

Pancho scratched his head. He knew he should have the answer... but he did not. He hated that.

The bear continued: "The law protects corporations so that they have no personal responsibility. And you know how we all feel about personal responsibility!"

"Oh yes!" Pancho answered quickly. He had learned much about the subject since coming to Cave Camp. The most important thing, if you have no leaders or rules, is personal responsibility. "Is that how they get away with destroying the forest?"

"That and all their other criminal activities." Judi shuddered in disgust. "So we fight them with all we've got, but the deck is stacked against us."

Pancho shuddered too. These corporations must be stopped, or held responsible. The pig, only shortly before used to exercising power on his old farm, now felt angry but helpless. What could he do?

"When can we do some forest protecting?" the pig asked.

"Soon," came the answer. "When the raven gets back." Judi sighed. "Enjoy the quiet while you can."

But Pancho itched for action. That afternoon, as he lay in the sweet grass, watching the clouds sail around, his belly full of acorn pie, he muttered to the sky, "I wish the raven would get here." As if to grant his wish, through the clouds burst a large black bird. She circled over the meadow where Pancho lay before landing on a rock near the makeshift kitchen. All the animals gathered round and Pancho ran to get a close position in the circle around the bird.

Quoth, the raven, paced back and forth on her rock until everyone arrived. She had big news and she knew the camp could not wait to hear it. "The corporation is planning another clear-cut," she croaked. "A couple of valleys over, they've already made the road!"

The forest protectors hissed and groaned.

"We have no time to lose!" screamed Bandit. "We must leave immediately."

But they all decided to wait until morning. Tonight they would prepare.

An excited Pancho begged to be on the sabotage committee; it sounded the most important and adventurous. The group included some bears, all of the raccoons, Bonkers the monkey, a weasel, and Pancho.

"What's our plan?" the pig kept asking, as the saboteurs scampered about gathering tools and supplies for the action. "Are we going to spike trees, destroy equipment, block the road?"

"Stop asking all those pig questions," the monkey snapped at him. "How do we know what we're going to do until we get there?" Bonkers rolled his eyes as if everyone should naturally agree with him.

Red put a paw on Pancho's shoulder. "It's okay," he said. "We'll take everything we need to do whatever we can." Red winked at his scruffy bear friend standing at Pancho's other shoulder, then added, "Arthur and I are always prepared if we have to chase a few humans." The two bears laughed wickedly.

Pancho felt reassured. "The plan is," he told himself, "to be prepared for all possibilities," and he had to admit that sounded clever.

Soon the pile of sabotage materials filled the burned-out tree trunk and spilled out onto the ground below. The saboteurs looked at it with satisfaction, but they all agreed it was too much to carry on such a long trek. "The string is good and so is this yarn," said Rascal, who really liked yarning trees more than spiking.

"The hammer and these long nails and this wrench," said Bonkers. "They are heavy, but important."

"This rock and this big wooden club can stay, we'll find some there. Food and water and bandages, just in case," advised Red. Pancho did not like the sound of that.

"Isn't that the dinner drum?" the hungry pig asked.

It was a little early, but the animals stopped their tasks to answer the drum call. Pancho could smell that the food was almost ready, but he also picked up another scent.

"Hey, it's Tex and Mex!" Riff Raff cried and started a rush of raccoons toward the two tattered old coyotes crouching near the drum. The visitors carried beat up guitars slung on their backs and certainly had the gift of gab. The camp animals greeted the coyotes with such pleasure that Pancho tried to keep an open mind.

"You fellas have great timing, not only are we just about to have dinner, but tomorrow we're going out on a forest action," Mischief said, grinning at Tex and Mex.

"We'd be grateful for the supper, but we'll have to pass on the adventure," Tex drawled. "Too old."

Pancho doubted that, but found their talk interesting, so when the acorn casserole arrived he took his plate and sat with the raccoons at the feet of the coyotes.

"Do you know where we spent last night?" Mex asked the raccoons. "Remember that farm with the big chicken coop?"

"Sure we do, we just raided that coop last week, didn't we, Pancho?"

"I did not raid any chicken coop," Pancho explained to everyone listening. "I would never attack chickens like that."

"We weren't after the chickens, we were after the eggs," Mischief said.

"Of course, so were we," added Tex.

"Is that any better?" Pancho's voice had that superior tone. "Eggs are baby chickens, just not hatched."

"No, not these, they're not fertile," puffed Mischief.

"And even if they were fertile, I don't believe they're chickens until they're hatched," said Mex.

"Besides, if we didn't get them, the humans would," Tex added. "Don't get me wrong, I've nothing against chickens."

"He loves chickens," Mex laughed. "but anyway you know that chicken coop farm? Well, it's gone."

"Gone?" Pancho exclaimed. "How can that be?"

"Well, the land's still there, of course," said Mex. "But no farm. The corporation foreclosed, they say. Don't know what they're gonna build, but the animals are gone, and the farmer too."

"No more eggs," Mischief sighed.

"Just like that?" Pancho couldn't believe it.

"Just like that. Guess I'll get myself more of that delicious acorn casserole," Tex stated as he made his way over to the food table. "Don't believe I've had a meal like this since the last time we had the pleasure of visiting here."

Pancho thought of the poor chicken coop farm. He had even considered staying there, if it were not for that boar. "Lucky I didn't," he mused. "Where would I be now?"

After supper the youngsters gathered sticks and bits of wood to build the campfire into a roaring blaze that would burn late into the night. All the camp drew close as the coyotes tuned and plucked their battered instruments. With a mournful howl the singing started. Tex and Mex sang the verses, but the refrains were a free for all of yips and yaps and yowls joined in by all. Pancho had heard better singing, but never sadder songs. The coyotes sang about the lonesome, wandering life of homeless vagrants. If the rhymes were not always quite right, you could sure feel the homesickness right in your gut. If he hadn't been surrounded by friends, Pancho would have gotten very maudlin. He looked around for Sabo, his old farm buddy. There she was, so moved she had to cover her ears. He scooted over to sit beside her and share memories of home.

The cat stood on tiptoe and whispered in Pancho's ear, "It's so sharp it's painful."

"My feelings exactly," sighed Pancho as he listened to the last sad strains of the song.

"Tell us a tail," screamed a young voice.

"A tail, a tail," echoed another.

"Okay, okay," chuckled Tex as his young fans gathered at his dusty feet. "What sort of tail? A long bushy fox tail? A bear tail, short and blunt? How about a cat-o-nine tail?"

"A cat-o-nine tail!" yelled a young buck. All the animals agreed.

"A cat-o-nine tail it is," Tex grinned as he put his guitar on the ground behind him. "This cat-o-nine tail is about bravery, heroism, and sacrifice. But it is honest and true: a true tail."

And Tex began: "Not so long ago, across the sea, the cats of Cat-alonia lived under the oppressive rule of a human who called himself the king. 'You cats must do this, you cats can't do that, you must obey this, you must believe that!' Power can be an evil thing, and government power, well, we know about that. The cats of Cat-alonia were sick and tired of being bossed around and abused. There was talk of revolt and of overthrowing the king. The cats of Cat-alonia wanted to be left alonia!"

Tex laughed at his own pun.

"But the power-hungry could not let that happen. The government said, 'You cats can't run things yourselves. You need our help. You don't have enough education. This kind of thing takes experts, professionals. You cats aren't strong enough to protect yourselves from the enemy.'

"Soon some cats were frightened. 'Maybe the government is right. Perhaps we can't take care of ourselves.'

"Other cats were angry. 'We cats can take care of each other. We will be just fine. And who is the enemy? The government, we think!'

"'Do not worry,' said the corporation. 'You will not be forced. See, you have a choice. You can vote for this ruler, or for that ruler.'

"The cats agreed. 'We will chose the nicest one. We will vote for a ruler who will be on the side of cats.' And that is what they did.

"'Oh no,' screamed the army. 'You cats made the wrong choice. It just shows you cannot run things yourselves. General Skanko will be in charge now. He will show you cats how things must be run.'

"General Skanko was very cruel. He was a corporate man, he was a government man, but mostly he was an army man. Skanko had all the soldiers and all the weapons, so what could poor Cat-alonia do?"

Tex paused and looked at his audience for response.

"Fight!" the forest protectors yelled.

"That's right," nodded Tex. "And that's just what they did: fight! Skanko had powerful weapons, but the cats were not alone. The bears from Bears-alona chased the soldiers out of the city and took their weapons."

A roar of approval came from the bears in the audience.

"While the strongest animals kept on fighting Skanko, who controlled other parts of the country, the other animals did something even more amazing. They began a new way of living together. They shared their food, bartered with each other instead of using government money, and rejected rulers and leaders. Animals from around the world watched in wonder, not to see the fighting, they had seen plenty of that before, but to see the new way of living. Some came all the way to Cat-alonia to fight to protect the new way of life.

"But General Skanko was ruthless and his army got stronger as foreign powers poured military aid into the Skanko war machine. Out-gunned and outnumbered, many animals were killed and others quit the fight. Some even joined with Skanko to be on the winning side. Cat-alonia fell to defeat and the new way of life was destroyed."

Tex took a breath and he looked around at the dejected faces of his animal audience.

"Cat-alonia and the animals who lived there suffered terribly and they still do today. But they showed the world something very important. Animals all over the world have hope because of them. They made a new and freer way of living and even though it was only for a short time, the world saw that it could work. Governments fear it, corporations hate it, and it sure does make the army mad, but the tail of Cat-alonia is an inspiration to animals everywhere."

Tex ended his tail.

Sabo seemed lost in thought. "Did cats really do that? Did it really happen that way?" she asked the coyote.

"Yes, Sabo, it really happened just like that," Tex answered.

"Wow, those were some cats," she said proudly.

4

Cave Camp was already bustling as Pancho opened his eyes. The different committees were huddled over their bowls of acorn porridge, getting organized. The squirrels of Nuts-To-Everybody were rushing about trying to get breakfast served so they could pack to move to the new site, where they would be the core of the support group. One stuck a bowl of mush under Pancho's nose as soon as he awoke, and, knowing Pancho's table manners, waited the thirty seconds required to slurp it down, grabbed the bowl, and ran back to the mess hall. Judi sat surrounded by birds of all kinds, rabbits, deer and other quiet and fast messengers. They constituted the Media and Information group; Sabo was supposed to be in it.

"Where is Sabo Cat?" Pancho asked after saying good morning to all. "Isn't this her affinity group?"

"Sabo went back to the farm this morning. She can spread the news there and bring back information to us. Besides," whispered Judi, "she just doesn't do well under stress."

Sabo went back to the farm, of course, thought Pancho. There is work to be done: time for her to disappear. He could not remember her ever spreading news on the farm, but maybe she did, just not to pigs. He didn't know.

Pancho scanned the scene for his fellow saboteurs. He saw them by the tree trunk packing-up and arguing over who got to use what tool first. Only the hammer and the wrench were real tools, and Riff Raff wanted that wrench and so did Bonkers, each offering the hammer to the other as conciliation. The argument was settled easily by the scruffy bear with the gravel voice who proclaimed he would carry both tools and everyone could share them as needed. No one contested the solution; the tools were heavy and the bear was big. Pancho wore a little pack with string and nails in it strapped around his belly and he noticed as he tied it on that he was trimmer than he had been in years, thanks to the acorns and exercise regime. All packed and ready, they stood in a circle looking at each other. Suddenly, or so it seemed to Pancho, he was being hugged by a scruffy bear on one side and a skinny monkey on the other. All the animals had their arms around each other in the circle and someone said "Ready?" Everyone yelled "Ready!" and the circle broke into a line as they followed the raven towards the valley.

While marching along in single file down the mountain trail, Pancho took a few minutes to get over his first bear hug. "Just think, a week ago I had never even seen a bear or monkey or raccoon." He looked down the line at his new comrades. "Now my favorite talks are with Judi Bear, my best arguments are with Riff Raff, and Bonkers is, I must admit, really funny." He felt happy and found himself humming a little fight song as they descended into the cover of the pines.

Nuts-To-Everbody brought up the rear of the march, half a dozen squirrels and a couple of chipmunks carrying a pot so big they could all sleep inside. As soon as the terrain permitted, they dropped the pot on its side and began to roll it by taking turns running inside. Pancho smiled at their ingenuity, but while his head was turned watching them he walked into a low-hanging branch. The weasel behind him snickered and the pig mustered what was left of his dignity, quickened his pace, and caught up with the bear in front of him.

They came out of the woods now and walked through grass so high even the bears had to stand on hind legs to see over it. The raven flew visibly overhead and the lead deer (for deer are wonderful trailblazers) knew where she was going. The others only needed to follow on the narrow, beaten-down path. Walking through the grass tunnel with no landmarks to measure progress seemed endless. The smaller animals began to tire and Pancho's stomach was growling when, without notice, the grass field opened and presented a wooded clearing with a little brook. The animals gathered together and put down their packs. Everyone crowded at the brook for drinks as squirrels distributed acorn cakes. "Sort of like K rations," thought Pancho, who had done some reading on military subjects. He munched at the hard biscuit. They had walked into the afternoon, so anything tasted good.

The raven perched on a fallen log and began to answer questions.

"How much further?"

"Just over this hill," replied the raven.

"Are there humans around?" The raven did not know, and flew off to check for danger.

The lead deer spoke. "I know this area, I feed here in winter sometimes. This is the best spot for camp. It is hidden and has water. Perhaps the squirrels should set up here."

"Sounds good to us," the squirrels chirped, and began foraging for supper. They had some big eaters, and this was unfamiliar territory. They had better get to work. A blue jay flew back to Cave Camp to tell Judi (who had stayed there because of her injury) and the others that the band had made it to the clearing and would camp there.

The sabotage group gathered by the brook to discuss their non-plan. The excited raccoons wanted to get going, but decided to wait for the raven's report; a human presence would alter their tactics. The bears, however, hoped to do some chasing. Pancho didn't know how this would all work out. He had never spent much time planning destruction: construction being his usual theme. "These others surely know what they are doing and the fact that Bonkers is swinging by his tail from the oak branch should not be interpreted as a lack of serious intent." Pancho sat on the bank and played in the water with his feet, hot and sore from the long march. He watched as the food committee sent a couple of media rabbits off to search the wider area for edibles. The birds circled overhead, keeping watch.

The big black raven suddenly crashed through their formation. She dive-bombed through camp, swerving a bit to nip the monkey's bottom and send him screaming to the ground. The animals rushed to hear the news as the raven took her spot on the log.

Quoth began by clearing her throat several times. To heighten the suspense she spent a few seconds preening her flight feathers back to their smooth condition. The animals watched her every move waiting for her to speak and the raven milked it for all she could. Finally, when she saw the tension and anticipation was at its peak, and just before it turned to frustration and anger, she began.

"I have just returned from my reconnaissance flight over the enemy's stronghold." She whispered very loudly for dramatic effect. "There are four large machines in a cleared area, a small shed and a larger shed on wheels."

"O-o-oh," the audience of impressed listeners gasped.

Quoth resumed, "I think there is one human there; I couldn't see into the small shed."

"Yes!" Two bear paws slapped each other in the air as the huge scruffy bear, Arthur, and a smaller golden one (inexplicably named Red) smiled knowingly at each other.

"If we start now, we should make it before dark. Looks like plenty of fun for all!" whispered the bird.

The sabotage group began to load up their bags of tricks. Both Bonkers and Riff Raff checked to make sure the wrench was indeed coming.

Pancho was still tying his pack as the weasel and raccoons began to climb the hill. "Wait, I'll lead you in," yelled the deer, whose soft voice could hardly be called yelling. The animals waited and she leapt to the front of the group giving Pancho a chance to get to the rear. The information birds flew on ahead and the other deer and rabbits fanned out to the sides, inconspicuously. It took them about five minutes to get to the hill-crest, where they spread out into a line peeking over boulders. From this vantage point the valley spread beneath them. In the fading light they could see the newly-cut logging road and the cleared area with the sheds and machines.

Pancho asked the raccoon to his left to explain what the humans were planning. "They will cut all the trees in the valley," Bandit hissed in disgust, "and haul them down that road they cut. The hillsides will be raped and ravaged and in the spring rains all the topsoil will wash downhill, filling the stream with mud. New trees can't grow because they are always washed away. Those butchers ..."

Red the bear put a paw on Bandit's shoulder to ground the excited Raccoon. "He's very emotional about this subject," growled Red. "We all are. But now is the time to be calm and rational." Pancho felt anxious as he looked at the valley and thought about its imminent destruction. Humans were truly evil creatures. He had learned that from his farm life, but he never had seen how destructive they could be.

"It's almost dark now," whined the weasel. "Let's go."

Somewhere down the line a bear growled "Okay, let's go," and the ragtag saboteurs eased down the hill, through the brush to the clearing below. They stopped behind a bush that was just a deer's leap from a large yellowish machine. Pancho could not identify it, but secretly wished they had owned such a mighty mechanism on his old farm. "It makes the road," said Bandit. "It's a bad machine, all machines are bad."

Bandit was worked up, so Pancho did not argue. Still, he thought, it's not the machine that's bad but what it's being used for.

Pancho's pardonning would not spare the yellow monster from the angry environmentalists. Everyone unpacked and laid out their tools and supplies. Surprisingly, Riff Raff did not complain when Bonkers grabbed the wrench and left him with the hammer. Instead the raccoons took off to spike some trees. This was a two raccoon job: one held the nail and the other hammered it into the tree.

Other animals busily wrapped yarn around tree trunks, making quite a tangled web, which would be somewhat effective at ruining chain saws and lots of fun as well. The wrench was hard at work on the yellow bulldozer's many bolts. Bonkers proved amazingly nimble at disassembling the machine. The bears and Walter, which was the rather sedate name of the weasel, had gone after the human. They tracked him down, locked inside the small shed with the pungent odor, but before doing anything they went to fetch Pancho to read the writing on the door.

"Port-o-let" he read aloud, shaking his head. "I don't know what that means, but at least it doesn't say 'danger' or 'dynamite.'"

"Let's go for it," said the bears, and, standing one on each side, they began to rock the small shed. They heard some screaming at first from inside Port-o-let, but, after a few gravelly growls of menace, there was only silence. Since the human wouldn't come out to be chased, the bears gave the shed an extra hard push, which toppled over. They began rolling the shed and its occupant down the freshly cut logging road like two kids playing kick-the-can.

Meanwhile, Walter was skulking around the large shed. It was a relatively new metal trailer and offered no easy holes at ground level, but weasels can get into anyplace they really want to. Up on the roof he discovered screened pop-up vents with one left just a little ajar. That proved enough. As Pancho watched in amazement, Walter squeezed through the crack and slid inside. It was simple for the weasel to open the locked door from inside, then Pancho and Walter began to trash the trailer. Pancho had more experience with things human, so he knew that some of the papers should be read before being destroyed. He began to stuff important looking files into a Macy's shopping bag he found in the cabinet.

Walter began going through the desk drawers and was decorating himself with anything he found that seemed interesting. He slinked over to see what Pancho was putting in the shopping bag. The weasel had paper clips on his ears, rubber-band bracelets and, around his neck, a key with a tag reading 'Pick-Up.' Pancho reached for the key and Walter shouted "Hey, this one's mine. There's lots more over there," pointing to the top desk drawer. Pancho examined the keys marked Dozer, Feller-Buncher, Dump T., and Tool Box; only the last made sense to him.

"Walter, humans lock up important things. Find a big box with a lock."

Walter slithered out of the trailer to look. Pancho grabbed the remaining files and all the keys he could find and put them in the bag. Outside, everyone was working on dismantling the machines. The raccoons had run out of yarn and nails, and the bears came back from wherever they rolled the human.

"Everyone, look!" Pancho showed the keys. He received only puzzled expressions in response. The pig realized they did not know about the magic of keys.

Then Walter called, "Pancho, maybe this is the box!" They all went behind the trailer and saw a very large, white metal box with a padlock attached. Everyone crowded in so close that Pancho could hardly turn the key. Snap, the padlock popped. A dozen paws threw the lid open and the animals stood in awe of what they saw: tools beyond their wildest dreams. Wrenches for everybody in all sizes, hammers, screwdrivers, and all manner of wonderful things they had no names for. There began a scramble of raccoon paws in the tool box and a race to the partly monkey-wrenched bulldozer.

Bonkers, however, was almost trance-like as he walked over to Pancho and looked at the keys. "What do the others open?" he asked, his voice full of mystery.

"I don't know," said Pancho, "but they may work the machines."

The monkey's eyes grew wide and he stared into Pancho's squinty pig's eyes intently. "Let's do it!"

Pancho laid the keys down on the ground. "Walter! Come here, we need to use your key," hollered Pancho.

Walter tossed the key over. "It's okay, I like the tool key," he yelled back. "It has a red tag." Then he busily returned to work on the dozer.

Pancho read the words on the keys to Bonkers. "Dozer, Feller-Buncher, Dump T., and Pick-up. Do you know what any of those words mean?" Bonkers shook his head; Pancho picked up the keys and walked over to the smallest truck. They looked all over the machine for places for the keys to fit and noticed several possibilities. Bonkers was good at working the keys and soon found that "Pick-up" fit in the door hole. As he carefully turned the key he did not know what to expect.

The door swung slowly open, a dim light came on, and they poked their heads inside. As Bonkers jumped into the seat behind the wheel and began to frantically turn knobs, Pancho noticed an owner's manual at his eye level in a pocket on the driver's door. Leafing through the greasy book he found the page describing the dash panel. Pushing his snout past Bonkers, he poked his foot at a small key hole. Bonkers fiddled with the key for a minute, then he moved the key clockwise and the engine turned over. Both animals jumped back, but the motor had died. Inspired, Pancho read aloud much of the manual to Bonkers, who seemed to memorize it instantly. The pig could read the words, but Bonkers really understood the process. "Walter," shrieked Bonkers, "Get over here, we need you."

Walter ran over and Bonkers began to explain the brake, clutch and gas peddles. "I can do the rest if you do the peddles, Walter. Pancho, get out of the way!"

And, after a few false starts due to coordination problems, they were off. The raccoons and bears watched in amazement as Bonkers and Walter lurched the truck forward and back, left and right, getting the hang of driving. Around the clearing they sped, taking corners way too fast. Then Bonkers got a not completely good idea. He backed up the little truck and aimed it directly at the big truck, preparing to ram it.

"Stop, wait!" It was not only Pancho who saw the problem in the idea; the bears ran forward and stopped Bonkers in time.

"Use the big truck to smash the little stuff, that's the way," said Red. "You'd hurt yourself otherwise."

"I was going to jump out the window before we hit," explained Bonkers.

"And what about me," screamed Walter. "I didn't even know where we were headed."

But Bonkers was already scrambling for the big truck, having decided it would be more fun to drive anyway. "Hurry up Walter, it's almost the same!"

The monkey found the key that fit, and with a less than fully enthusiastic weasel in position began to move the big dump truck. The only difficulty proved to be a stiff and temperamental gear shift. Whereas Bonkers could operate the pick-up shift with his tail, this truck required the power of a hind leg as well. Bonkers was like a monkey possessed and nothing could stop him. Pancho grabbed his shopping bag and ran for higher ground as the animals scattered to avoid being crushed.

Bonkers pulled back as far as he could and sped headlong into the unsuspecting pickup. The crash made a stupendous noise. Bonkers pulled back and then crashed into the truck three more times, the third time going right over it, leaving a mere pile of metal. The dump truck seemed uninjured and unmoved by this violence against its baby brother. Bonkers prepared to assault the trailer. The blow caught the trailer's end, knocking it off its blocks and sending it rolling until it tumbled down a small ravine behind the clearing.

This pleased everyone no end. Cheering and jumping up and down, but still keeping a safe distance, the animals watched Bonkers take aim at what Pancho had deduced must be the feller-buncher (since the Dozer key fit the other machine). A frightening looking machine with huge metal jaws in front, it proved no match for the monkey and weasel in their dump truck. Crunched and mangled by a half-dozen rammings, the tangled metal eventually got pushed down the same ravine. Only the dozer remained, and though it was mostly in parts now, Bonkers was on a roll. They ran over different parts of the machine just for good measure.

Never had the animals created so much havoc. Bonkers and Walter were heroes and jumped from the truck to dance a little victory dance.

Pancho climbed into the high cab of the Dump Truck. He thought the truck was strange looking and it must be called Dump for some reason. The pig could find no book inside so he began to turn knobs and pull levers. Suddenly the back of the truck tipped up and all sorts of heavy things fell out onto the ground, almost crushing some of the animals partying closest to the rear of the truck. Alarmed, Pancho jumped out of the cab and rushed to check on his buddies who, since no one got hurt, were busy examining the chainsaws.

Bandit was beside himself. "These are the most horrible of the machines, even though they are small. The sound alone makes your blood run cold."

"Okay, Bandit," said Red. "We'll kill them. You say how."

Bandit sat for a long time thinking, but could only come up with ramming them with the dump truck. Quoth had a suggestion. "I know a place on this logging road with a cliff so high they will be smashed by the fall. We can ram them a bit, then put them back in the dump truck and Bonkers can drive them to the cliff and dump them down." This sounded good to Bandit and especially to Bonkers, who was not done driving yet, so they ran the truck back and forth over the chainsaws until they were crushed and bleeding oil. Then they loaded them back into the truck and off they went, led by the raven down the road to the cliff. The other animals stayed at the clearing, gathering up the best of the tools and preparing to hike home for a late dinner.

A tremendous crack shook the forest and, for a few moments, a flare of light pierced the night. The animals froze and stared at the sky until the light faded back to darkness. They slowly turned to climb the hill; the euphoria of the evening turned to dread as they slowly trudged over the hill and back towards their base camp.

As they crossed the brook on the edge of camp they could hear Quoth the raven telling her tale in the most dramatic style possible. When they got closer, there hung Bonkers swinging from the oak branch and Walter showing off his new jewelry.

When Bonkers and Walter saw the weary saboteurs wading across the brook they ran to meet them. "It was great, you should have seen it," chattered Bonkers. "It was great! It was great! We put a rock on the gas instead of Walter and sent the Dump T over the cliff. I jumped out the window just in time."

"Pow, it exploded!" added Walter. "And it caught fire." The story was elaborated and redecorated all night, retold over steaming bowls of Acorn Surprise.

Pancho gulped down the first two bowls, but by his third he realized it was not just his hunger that made the food taste so good. The "Surprise" in the acorns was apples.

5

Dawn broke too soon for the saboteurs, but the group wanted to head for Cave Camp as soon as possible. When the corporation discovered the destruction of its machines it would be best to be long gone.

The acorn fritters carried that delicious apple aroma and Pancho asked Mac, today's squirrel chef, where he had found apples. "The rabbits found them," and since his paws were busy, Mac nodded in the direction of two rather mangy looking rabbits talking to some jays.

Pigs have the undeserved reputation for slovenly personal hygiene. This is untrue of pigs in general and Pancho in particular, who prided himself on good grooming. Rabbits, on the other hand, are usually thought of as fluffy and clean, but certain jack rabbits could not be further from that mold.

"Thank you for finding apples yesterday. They made our victory dinner extra special." Pancho wanted to start politely, having never had a conversation with Blackstone and Hamilton before. To his surprise Blackstone, whose left ear was broken and fallen over midway, answered him with almost Shakespearian elocution.

"We were ecstatic ourselves with the discovery and acquisition. The cuisine provided by our hard-working and well-meaning associates does, alas, wear on the palate. Any addition or compliment to the lowly acorn is welcome, but I fear it will be a long while before we have the pleasure of savoring the golden delicious again." Blackstone shook his head sadly and his floppy ear beat against his nose. Hamilton continued, "Still, we must give credit where credit is due. The apples were located by divine

providence in the form of a young buck with the unfortunate name
of Bambi."

"Surely, Bambi isn't his real name." Pancho said, overwhelmed with pity.

"I really believe it is," sighed Hamilton. "Too, too cute."

As everybody started to leave Pancho grabbed his little pack,
now empty, and stuffed it into the shiny blue shopping bag,
decorated with a picture of a carnation and the words "White
Flower Day." Pancho did not know the significance, but it seemed
a pleasant sentiment.

Many souvenirs of battle were making their way back to Cave
Camp. Almost everyone had a wrench or screwdriver. Bonkers had
found and proudly wore a cap that said CAT in large letters on the
front. Walter had started a trend with the keys. Bonkers wore
Dump T. around his neck and Pancho wore Pick-up. Walter had
Tool Box and was still accessorizing with his office supplies. But in
the shopping bag hid two more keys. Pancho wanted to give one
to Judi, but the other one, well, he did not want to start a fight.

Bandit wore chainsaw chains crossed on his chest like a
bandoleer. Nuts and washers from the dismantled doser made nice
necklaces for deer and even for some birds who used them as
ankle bands. The squirrels had an almost-new flowered bedsheet
thanks to the thoughtfulness of Red, who had grabbed it from the
back of the crushed pick-up. The path home felt longer and
steeper than the day before. As he dragged the shopping bag
behind him, Pancho hoped the files and papers inside really were
important.

After dinner Pancho finally got Judi alone and gave her the
brass key with the tag Feller-Buncher attached. She looked
impressed. "Did you really crush a feller-buncher? They're such
destructive machines! What they do is, after all the big trees are
cut, the feller-buncher grabs the smaller trees and cuts them down,
really fast, like mowing a lawn. That way when the humans are
done, they've gotten every piece of wood, and nothing is left to
grow at the clearcut. But they are expensive, I hear. The
corporation will be really mad when they see what we did!"

She smiled and slipped the key around her neck, arranging the
knot in the string to the back. "Thanks Pancho. What's the rest of
the stuff in the bag?"

Pancho showed her the files. He had not gotten a chance to look at them himself yet. Judi could not read very well, but she quickly snatched a large topographical map from among the papers. "I know where this is," she said, "and look, here and here." The map displayed future logging sites. "Wow, we really needed this!"

Pancho began scanning the files: dates and surveyors markings, permits to log, contracts and business letters. Pancho could read them but not grasp their big-picture significance, since he knew so little about forests and logging practices.

"We need to show this to our legal experts," said Judi.

"Who," asked Pancho in amazement, "are our legal experts?"

"Blackstone and Hamilton, of course." Judi tossed it off as common knowledge. "They are very highly educated, graduated from Harevard." She smiled.

Pancho shook his head. "I can't believe I've avoided talking to them for weeks and they turn out to be so interesting and accomplished. I never would have guessed."

"You can never tell," said Judi. "Then sometimes you really like somebody right away, and they turn out to be a spy."

"Speaking of which," joked Pancho, "where is Sabo?"

"I expect she'll be back tomorrow, now that the action's over." Judi had noticed this tendency as well. "Sabo's okay, " she added, "remember, don't be too quick to judge."

The next morning after breakfast (acorn pancakes) Pancho dragged the bag of files over to the legal experts. He had removed the key and little belly pack because he wanted to give the files to the rabbits and no longer worry about Timber Harvest Plans, whatever they were.

Blackstone and Hamilton saw him coming and said "Finally, Pancho, are you going to show us what you have in your shopping bag?" Pancho opened the bag and revealed the stack of maps and documents. The legal experts became all business. Glad to be rid of the paperwork, Pancho found a nice spot to lie down.

While taking a well-deserved rest in the grass, Pancho was disturbed by a commotion near the cave. Sitting up to look, he saw Sabo running through the camp as though her tail were on fire. She noticed Pancho's head pop up from the tall grass and raced in his direction, eyes bulging from her black face. She panted so hard she could not speak. Pancho jumped to his feet, alarmed to see Sabo in this state; perhaps the dogs from the farm had chased her, too. He got a bowl of water and when she had drunk from it and caught her breath she began a horrible tale. "Things are very, very bad on the farm," she sputtered. "The pigs have seized control and the other animals are like prisoners. The pigs are murdering every animal who disagrees with them."

"I must go back," Pancho said, suddenly snapping back to his former farm life.

"No!" Sabo screeched. "You can never go back. They have told lies about you. Everything bad that happens is blamed on you and anyone that defends your name is killed as a traitor. You can never go back, and neither can I." Sabo collapsed, a heap of black shiny fur in the green clover. Pancho stroked her back and let the story sink in. She recovered enough to comment: "This is what happens when you have leaders. Sooner or later, even if they start out with good intentions, it comes to a bloody end."

Sabo did not spring back. She limped around the camp and would not eat. All the animals were worried, they had never seen her like this. She lay near Judi, but would not talk even to her. Pancho knew Sabo was in shock, but had no way to help her through. Bonkers took the cheering-up of Sabo as his personal duty. Often co-conspirators in camp pranks, Bonkers looked on her as a soul mate. He tried all her favorite antics, funny faces, mimicking of other animals, but nothing made her smile.

One day, Bonkers calmed down. He no longer tried to make Sabo smile. In his paw he carried the cap he had taken from the dozer. He put the orange cap down next to the black cat and showed her the letters on the front that Pancho had read to him. "C...A....T, cat. See Sabo, it's for you." Sabo reached her paw out and touched the brim. She looked at Bonkers and then at Pancho and burst into tears. She sobbed and sobbed. Bonkers and Pancho were devastated, but Judi patted the cat and let her cry. "That's good, Sabo, just let it out," she said, and she nodded a knowing smile to the pig and monkey, who stood speechless.

After that Sabo did perk up. She began to eat and talk, but she seemed changed. She had seen something horrible and would never forget. Once or twice, to please Bonkers, she tried to wear the baseball cap, but it was much too big. She tacked it to the wall of the cave and told Bonkers it hung there to remind everyone of their glorious victory. By doing that, she began a tradition: after every action the group brought back something for the cave wall. Ever since her return Sabo stayed very close to camp. She never wandered out alone as she used to do. Pancho thought this behavior unhealthy, not Sabo's natural way. Maybe if he invited Sabo to take a walk with him she would go. Maybe they could go look for the apples (this had been in the back of his mind for days). Pancho remembered the rabbits had told him a young buck named "Bambi" had found the apples. How could he forget that name? He began to ask around for Bambi, and in minutes had the deer pointed out to him. Bambi acted as if he were about to be punished when Pancho asked to talk to him. He was little more than a fawn, really, and had just recently lost his spots.

"Bambi, I'm Pancho."

"I know," said the deer in a muffled voice.

"Bambi, the rabbits, Blackstone and Hamilton, told me that you showed them where to get apples."

"I don't think it's stealing if they're on the ground," the deer replied.

Pancho calculated his next words. "We take acorns off the ground and off the tree and that's not stealing. Apples are no different than acorns. Why would it be stealing?" Pancho guessed the answer before it was mumbled.

"Because of the fence."

"Well, maybe the fence is the thing that is wrong, maybe the fence is like stealing."

Bambi was silent, puzzling.

"If you could take us there, Sabo and me, we could look at the situation and decide what is stealing and what is hungry animals fighting for the forest."

"I guess so," was the reply, "but my mother won't let me cross fences, she says you can get shot."

"She is right," Pancho said. "Shall we go?"

They collected Sabo and started down a path only a young deer would choose. They made very good time and soon stopped to rest by what must have been the very same brook they had camped at the other night, only further downstream. "Bambi, I have wanted to ask you, is Bambi your real name?" Pancho wished he had not asked when he saw the deer blush.

"Yes, and I hate it!" he answered.

"Well, why not change it?"

"Yes," inserted Sabo, "Pancho changed his, didn't you, Pancho." Sabo had reverted back to her old, teasing self.

"You changed your name?" asked Bambi. "From what?"

Now it was Pancho's turn to blush, his white face turned red as a beet. "It was a terrible, silly, undignified name" said Pancho. It just wasn't me."

"Tell him," pushed Sabo. "Go ahead."

"Promise, no telling?"

Bambi nodded and the pig tiptoed up to whisper in his ear.

If you have ever heard a deer laugh, you know it is quite contagious. Soon the cat and pig were rolling on the ground with the deer.

"I can sure see why you changed that," he chuckled. "Pancho's better, it's a good name for you."

"Well, what's a good name for you?" Sabo asked. "How about Hercules?"

"No, no, no," said Bambi. "Something normal, something plain. Tom, Bill, John."

"John?" said Pancho. "John Deer? Wait a minute," and he pulled from his little pack the dozer key. The key was silver and, embossed on the top, was a picture of a leaping stag and the name John Deer. "Here you are John Deer. This must be yours."

Never had they seen a deer so excited. These keys had been the hot item in camp all week and now he had one, and personalized too. "Wow, thanks, this is great." He leapt higher than the deer on the key. "I'm sure John is the right name for me now."

"And I know why I kept that key," thought Pancho. "To the apples?" he asked.

"Right over here," shouted John. The pig and cat had to race to keep from being left behind. "Just follow the brook."

6

F resh air, new terrain and good company seemed to re-awaken the old Sabo. The cat bounced along the bank swatting her paw at the occasional dragonfly; her tail twitched with pure joy-of-life. Pancho splashed along in the shallow water. This was the sort of friendly outing he had never seemed to have time for on the farm. The air felt still and warm and the brightness of the sun played checkers with the shadows of leaves. Colors seemed brighter and smells more alluring than on ordinary days. Pancho closed his eyes to inhale and there it was, mixed with the mossy dampness, the smell of nearby apples! John Deer had bounded on ahead. The energy of youth and longer legs had carried him to the edge of the wood, within sight of the fence, where he stood like a lawn statue and waited for the others to catch up. The cat and pig emerged from the trees, but because of their height or lack thereof, they could not see the fence.

"John, where are you?" Pancho searched the brush. "Where is that deer?"

"Boo!" John whispered loudly in the pig's ear. John had stood so still they looked right past him. Sabo jumped into a nearby bush. Her nerves were still raw; she got spooked easily.

"Come on, scaredy cat," coaxed John, "it's just me."

Sabo crept out trying to look nonchalant, but the hair on her neck lay not entirely flat. "See," said the deer, "there is the fence." The smaller animals had to creep a bit closer to see the very long fence, somewhat in need of repairs, stretching as far as they could see in both directions. The brook ducked right under the wooden rails and flowed her winding way through the vast orchard. Everywhere the animals looked they saw fruit trees and nut trees: apples and pears, peaches, cherries, walnuts, almonds, pecans, and others Pancho was unable to identify. Unlike the fence, these trees wanted for nothing; they appeared pampered and bore fruit abundantly. A few apple trees near the fence had reached their branches over to the wild side.

This was where John came to get fruit, "But," he carefully explained, "only if it fell to the ground."

"Your mother has raised a very ethical child," Pancho complimented him, "but how can it matter if the apples are on the branch or on the ground. Sooner or later they will all be on the ground. Right now there are only a dozen or so apples on the ground. Probably tomorrow another dozen will fall, but we will not be here to gather them. If we pick them we are only gathering tomorrow's apples today and sparing them the bruises of the fall."

Pancho spread a cloth on the ground and began to place the apples on it. Sabo climbed the tree and shook the branches, raining the apples down faster than Pancho could pick them up.

"Well, I guess you are right, they were going to fall soon. But I don't think we should cross the fence," said John as he helped to collect the apples.

"Of course, you're right, and we have plenty of apples right here. However, if we wanted to gather pears or cherries or pecans," the pig could almost taste them as he talked, "we would have no choice but to cross the fence."

They quickly gathered the apples. When the cloth was full Pancho tied it like a hobo bundle and hid it in a bush. Then the three friends ate all they could of red juicy apples, dropping the cores on the ground to be covered with ants.

Looking down the endless fence, Pancho mused aloud. "Wow, how big is this farm, do you think?"

"It's huge, gigantic!" offered John. "The brook goes right through the farm. I've followed the fence to the other side where the brook comes out. It's far." Then, out of the blue, he added, "I've never had a pear."

All adolescents have a need to push the boundaries of parental control and John was no exception. But Pancho did not want an angry doe on his back. "There is nothing in this world quite as wonderful as a perfectly ripe pear. You stay here and I'll get you one."

The cat and pig slipped through the fence and walked slowly through the fruit forest. The trees were arranged in sections and they had to pass many apples and peaches to get to the pears. There seemed to be no fruit lying on the ground on this farm, but they picked a likely tree and Sabo climbed it.

"We might as well get a pear for each of us," Pancho said, as Sabo swatted at the heavy yellow ornaments, shaking them loose. Pancho scrambled on the ground, rounding up the pears that had rolled to the sides, when under his snout there appeared an orange fur paw on top of the rolling pear. Pancho jumped back in reflex as he looked up to see a large but matronly golden retriever smiling at him. When she saw the cat's terrified eyes and the pig shaking as his back pressed the pear tree, the dog crouched down in the subservient position usually reserved for rolled newspapers. Strangely, this body language worked and the dog began, "I won't hurt you, don't be afraid. Is there something you want?"

Pancho's fear had given way to guilt; Sabo slid down from the tree, hoping not to be seen. It would be hard to make up a believable lie at this point. Unable to articulate, he held up the pears and smiled sheepishly.

"Oh," said the dog, "the pears are delicious this year. You know, there is nothing in the world as wonderful as a perfect pear."

Pancho started to say that it was amazing how he had said the same thing only moments before, when he realized that the dog must have overheard their conversation. "I'm very sorry to have taken these pears, please have them back." Pancho offered them to the reclining dog.

"Oh, nonsense, I insist you take them. Your little friend has never tasted a pear. My name is Goldie and you are guests on our farm. Help yourselves to whatever you require."

The word "require" sort of bothered Pancho. It implied a need, which in his case, stuffed as he was on apples, could hardly apply to pears. "Thank you very much, my friend John will be delighted to taste his first pear. I am Pancho and this..." He looked for the cat, who peeked from behind the tree trunk. Beckoning her out, he added "...is Sabo."

They began to move slowly in the direction of the fence. The young deer pacing on the other side assumed his statue pose when he saw the dog coming. Goldie carried a pear carefully in her mouth, so gently the skin was unbroken. She placed it on the ground and pushed it with her nose under the fence toward John. The deer rolled the fruit in the grass to dry it off before taking a preliminary nibble. It was love at first bite and he gobbled the pear, core and all.

"Here, there are plenty more," said Goldie, gesturing to Pancho to lay down the ones he was keeping for himself.

"These are fabulous, terrific, the best things I ever ate!" John was at an age when he could never seem to get enough to eat.

"And they are very healthy for deer," said Goldie.

Pancho felt a bit bolder now, back on the safe side of the fence. "Does the master of the farm approve of your giving his fruit to the wild animals?"

Goldie laughed and looked at the pig, cat and the almost fawn. "You don't look so wild to me and," she hung her head sorrowfully, "we have no master."

"Really," asked Pancho, "no humans on the farm?"

"No, not anymore. We had humans once but first one died and then another. It's a long story." She changed the subject. "Would you like to see the farm? I'll give you a tour."

Pancho looked at Sabo, who shrugged her shoulders. Then they both looked at John. "John is a good son," said Pancho, "and his mother does not want him crossing fences and getting shot."

"I should think she doesn't," Goldie said to John. "I don't want you to disobey your mother. I was a mother once myself. But there are no guns on this farm. I'll tell you there are guns on the next door farm and most other farms, but you are perfectly safe on this one. Still, you must use your own judgement about what is right."

John thought about his mother's rules and also how the animals at Cave Camp said they had no rules and no rulers. "I'm my own buck. I have no rules and no rulers. I even changed my name today. If you say there are no guns ... let's go!" and John leapt over the fence and into adulthood.

The others followed, Goldie and Pancho walking abreast and Sabo cat trailing behind. Sabo was not in the habit of strolling with strange dogs and although this one seemed very sweet, better safe than sorry. John, however, skipped way ahead, not particularly interested in a formal tour. They could tell by his excitement he had been itching to jump that fence for a long time. They walked through acres of trees bearing fruit of every kind and then through an area of new baby trees too young to bear fruit. "We planted these two months ago," said Goldie. "They are doing very well."

"Who planted them," Pancho asked, "Dogs?"

"No," smiled Goldie, it seemed she always smiled. "Mostly horses and goats. They are really fond of fruit. But we all helped."

As the animals emerged from the trees the view made them gasp in delight. The meadow before them was wide and gently rolling. The green grass sparkled with camomile flowers and dandelions, and the brook wound through it all, punctuated with the occasional boulder or willow tree. Healthy lambs and kids kicked up their heels, waving to Goldie and the visitors, who emerged from the orchard shade into the full afternoon sun. Pancho's eyes welled up with tears. This was the farm of his dreams, this is what he had wanted for his old farm home. Even Sabo seemed moved. She, too, had been born on a farm.

"What a beautiful meadow!" she purred, falling under its spell, chasing butterflies in the sunlight. John began cavorting with the other youngsters; within minutes they were like old buddies. For him the novelty of the place, not nostalgia, caught his interest.

Pancho turned to Goldie and begged, "You must tell me how you did it, how does it work so beautifully here. Please tell me how you made this farm."

"It's a long story," she said again.

"I really want to hear it," Pancho pleaded. So they sat under a willow by the brook and tossed dandelions into the water as Goldie started her tale. Pancho sat frozen, his mind a-whirl with ideas.

"We didn't make the farm, it existed before any of us were born. Our human Margaret was born here, and her mother, too. Margaret was already old when I was born. Her husband was long buried under the oak and she had no one to talk to except us. Then she became sick and had to stay in the house in a bed. Her chores went undone and we all were depending on her." Goldie looked at the rippling water and seemed lost in memories. "Then one day someone said, and I can't for the life of me tell you who, but someone said, 'Let's do it ourselves,' and it seemed so right and proper. We did it to help Margaret of course, but also to help ourselves, because if no chores were done we would starve." She looked at Pancho and smiled that golden retriever grin. "To tell the truth it was easy and fun. We found we already knew how to run the place, we knew the routines and actually we improved a lot of things. We began to change things."

Goldie paused to watch as a mother quail and her chicks raced through the meadow. Her eyes showed her interest, but she made no chase. Pancho was caught by her story and wanted to bring the dog back to the subject. "What changes?"

"Well," Goldie wrestled her attention back, "one improvement I particularly remember: Margaret always kept her kitchen garden fenced to keep us animals out, but she spent a lot of time fighting the bugs, snails and slugs for ownership of the vegetables. Well, after she got sick and we were tending that garden, the ducks made a good suggestion. They liked to eat snails and they would be careful not to step on the little plants while they did it. It turned out great for us all, and now the ducks are mostly responsible for that garden patch."

Sabo finished chasing grasshoppers and decided to nap. She curled up nearby to listen to the story.

"By the time Margaret died, we had gotten quite efficient at running the farm. We found the more we thought about things, the better we made the place. With so many different abilities from all the animals and so many of us, we hardly have to work at all!"

Pancho interrupted. "How did that happen? It seemed the opposite on our farm!"

The dog paused and thought. "It may be the magic of the land. Some think Margaret's being buried in the ground here helps things grow more abundantly, but I think it's probably the sisterly love we have for one another."

Pancho did not believe in magic, although this was an exceptional parcel, very large and unspoiled. "Sisterly love?" he asked, unsure of this concept in relation to economics.

"You know, caring about each other," Goldie answered simply.

"And your leader?" Pancho asked. "What is he like?"

"Leader?" Goldie thought a bit. "I guess Margaret was sort of our leader, but she died," she shrugged, "the leader thing just never came up."

Pancho raised his eyebrows. "But it's so organized here ... who?"

"It just hasn't been a problem, I guess we all organize ourselves." Goldie was tired of explaining. Pancho had more questions ready for her when she exclaimed, "Well, look who's coming! It's Carlos and Juanita. You'll be very interested in them. They were freedom fighters in their old country." Pancho looked across the meadow at the odd animals approaching them. They looked something like large hairy goats, but not quite.

"What are they?"

"They call themselves llamas. They are teaching me Spanish." Goldie started wagging her tail. "Hola, amigos, buenos tardes."

"Buenos tardes, Goldie," said the soft-eyed caramel colored llama.

"This is Pancho, this is Sabo," the dog gestured toward the sleeping cat, who opened her eyes as her name was mentioned, "and down there in the far meadow is John, the young deer."

"I'm Juanita and this is Carlos. So, you're the forest protectors we've heard so much about."

Pancho looked surprised because this had not yet entered the conversation with Goldie. "You know about us?" Pancho glanced at Sabo, who shrugged.

"Your media birds have been chattering up a storm lately. Did the monkey come with you? We were hoping to meet him." So Bonkers had achieved celebrity status.

"No, he didn't come today. Perhaps another time, or if you want to, you could visit us at the Cave Camp."

Pancho was just being polite, but the llamas were ready to go. "That would be great fun!" Juanita's soft accents made Pancho think of far-off lands.

"Carlos, could you go get the packs?" Carlos nodded his shaggy white head and turned toward what must be the barn and took off at a trot. "We have been following your exploits and we all support the cause. Goldie, could you please..."

"Water the corn for you?" Goldie finished Juanita's sentence. "Sure, why not."

Carlos came trotting back carrying two colorful woven packs. "We can't visit empty-handed. Pancho what do you think we should bring? Fruit and nuts sound good?"

"Perfect," smiled the pig, suddenly noticing the sun low in the sky. "I suppose we should be going soon. But we didn't see the rest of the farm."

"Then you have an excuse to come back." Goldie and the llamas packed the pouches with the best of the fruit.

Pancho quietly whispered, "Save some room. We already have a bundle of apples outside the fence."

"Oh, we'll just toss them on top," Juanita remarked. "Carlos is so strong he wouldn't even notice another bag of apples."

Carlos seemed embarrassed but pleased by her comment; still he said nothing. Pancho whistled for John Deer and signalled for him to come. If you did not know pigs could whistle, some can, and very loudly. John was not ready to leave, but when he saw the llamas and fruit he changed his mind. With his shiny key swinging around his neck, he led the way back to Cave Camp.

7

Returning as they were, bearing gifts, the animals received a hero's welcome. The fruit tasted delicious served with the acorn patties and the squirrels stored the precious nuts for eating later. John explained his new name and showed off the key to his friends. His mother neither asked nor was she told about the fence leaping. Carlos and Juanita took center stage as they shared stories of the old country with Bonkers. Pancho was skeptical that the monkey had ever been to the exotic places the llamas were talking about, but Bonkers as usual kept up his part of the conversation. Even Carlos got excited enough to speak as he told them about the destruction of the rainforest.

Riff-Raff thought they should all go to protect the rainforest, but Juanita explained how far away it was. Nevertheless, someday she and Carlos would like to return.

To the animals at Cave Camp the llamas seemed very worldly and well-traveled. Pancho was impressed with their expanded knowledge of the world and its possibilities. Until recently Pancho had not been off the farm on which he was born. Now he roamed the forest, even visited another farm today, and felt free and full of adventure. Hearing Juanita and Carlos talk of foreign lands with strange types of animals and the largest river in the world, he experienced the enlarging of the universe and the shrinking of the pig. The feelings struggled within him: the world so big with so many adventures and so many problems and Pancho the pig, so small, ineffective and inexperienced.

Judi noticed him pull away from the group and came to sit by him. "The llamas are great," she said. "It's always good for a group to get some new energy. And Sabo seems much better since your little outing. Hey, Pancho, are you okay?"

He sat staring at the grass. "I feel so helpless and lost suddenly," he said. "I can see so much that needs to be done in the world and I'm sure there's more I can't even imagine yet. I feel like I can't do it all and I don't know even where to start!"

Judi was a little surprised at him. "Of course you can't do it all, as if you were the only animal in the world, pretty egotistical, I'd say." She looked him in the snout. "And what do you mean you don't know where to start. You've already started, we're doing something important right here and your old farm was an important step, too. Just keep taking steps, that's all, and let others take steps with you."

She changed the subject. "Maybe the llamas want to go on tomorrow's forest action. Should we ask them?"

Tomorrow's action came as news to the pig. "What action? Where are we going?"

"Back to the last site! It seems they brought in new equipment and Blackstone and Hamilton say they are setting up a staging area for the whole clearcut plan."

"How do the rabbits know about the plan?" Pancho hated feeling so out of the loop.

"The papers you gave them in the blue bag," Judi explained, "everything was in there, they said."

"Oh," Pancho felt a bit more included. "Shouldn't we have a meeting if we are going tomorrow?"

"We already had one. You and Sabo weren't here so I think you're on Security and Sabo is Media again."

"What! I don't want to be on Security. I want to be on Sabotage!"

Pancho began to act like a piglet, stamping his foot and whining. "Hey, everybody wanted to be on Sabotage and you weren't here. Besides, Security is important, especially when you hit the same spot twice in one week."

"You're right, Judi, I'll give others a chance and at least I'll be close to the action." Pancho decided to make the best of it and was about to check in with the other security animals when Bonkers bounded over.

"Guess what, the llamas are coming with us tomorrow. They're going to be on Sabotage and show us some new techniques!" Bonkers was all smiles and Judi returned his expression.

"That's great. Welcome aboard!" she shouted in the direction of Juanita and Carlos. Pancho's eyes narrowed to slits in his moonlike face. He wished those llamas had never come to Cave Camp, but it was hard to complain since he had invited them.

The preparations the next morning were much the same as the other day, with two big differences: this time there were a lot more tools and there were two strong llamas with big packs to be filled. The amazing ability of their new comrades to carry heavy and clumsy burdens down rocky, narrow paths was a windfall. The Nuts pot was strapped on and toward the end of the hike some of the squirrels had hitched a ride on Carlos' back. Even Tex and Mex decided to come along this time, not wanting to be left all alone and without the food contingent. They made a quick and less exhausting trip and, at their temporary camp, had time for a strategy meeting.

The birds watching the clearing site all day were full of information. During the day there were many humans there, but now most had gone away, leaving two guards. The corporation had bought lots of new machines, but no new trailer, not yet anyway. The guards had put up a small tent and had started a fire to cook supper.

"If they keep the fire going after dark they'll see us," Carlos said to a fascinated group, "and they probably will because two guards means they will take turns sleeping and watching."

"How about just scaring them off," asked Red and the large scruffy bear nodded approval.

"They're sure to have guns," Pancho reminded the bears. "We must be very aware of guns."

Suddenly Quoth the raven flew in, making a dramatic entrance. She was out of breath, or perhaps just pausing for effect. When she had their complete attention she announced, "They have a dog!"

It was so quiet in the circle you could hear a nut drop. In fact, the silvery squirrel had dropped a whole bag of nuts when he heard the news.

"What kind of dog is it?" Juanita asked.

"It's no chihuahua!" the raven quipped. "Big. Big and vicious, that's what kind it is!"

The animals thought quietly for a minute, then three squirrels from Nuts-To-Everybody came forward.

"What does a dog like to eat?" the silvery one asked.

"Squirrels!" squawked the raven, "and rabbits and pigs and deer and birds. We're not having him to dinner!"

Everyone laughed at the gentle squirrels and their innocent minds. "But if we could find something he liked to eat," said Mac, the head squirrel chef, "we could drug him. In fact, we could drug them all." That said, the squirrels went back to their quiet work preparing supper for the camp.

The animals looked stunned at the suggestion. They all watched the squirrels preparing the food and the same thought circled the meeting. All along they had completely trusted the food from the squirrels. No one had ever considered they might be drugged.

Mac felt their eyes on him and said, "Hey, relax, it was just an idea," and then, a bit defensively, "none of you have even gotten indigestion from one of our meals." The animals laughed at that erroneous remark. "Well, nobody's really gotten sick or anything." Mac acted offended and Red spoke up for him.

"Mac, you and all the Nuts are great and we really appreciate you, don't we." He turned to the group who clapped and cheered in genuine approval.

"And your suggestion, well, we never thought that way before, but it just might work."

Mischief and Bandit nodded. In fact, the more they thought about it, the better it sounded.

"What did you have in mind, Mac?" asked Red.

"I'm not sure, but the woods are full of plants that can do all kinds of things: make you sleep, hallucinate, even kill you." The soft spoken squirrel began cracking acorns as he spoke. The animals nodded in recognition. They all knew dangerous plants and had been taught early what not to touch.

The squirrel continued: "Flora and I are herbalists, you know, and we could make up a sleeping potion, I'm sure." He looked at the round, furry Flora.

"The heliotrope is in bloom right now," she added, "that makes it easy to find."

"So if you could get them to eat it, the humans and the dog could sleep through the whole action." Mac smiled, proud of his idea.

"It'll be dangerous, but we could get the sleeping potion into their food." Mischief said, rubbing his paws together as he smiled at Riff-Raff.

"Amigos," Carlos spoke up, "If we are going to risk getting killed, and we are since they have guns, we should poison the guards, not put them to sleep for the night."

"Si, they are our enemies," Juanita added. "If they live, we will just have to fight them another day."

"They won't hesitate to shoot us with those guns of theirs," Pancho agreed with the llamas, "but what about the dog? How can we know he's an enemy? Maybe he's just a slave to the men."

"Some dogs are very kind," Sabo added, but then wondering why she was defending a dog.

"Okay, drug the dog, but I say kill the humans," yelled Bandit.

Judi stepped forward. "This violence will backfire on us. Besides, maybe the human guards are slaves of the corporation?"

"You mean maybe we could talk to them and convince them to fight for our side?" Pancho snorted. "Ridiculous! Humans are evil."

"I completely agree," said Juanita, "it's in their nature to be selfish. I wish it could be otherwise."

"Nevertheless," Judi stood her ground, "we don't need to stoop to their level. What would be the difference between us? Animals are better than that!"

Judi's reasoning prevailed this time. The animals decided that sleeping drugs would be best. Flora and Mac scampered off to look for the flowering plant whose root would be used for the potion. They did not have much time to search, but they did find one root, enough to sedate the men. The dog would have to be given a hallucinogenic mushroom. After all, the dog did not have a gun.

Pancho sat on a log, turning thoughts over in his mind. He had never thought of poisoning anyone before. Death in the heat of battle was one thing, but this premeditated stuff felt a bit sneaky. He was glad they decided against a cold blooded killing. Yet he really did not consider human lives to be as valuable as animal lives. Humans had been nothing but trouble for all the other animals since they arrived on the scene. "And humans think nothing of the mass slaughter of farm animals," Pancho justified his thoughts to himself. "Why should we care about two humans who stand in the way of forest protection?" Still, he would just as soon avoid watching another creature suffer, even a human. This way they could feel a bit superior in their actions.

Bandit and Rascal volunteered for the dangerous mission. Rascal, the fastest runner, would run through the clearing so the dog would chase him. Then Bandit would run over and drop the sleeping potion in the pot of food on the fire. As the dog got close to Rascal he would drop the dog's magic mushroom and hopefully the dog would eat it. Then they would wait for the drugs to take effect.

Mac made a special acorn burger with the mushroom hidden inside, chopped up. He added extra salt because dogs like salty food. Then he wrapped the sleeping potion in a leaf. "Just drop it in the pot still wrapped in the leaf," he explained to Bandit.

Most of the animals decided to go and watch, but Sabo and Judi stayed with the coyotes at what they now called Brook Camp.

Plans never are as perfect as they seem. As soon as the saboteurs peeked over the hill and down into the clearing they knew they had problems. It was not dark yet, but the guards had started eating their supper and the dog was nowhere in sight.

"We have to hurry, hopefully they will eat second helpings. Go! Hurry!" Carlos urged.

Rascal looked at him. "But I don't know where the dog is."

"He'll find you, don't worry. Got the burger?"

Riff-Raff tried to be encouraging. "Are you ready, Bandit?" The raccoons nodded, hearts thumping. Rascal took a deep breath and ran out into the clearing. He zig-zagged around all the equipment and ran right past the men, but saw no dog.

The men saw him racing around and one said to the other, "What's with that raccoon? Sure is acting strange. Do you think he's rabid?" Of course the animals could not hear what the men said, but they could see one grab a rifle from the tent. Rascal continued running back and forth, looking for the dog.

The sound of the rifle-shot finally woke the sleeping doberman, who was chained to a new feller-buncher. The first shot missed Rascal, but the second did not. The raccoon flew into the air when the bullet hit, falling down near the bushes.

Without a thought Riff-Raff raced over and grabbed the acorn burger out of Rascal's clenched paw, running for the dog. Dodging gunshots, he tossed the food in the dog's face and dove to safety on the other side of the clearing. "We did this backwards," he thought angrily as he ran back out to draw fire from Bandit, who carried the sleeping potion. The distraction worked. Both men had their rifles out now and began stalking Riff-Raff. They did not notice Bandit trying to get the lid off their stew pot. Riff-Raff took a shot in the hind leg and ran into the bushes. Out ran Mischief to take his place distracting the riflemen.

Pancho put his paw to his head. "Oh no, if we don't watch out, there will be no raccoons left." He looked over at the dog, who was watching the chase and barking in between chomps on the burger. Bandit dropped the leaf-wrapped potion into the pot and ran off in the other direction, but Mischief did not know his buddy was safe. The raccoon ran back and forth like a duck at a shooting gallery. "Bushes, Mischief, bushes," Pancho chanted under his breath.

Suddenly a shower of stones came from behind the guards. At the sound, the men swung around and began firing at the rocks. Red reached his long paw out of the bush and grabbed Mischief, pulling him to safety. As Pancho glanced in the direction the rocks had come from, he saw the two llamas sneaking back to join the other animals.

"Those humans had better be hungry after all that exercise," Mischief said, his adrenalin still pumping. And it seemed they were. The guards did not notice that the lid was off the pot. They did not see the leaf in their stew; they were too busy talking about the crazy raccoon.

"I guess they can't tell one raccoon from another," thought Bandit who was close enough to hear their talk. Eating their stew, the men swore they had hit the raccoon several times. Across the clearing, the animals gathered around the body of Rascal. Red picked him up in one arm and the wounded Riff-Raff in the other and carried them over the hill to Brook Camp. As night began to fall the other animals watched the clearing and waited for the drugs to do their work.

At Brook Camp the rifle shots had forewarned of tragedy. There had been too many shots for them to be all misses. When Red carried in the raccoons, Sabo lost her cool. She relapsed into her depression, climbed a tree, and hid for the rest of the night.

"The plan didn't quite work out like we thought," Red said sadly. He left the rest to Judi and the squirrels. After bandaging Riff-Raff and laying out Rascal's body for good byes, they waited for it all to be over.

Riff-Raff said to them, "I don't think anything bad can happen now, just the sabotage," and he fell asleep. But the squirrels knew Riff-Raff was badly hurt and not out of the woods yet. The night was young, and many things could go wrong.

The doberman began acting funny, chasing his tail and rolling on his back, then barking in sudden fits at nothing. The men could hardly keep their eyes open. One gave up and lay down by the fire to sleep. The other propped himself up against a rock with his rifle across his knees. He tried to stay awake, but the sedative won out. His head dropped onto his chest and his breathing became slow and regular.

The dog started digging a big hole for no apparent reason. The sun set and the sky turned from orange to black. Pancho stood at his high vantage point to keep watch. He saw the big scruffy bear poke the men to see if they were indeed asleep.

It had gotten too dark to see anything, at least for the pig. "This is why I'm not good security," he thought. Then his sensitive nose picked up something. "Humans," he whispered to John Deer. "I smell them."

John silently crossed to Red. "Humans! Pancho smells them," he whispered.

Red looked around, but saw nothing and whispered back, "probably those two down below." John relayed the message to the pig, who felt uncertain.

"Maybe," he thought, "but it sure smells close," yet he could see nothing and soon the smell became faint.

Below the animals of the sabotage group worked hard with their new tools. They made a lot of noise, probably because of the dark, moonless night. There were bumps and bangs as machinery crashed to the ground. Bonkers tried his keys on the different machines. Pancho had told him that wouldn't work, that the new machines would have new keys, but the monkey wanted to drive. He climbed into the seat of a new Dump T. and got frustrated when the old key did not work. He started playing with knobs and switches. As he gave one knob a particularly hard pull, two beams of light shot out from the front of the Dump T., lighting the clearing. The light caught Mischief, Juanita and Red on one side and three humans on the other. Everyone froze.

Mischief came to his senses first and ran for darkness. Juanita and Red noticed something else. Red held up his wrench and the humans held up their hands, which also held wrenches. Juanita was not afraid of most humans, so she spoke: "Who are you?"

"We're environmental activists and we're here to disable the logging machinery." The young bearded man spoke softly so as not to frighten anyone, or perhaps to reassure the large bear only feet from him.

"We got here first," growled Red. "We get to do it."

"Did you guys do it a few of nights ago? That was really something." The higher-pitched voice meant this was probably a female.

Bonkers leapt from the cab and jumped into the spotlight. "I drove the Dump T. over the cliff," he boasted, and soon the other animals crowded into the light. The humans stepped back when they saw how many there were.

Pancho's head began pounding. From the distance he wondered why the animals were talking to humans. Either attack them or run away!

"How many are there of you humans?" asked Red.

"Five, just us here," said the woman, as two more men stepped into the lighted area. "There are more, but they aren't here tonight."

Juanita had realized how hard the dismantling would be. "Did you humans have a plan to destroy the machines," she asked and Red shot her an angry look.

"Well, yes, we were going to blow them up," answered the bearded man pointing to sticks of dynamite in his pocket.

"Yes! Yes! Yes!" shouted Bonkers.

"No! No! No!" thought Pancho.

"Won't that start a fire?" The question came from John Deer.

"Probably not, if we drain the gas tanks first," answered the man.

"Okay, let's do it!" voted Bonkers.

"Okay," each of the animals said, polling themselves.

Pancho could contain himself no longer. "No," he yelled from his post. "Stop talking to those humans. They are the enemy. It's a trick or something. Animals will be hurt."

The animals listened and began to backup.

Then Juanita yelled to Pancho, "I think it's alright. We're on the same side tonight."

"It's true," the man yelled. "I promise, no animals will get hurt."

Pancho was outvoted and outraged. It seemed everyone else wanted to see the machines explode, no matter what that did to their safety or principles.

The corporation had many more machines now than a few nights ago, which made for quite a number of explosions. The doberman began howling at the non-moon and Red decided he could be unchained and led to Brook Camp, where he could be rechained until he came to his senses again. Unfortunately, Red chained the dog to the tree where Sabo was hiding, adding greatly to her anxiety.

Pancho remained at his post during the dynamiting. The animals were all warned to keep well back for fear of flying metal. The first few explosions proved exciting and relatively small. Everyone tried to be careful and Pancho almost took back his reservations. The machines were very thoroughly destroyed. It was quick and easy (and for some, lots of fun).

To explode the big truck they needed extra dynamite. The human with the long black beard emptied the gas from the fuel tank and set the fuse. All the environmentalists backed up, but not enough. No one knew this truck had a second fuel tank.

The huge explosion caused metal pieces to fly in a much wider circle than they expected. The black-bearded man was killed by the hood of the truck hurling through the air. Many animals were injured and one, John Deer, was killed by a piece of the engine.

A fire engulfed the rubble that was once the truck and began to spread on the ground, following the trails of spilled gasoline. Everyone needed to get to safe ground quickly. The scruffy bear scooped up as many injured animals as he could carry. Red picked up the limp deer's body and they all headed over the hill. The flames leapt to the tent where the drugged guard lay sleeping. His bedroll caught fire, but he never woke up. Bullets sound like firecrackers when they explode in the box. The second guard was hit and killed by the flying bullets.

The humans were struggling with their dead friend when Carlos appeared at their side and offered his back. The body draped over his fur much like the packs he often carried. Carlos led the humans to Brook Camp. This time, Pancho hated being right.

8

No victory party was held that night. Brook Camp whispered, hugged and wept. Pancho protested everywhere and to everyone the presence of humans in their camp. But the humans were in no condition to leave yet. One was dead, two injured and the others frightened almost into paralysis. When they heard about the drugging of the guards and their death in the fire it was more than they could take.

"No one knows about you," the woman told the animals. "Everything you do is blamed on us. When the bodies of the guards are discovered we will be called murderers and no one will believe the truth."

"We can help you hide," Judi said sadly.

Pancho grabbed her arm and squeezed it. "Do not take humans into Cave Camp!"

"There are lots of hiding spots. Stop squeezing me, Pancho. Cool out!" Judi was tired, they all were. "These humans fought with us and died with us. They are at risk because of us. We can't be prejudiced against them just because they are human."

"If we associate with them, we will become like them."

"How do you know they won't become like us?" replied Judi. "Do you think we are so weak in our convictions that we will catch human behavior like catching a cold?"

Pancho watched the animals and humans making plans together, sickening at the sight. Still, he stayed and listened, the way one watches a disaster, with morbid fascination. A hollow tree was chosen as a message center so the groups could communicate if necessary. At a cave nearby the humans would stay hidden for some time; the deaths would not blow over quickly. Birds would be sent to inform the animals of the situation; squirrels would help with food.

Pancho moved to the grassy clearing where bears were digging a grave and began to help. Pigs are good diggers, better than bears. The physical activity, grim as it was, helped to clear his head. He started to romanticize his farm memories as though he had actually done the manual labor of planting and harvesting, instead of just supervising. He could see himself digging up a field for planting instead of a grave for a human. "I'm a farm pig," he thought, "not a wild boar. I can't see a successful end to this fight. And now humans are involved with us."

He dusted the dirt from his feet and stood back with the bears to look at the finished grave. Humans buried their dead underground, a strange custom, Pancho thought. Animals left the bodies of their loved ones as food for others, as part of life's circle, a final generous act. "No matter," Pancho shrugged. "They can't hide from the worms. But still, it's so selfish, so human..."

The humans laid their friend's body in the hole the animals had dug. Rascal and John Deer were put nearby on a grassy patch of land near the brook. Everyone gathered around to watch and cry. Some speeches were made, but they sounded weak and forced. Pancho took the key from his neck and placed it on John's body. Bonkers gave a wrench to Rascal, and the humans put a photograph in the hand of the dead man. They covered the grave with dirt and then with grass and leaves. No marker was placed; searchers would never discover the grave. Everyone sang a song and held hands in a ring, but it was too soon for the reality to hit them. No one really felt what had happened, yet.

The campfire that night was small and barely glowing. No one felt much like singing, but Tex and Mex gathered the animals and the humans around for a tail.

Sabo listened from the tree limb where she clung, unable to descend because of the chained dog below. Pancho sat alone, behind the bears, so he could not see the humans. Unfortunately, the big furry backs also blocked his view of the storytellers. He closed his eyes and listened, hoping there would be something in the coyote's story to make him feel better. There wasn't.

In his quiet, lonesome voice, Mex began:

"Life is full of dangers and hard choices," the coyote explained. "All young animals in the wild learn very early: Don't eat that mushroom, run from hunters, if your foot gets caught in a trap..."

"Chew it off," the animals recited back to him in monotone.

"And you must chew it off or face a fate much more horrible. These are life's realities. The world is sometimes cruel, events may seem unfair, and all living things must die," the coyote said, and poked at the fire with a stick. "Some things cannot be changed, but some things can. Life is hard enough. We must work together to change the things we can, to make this world a kinder, fairer and more nurturing place. Everyone at this campfire knows life's realities and each of us has dreams of a better future."

The animals nodded slowly. Mex was really bringing them down, and they had started pretty low. "I hope you have a point," Red mumbled. "I thought we were going to have a tail."

"We are going to have a tail," said Mex defensively. "And I always have a point." He waved the glowing end of the stick in the air. "All of us, even these humans, understand why the corporation must be stopped. We have an obligation to stop evil when we see it or we are just as guilty as the corporation itself. Our motives today were pure. The intent was good. Yet fate played its hand. Outcomes are not predictable. But were we wrong to try? Some will say yes, but I say you must always try to do the right thing." The coyote looked at his audience who stared at the ground. Time to change the subject.

Tex took over. "Human's are always thinking, they love ideas. Some ideas start out big and end up small: 'The world is flat and if you sail far enough you will fall off the edge.' Some ideas start off small and end up big. The idea to make a corporation was the second kind. It started small and hasn't stopped growing yet.

"The idea began with wicked intent. 'How can we get all the income from a business, while avoiding all the losses?' was the greedy question. 'How can we commit crimes and legally avoid taking responsibility?' puzzled the group of evil men.

"Because the conspiring men had small minds, it took a group of them thinking hard to come up with this fiendish scheme. 'We will make masks of paper with the eyes cut out. When we are wearing our masks we will not be ourselves, we will be something else altogether. We will be a corporation. When we take off our masks we will be ourselves again. Anything we did while wearing the masks was done by the corporation, and when we take off the masks, we cannot be held responsible. The idea is to keep putting on and taking off the masks, as is convenient.'

"Now you may think this silly idea would never work. That the animals and other humans would see right through those masks for the fraud it was. But like the Emperor's New Clothes, no one said a thing.

"The evil men put on their masks. 'Now we are the corporation,' they said. 'Let's make some money!' The corporation decided to bring gold from across the ocean in ships. This was a dangerous and risky business, but the potential profits were high. The corporation, the merchants in their masks, borrowed money to buy five ships and sent them off across the sea to fetch the gold. Four ships returned full of treasure. The corporation gathered the gold and split it up among the mask wearers. Then the evil men took off the masks and carried the sacks of gold to their private homes. The fifth ship became lost at sea, the victim of storms or pirates.

"The men put on the masks again to answer the claims of the men who had loaned money to buy the ships and gold. 'You owe us money for five ships, but you paid us only for four,' the men who had loaned the money complained.

"The corporate masks answered, 'The fifth ship was lost with its treasure on board and so we have no money to pay you.'

"'But what about all the treasure from the first four ships? That was much more than the money you owe for the fifth.' So reasoned the money lenders.

"'We have no money. The corporation is bankrupt,' said the masked men as they removed their masks and tore the paper to shreds. 'We are merely individuals now, not the corporation. The corporation is dead and has no money, so there is nothing more for you to collect.' The evil men headed home to their piles of gold.

"The men who loaned the money had no choice. The corporation had borrowed money and now the corporation was bankrupt. Just because the former owners of the corporation were very rich did not mean that the corporation had any money at all."

"That's not fair," said Red, "is it?"

"No, it's not fair, but it's legal," the coyote continued. "So what do you think happened next? Well, you may think that the men who loaned and lost the money would complain that this was unfair. That they would demand an end to the corporation idea." The animals nodded yes, but Tex nodded no. "What happened was just the opposite. The men who had lost money got together and made themselves some paper masks. They were shrewd businessmen and they could see a great money making idea in the wearing of the corporate masks. Soon all the rich men had made masks. These masks were not to hide the true identity of the men, like some masks. They were just pretend, and everyone agreed to pretend together that when the masks were on a man was no longer responsible for his debts or his crimes.

"Rarely do you see such cooperation among men, especially rich ones, but they all agreed this mask idea held the answer to their dreams. At first the animals and poor humans paid little attention to the mask game. Why should they care? They had no money to lend, no gold to ship across the ocean, no capital to hide. No, they were just the sailors on the ships that went down, the miners caught in the collapsing shafts, the farm workers sprayed with poisons while picking the corporate crops. But when disasters struck and workers were killed or injured, the corporation owners took off their masks and disappeared."

"That really makes me mad," Bonkers said, jumping to his feet. "How can they be so cruel?"

"Do you want to know what's even worse?" Mex howled. "The profits of corporations are privatized, that means each masked man can take them home, but the losses are socialized. That means the poor animals are paying to protect the corporations from any money loss. The poor are paying for the privilege of being tricked, robbed and abused."

Bonkers was irate. "What kind of suckers do they think we are? Why did animals let them get away with it?"

"Animals and poor humans were confused about how to deal with these growing corporations. On one paw the corporations provided the jobs and meager wages that the workers depended on to survive. On the other paw, as soon as trouble came, and often from corporate neglect, they disappeared into a pile of useless paper.

"The corporations grew even larger, swallowing each other whole, forming new and more powerful alliances, taking over all commerce. Piles of paper masks covered the desks of the richest men. The government, the courts, the army all cowered at their demands. 'We need more tax breaks, more free land! Break the unions for us, let us cut those trees without paying for them!' cried the masked men. And the world obeyed. Anything the corporations wanted they could get." The coyote Tex paused to take a breath. He waved his paw at Mex to pick up the tail.

"When something in nature starts to grow, it knows when to stop. A squirrel will never be as big as a bear. A daisy plant will never grow as big as a redwood tree. Yet even the giant redwood doesn't grow forever. It knows when to stop. When something in nature grows out of control and won't stop, we call it a cancer. And we know what happens when you have a cancer. If you don't deal with it you will die.

"The corporation is an out of control cancer, growing bigger every day. The longer we wait to stop it, the less our chance of survival." Mex looked at the wide-eyed animals and humans. "If you have a cancer growing on your foot and it keeps growing, climbing up your leg ... I know it's horrible, and painful and scary, but what must you do if you want to survive?"

"Chew it off," they answered.

* * *

Activity restarted even before dawn overwhelmed the starlight. The camp broke up quickly. The humans were hidden somewhere; Pancho did not care where. He felt like a surgeon had come in the night and cut out his heart.

Sabo slowly crept down from the tree and joined Pancho. "I want to go to the farm," she said.

"Our old farm? We can't," said Pancho in a monotone.

"No, the other farm, the apple farm. Come with me," she pleaded.

"Yes, okay, we'll go," he stated without enthusiasm. Maybe that was the best idea, he did not know. At least it was something.

The doberman awakened completely confused. He couldn't believe he was having his options explained to him by some fancy talking rabbits. He opted to go his own way in peace. He had no political views and was just following orders, so it seemed. They unchained him and gave him some breakfast, which he sniffed with great suspicion before eating. He seemed anxious to leave, saying he wanted to check out the damage and then disappear.

"Don't eat the beans in the pot," cautioned the rabbits as he trotted away, never to be seen again.

Pancho and Sabo joined a group of animals and sat with them, eating bowls of acorn mush. Pancho started casually: "Sabo and I are going on a little fact-finding tour of some of the neighboring farms."

No one was fooled. Juanita said, "Oh good, will you..."

Pancho joined in unison, "... water the corn."

"Sure, no problem," he answered. "So you're not going back?"

"Not right now," she said, "but say 'hola' to everyone for us and tell them about our adventure."

Judi took Pancho aside. "I know you're upset, I'm sorry I was short last night. Don't leave mad."

"I'm not mad, really," he said, hugging her. "Sometimes I just feel if I bend any more I'm going to break."

Judi laughed. "You won't break, but you may start to dance!"

He smiled; it sounded easier than it felt. "Sabo wants to go and it will be good for me too."

Judi nodded, then looked at him for a long minute. "The enemy of my enemy is my friend," she said.

Pancho stared back blankly.

"It's not a riddle," she joked. "I think it is the only way we can win." Pancho opened his mind a crack and Judi stuck her foot in the door. "Look," she explained, "who is the enemy of the forest."

"Humans," responded Pancho.

"Not really," said Judi. "I would say it is not the humans who fought with us last night, or even the humans that actually log the forests. The real enemy of the forest is the corporation that makes all the profits from the destruction. Really, just a few humans. That leaves most of the other humans as potential friends."

"The guards," asked Pancho, "were they potential friends?"

"I suppose they had the potential, but it would have taken a lot of work for them to come around," Judi admitted. "I'm just putting out a theory, something to think on."

"The enemy of my enemy is my friend," recited Pancho. "I'll think about it."

"Let's go," whined Sabo, "bye Judi, see you around."

"Keep in touch," she replied, waving, as the cat and pig wandered away, following the brook.

9

Water mumbled over the rocky stream bed, providing the bass notes. The bright day had inspired the songbirds to vocal gymnastics, and the insects hummed along. The cat walked silently as always, but her head hung down and her tail dragged the ground. Pancho walked unaware of nature's morning concert. His head pounded and the drone of an energetic dragonfly dive-bombing the stream felt like a dentist's drill.

Lost in thought, they stumbled along the bank. They did not speak, there was nothing to say.

Pancho glanced at Sabo. I suppose she's headed for another depression, he thought. Maybe this time I'll join her.

But Pancho was too angry to get depressed. Angry at the violence that seemed to be part of all change. Angry that humans had become part of the forest protectors, and angry at life not going the way he had planned.

They followed the bank for about an hour, paying little attention to the surroundings, when they came to what appeared to be a fork in the stream. The cat stopped and stared like a zombie at the two waterways. A breeze blew and the water seemed to flow backwards; it was hard to tell which was the main stream. Pancho did not remember the fork from their last trip, but then they had been following John, poor John Deer.

The pig broke the silence. "They probably end up in the same place," he said to Sabo. "This way?" He pointed his muddy foot towards the right. The cat shrugged and followed behind Pancho, who suddenly felt chatty. "I'm sure we're nearly there. I can't wait to taste those apples. We'll get to see the rest of the farm, I'm sure it's great."

As they walked Pancho day-dreamed aloud about the farm and
Sabo began to brighten up. She still said nothing but her tail no
longer dragged and she swatted at a butterfly that ventured near,
so he could tell she was feeling better. The surroundings were not
really familiar, yet Pancho could not be sure since he had only
been to the farm once before. They followed the stream branch for
a short while, then the wind suddenly shifted. The sensitive noses
of pig and cat were snapped to attention. "Dogs," they hissed in
unison, but before they could get a second whiff the wind turned
again and they could smell only clover.

"That couldn't be Goldie," said Pancho. "Too strong a
scent."

"Be careful," cautioned Sabo.

Pancho nodded in agreement, but as the smell was gone, they
continued along the water.

The stream went into thick brush which slowed travel to a
crawl. "Get on my back," said Pancho. "We'll do better if we walk
in the stream."

So with Sabo on his back and holding on a little too tightly
with her claws, they waded in the water through the undergrowth.
Pigs feet are not the best on slippery rocks, but before long they
reached more open terrain. As soon as it looked possible, Sabo
leapt off Pancho's back to the safety of terra firma, leaving pink
scratches on the white pig skin. Pancho made a mental note: no
more piggy-back rides for Sabo, and rolled in the water to calm his
sores.

"What's this," he asked aloud to no-one, since he knew well
what it was. Out of the water he pulled a soggy cardboard box
marked '9mm Ammunition.'

"Somebody's doing serious hunting!"

"And look at this!" Sabo pointed a rigid paw at something
round in the grass. "A hand grenade. Where are we?"

They crept forward slowly. The stream turned sharply to the
right over a low hill. As they climbed to the top the wind shifted
again. Noses and eyes moved in ensemble: dog kennels. Below the
hill, and behind a high chain-link fence, the stream flowed into a
huge field of German shepherds. They were separated by fences
from each other into small packs of dogs; each group marched in

its own formation. From the hill top it looked like a dance; the pig and cat felt safe enough to watch unnoticed.

"What are they doing?" asked Sabo.

"Maneuvers," the answer came from behind them!

The pig and cat jumped, then saw a large wild turkey and her chicks a few feet from them, scratching through the grass.

"Wow, we didn't notice you here," Pancho said as he tried to calm his pounding heart.

"I know," said the turkey, "that's why I always bring my chicks here to feed, everyone's so distracted by those dogs they never notice what else is going on."

"I'm sure you're right about that," Pancho said looking back at the kennel. "Why are they doing maneuvers? Are they planning an attack on something?"

"Oh, probably," said the turkey as she herded her chicks up the hill. "I think the planning is their favorite part. But they do have weapons, so they could attack something, I suppose."

Pancho and Sabo watched the marching drill in fear. Dogs, with guns! That is every cat's nightmare and not such a happy thought for pigs either.

"Lately they're really upset," continued the bird. "The owners of the kennel have started raising poodles as well as shepherds. That means less room for the shepherds, and they are very territorial. Look over there, you can see the poodles."

They looked and saw a few small curly-haired animals watching the shepherds' drill. The poodles were separated by a strong-looking mesh fence from the other dogs, but were still clearly intimidated.

"Those poodles don't really look like dogs," said Sabo, "they look more like little sheep."

"But they are dogs, just like the shepherds," the turkey said as she pecked seeds from the tall grass. "Those dogs don't know who their friends are, or could be," she paused to count chicks, "or who their real enemies are. And they don't know beans about freedom."

"How do you know so much about these dogs?" Pancho was always a bit wary of strangers with too much information.

"I live here in the summers and I keep my ears open, and my eyes too." She spread her wing feathers as if to shake off Pancho's insult. "The dogs talk about freedom and rights. But what it really amounts to is the freedom to be the only dogs in their kennel prison. Instead of joining with the poodles to fight their real enemy."

"The owners of the kennel?" Pancho was following the turkey's line of thought.

"Sure, that's a start, but who owns the owners?"

"The corporation?" Pancho offered.

The turkey smiled. "It's so much easier to fight poodles."

The marching stopped abruptly and the dogs stood at sharp attention as only German shepherds can. In each group one dog started barking and the others listened. Pancho listened too, but could not make out what was being said. Suddenly all the dogs began to bark together, louder and louder. Sabo had to cover her ears and the turkey chicks ran to hide beneath their mother. But still Pancho could not make it out.

"What are they chanting?" Pancho screamed to be heard over the racket.

"Life, liberty, and the pursuit of happiness," replied the turkey in a loud squawk.

"Life, liberty, happiness? Well, I believe in that too," Pancho shook his head in confusion.

"Of course, everyone does, for themselves, at least. The important thing is to believe in it for all living things, then you're on to something," said the turkey.

To himself, Pancho said, "turkeys are much smarter than I ever knew." He watched the soft brown and gold chicks snuggle against their mother's belly.

"I really wish they didn't have those guns," Sabo said. She hated loud noises. "It shouldn't be allowed."

"That's part of the liberty, and they could be right, they may need them. I just wish they'd point them in the right direction." And that said, the turkey turned to hustle her small family down the hill.

"Wait, please wait," called Pancho. "We haven't really met. I'm Pancho and this is Sabo." Now the dogs' chant had subsided and they were able to talk in a normal tone. "We are a bit off our path. Could you show us the way to the apple tree farm? We were following the river, but got confused at a fork back a ways."

The turkey started chuckling. "The wind fooled you? It's always changing direction — confuses everyone. When it blows upstream it makes the river look like it's flowing backwards."

She shook her head slowly, side to side, and the loose red skin under her beak swayed hypnotically. "But if you look closely at the river you can see the current underneath the surface. It's too strong to be changed by the wind." The turkey cocked her head to one side as if to size up the pig and the cat. "Apple farm? I think you mean the old Circle H. The river flows right through that place. Well, you could go back and follow the branch to the fork, but actually it would be quicker to follow the kennel fence. The Circle H is right next to the dog kennels." The mother took a few more steps down hill, following her eager chicks. Then she glanced back and said, "They call me Emma. I'll be seeing you around. And don't worry so much about the dogs, they're not really the enemy."

Pancho and Sabo watched Emma and her chicks waddle off into the underbrush, then turned to face the kennel fence. Despite the turkey's calming advise about the shepherds, the pig and cat chose a more difficult but emotionally comfortable path a few hundred feet from the chain link barrier.

"No sense being seen or smelled if we don't have to," Pancho said, and Sabo quite agreed. Keeping the fence in view, they walked through tall grass that seemed dry and crackly for the time of year. "It's strange such a desert-like terrain could be next to such a fertile one," thought Pancho, and his stomach growled as he pictured the fruit trees of the nearby farm. "I hope we really are close," he mumbled to himself as they began to climb a hill.

Then they noticed the dogs' fence ended on the hill crest. Exchanging grins they sped up their climb and soon were looking down to the green meadow, the fruit orchard, the pond, and there lay the river, flowing in just as it was meant to! As he huffed his way down the hill trying to keep up with an agile feline, Pancho made a mental note about the tricky nature of the wind—Always check for the true current—as he squeezed under the wooden crossbeam of the fence and raced Sabo to the fallen apples.

10

nwinding in the apple shade of the orchard, munching fruit, Sabo's black fur shining like a bluish ball where she lay curled in the sunlight, Pancho sighed the contented sigh of home and safety.

"But you're not home," he reminded himself, "just a visitor here." Still, the smile would not leave his snout as he gazed at the greenery for signs of Goldie. From the corner of his eye he saw something dart behind a pear tree and he squinted his pig eyes to see in the dappled light, but he saw nothing moving now and he was much too comfortable to get up and investigate. "After a little rest we'll walk to the pond," he mumbled, "see who's there..." and closed his eyes.

Cats are well known for their napping ability, put pigs are a close second. Pancho was not only a good napper, but an excellent snorer as well. The fruit quivered on the branches above his head as the growling sounds of a sleeping pig echoed through the orchard announcing to the whole farm the presence of the visitors. Pancho and Sabo slept for most of the afternoon. Sabo kicked her legs as she dreamed of chasing mice (just for fun of course) through the meadow of camomile. And Pancho dreamed he was being fed apples by a pink, plump sow he once met, many years ago, at a 4-H competition. He was just getting to his favorite part (of his favorite dream) where he gets to explain the wonderful plan he had devised, to the amazement of his female companion, when a harsh hissing in his ear jarred him awake.

"Wake up!" Sabo gave a little scratch for emphasis and Pancho bolted upright to see a crowd of animals encircling them. Pancho searched the faces for a golden retriever, but Goldie was not there.

In the front a black sheep and a white, aging goat stood scowling. Pancho grinned and extended his foot in greeting. "Hello, I'm Pancho and this is my friend Sabo." The cat gave a sheepish grin, if that is possible, and backed up a step.

"We're friends of Goldie," Pancho looked at the black sheep for approval, "and also Carlos and Juanita," he added hopefully, to the goat.

The goat took a step toward Pancho and brayed, "and just where are Carlos and Juanita? We haven't seen them for days. What have you done with them?" He stared right into Pancho's eyes and caught him off-guard. For once, Pancho was speechless. "Won't talk, eh?" the goat turned to the crowd and announced, "Police Agents!" Some of the others gasped as the black sheep moved forward and looked at Sabo. "What do you know about this?"

The cat found her tongue. "We are forest protectors from Cave Camp. Carlos and Juanita are there at Cave Camp."

The big ball of black wool turned around to face his audience. "Spies, from Cave Camp," he spit out.

"No, we're not," Pancho shouted back, "and we're not police agents. We're friends and we were invited by Goldie."

"Very convenient," cried the goat. "Goldie isn't here right now."

Across the meadow, at a gallop, came a light brown Jersey cow led by a frantic duck. "Oh, for Pete's sake!" she huffed loudly before she had quite arrived. The goat and sheep stepped back into the crowd. As the cow approached the orchard she slowed to a stately walk and looked over the situation. Everyone stood in silence. "What's going on Bob?" she asked the black sheep.

Bob did not meet her gaze, but instead stared accusingly at Pancho. "They're spies from Cave Camp."

"Or police agents," chimed in the goat.

The cow turned and looked carefully at Pancho and Sabo. "Are you spies or police agents?" she asked in a serious voice.

"No!" the pig and cat screamed together.

The cow turned to the crowd of animals and said, "They say they're not police agents or spies."

The crowd of animals began to wander off but the goat and Bob the black sheep stayed to argue. "Of course they say they're not spies!" The goat and sheep rolled their eyes at each other.

Pancho explained again, "We're friends of Goldie and Carlos and Juanita."

"Where are Carlos and Juanita?" The goat jumped forward at Pancho as he spoke.

"Fighting for the forest at Cave Camp." Pancho directed his reply to the cow who turned to the goat and said:

"You know they went to Cave Camp. What's the matter with you, you old goat?"

The goat mumbled "sympathizer" under his breath and turned away.

"Goldie will be back soon," the cow said to all the interested animals. "If they are Goldie's friends we should treat them kindly until she returns." She looked at the sheep. "You have pretty strange friends, Bob, but we don't accuse them of things when you aren't around." Bob grumbled and said something about it being very unnatural for a cat and a pig to be traveling together, then he walked off in the opposite direction of the goat.

"Those two never agree on anything, except when they decide someone is a spy." The cow smiled and watched the sheep and goat walk their separate ways. "It's one of their big joys in life," and she chuckled like she had just separated two little calves from a squabble. Pancho felt more like he and Sabo barely escaped a lynching.

"They're really harmless, no one listens to them when they talk like that. Come on now, it's Pot-Luck time! Are you hungry?"

The soothing moo of her voice and her soft brown eyes had put even the nervous cat at ease and Pancho answered for them both: "Always!" and they headed through the meadow toward the barn.

Even though the cow was ambling along, the cat and pig had to move at double-time to keep up with her. Pancho noticed, from his rear view vantage point, a brand burned into her back flank: Circle H.

"Excuse me," Pancho started.

Rosy the cow turned and smiled at them, "my name is Rosy, I'm sorry I forgot my manners."

"Pancho and Sabo, pleased to meet you," said the pig. "Rosy, I couldn't help but notice that barbaric brand. Certainly you don't brand on this farm?"

"Oh, not anymore," she said as she looked at the burn mark, "I almost forgot it was there. When I was younger I thought of changing it to a flower or some other design, but now, I don't know, it's like history." The cow started walking again, but slowed her pace for the smaller animals. "We heard about what happened at the action last night."

Pancho and Sabo exchanged looks of surprise.

"Birds," Rosy continued, "can't wait to tell whatever they know." She hung her head down to say, "we are all very sorry for your losses."

"Thank you," said Pancho.

"It wasn't worth it," said Sabo, thinking of it for the first time in hours.

"Oh, don't ever say that," said Rosy. "It's a vital cause. In fact, it's worth everything. And I think your fallen friends knew that."

It surprised Pancho to hear such militant talk from an old cow. He replied, "Why don't you join the forest protectors if you feel so strongly."

"Well, I'm an old farm animal, probably not much good in the wild, more trouble than I'm worth," she chuckled. "Besides, I'm sort of a farm protector."

Looking around at the peaceful meadow bathed in pink twilight Pancho could see why she would say that. "But does the farm need protecting? Is it threatened?"

"I think so, we can see it coming," she brightened, "but not tonight! Here we are at the barn and just in time for Pot Luck."

The barn had been red many years ago, but had peeled and chipped to a weathered grey. The wide doors were propped open and Pancho could see all sorts of animals inside scurrying and chattering as they prepared the supper. Hay was spread on the barn floor and bales were used as tables. All kinds of food were piled high in pails and baskets, set out buffet-style, all you can eat. Pancho and Sabo held their breaths at the sight of such bounty. After a diet of acorns, this looked fit for ... "hungry animals, who have had a hard journey!" Pancho finished his thought, and they cautiously entered the feasting hall.

Lanterns were hung from rafters to light the food tables and the animals lined up starting at the salad. Pancho felt the dozens of eyes watching him and Sabo. "When do you think Goldie will be back?" he asked Rosy.

"Soon, she's just next door at the dairy. She won't miss Pot Luck. Come on, fill your plates," encouraged the cow. And they did; not exactly plates but big cabbage leaves, piled high with grains and vegetables, fruits and even honey. Cleanup would be easy when they finished: they would eat the dishes.

Rosy knelt in the straw to eat. Pancho sat next to her on a hay bale with Sabo at his feet. Pancho, as usual, finished first and began to ask questions. "What's at the dairy?"

Rosy replied, between mouthfuls, "They have a service on Sundays that Goldie and some of the others enjoy."

"I would think you would go, I mean since it's a dairy, with other cows and all." Pancho could not imagine what cows might have to speak about that would be of interest to a dog.

"I guess I'm just not a joiner," said Rosy. "Help yourselves to seconds; the line is empty."

Just as Pancho got up for more, Goldie came into the barn, smiling blissfully. She said hello to several animals on her way to the buffet and almost bumped into Pancho as he got more corn.

"Pancho! How nice of you to come back to visit." Goldie seemed far away and dreamy.

"I'm glad you're back too," said Pancho, not sure she was completely back.

"It was such an inspirational afternoon," Goldie sighed. "The Sacred Cow talked for hours and then we sat in silence and chewed cud. I can't chew cud, but I'm working on it," she said proudly. "You really should come next Sunday and hear her talk, she's so peaceful."

"Well, perhaps," Pancho didn't think it was his sort of event so he switched subjects. "Did you hear about last night and the forest action?"

Goldie nodded, and Pancho continued. "Carlos and Juanita are fine, don't worry, but it was so upsetting for... for Sabo..." he whispered the cat's name and tilted his head in her direction, "that we wondered if we could stay here, at least for a while."

"Hey, move on, you're holding up the line!"

Pancho turned to see two young German shepherds elbowing their way to the food. Goldie and Pancho filled leaves and went back to Rosy and Sabo, who were talking horticulture.

"I think those dogs are from the kennel. Look at their fur." Pancho referred to a strange style of clipping he had noticed earlier on the marching dogs.

"Yes," said Rosy, "they are our neighbors and they are invited to Pot Luck. They always bring something." Pancho remembered an unappetizing metal bowl of dried kibble at the end of the buffet.

"The dairy cows are invited too, but they fast on Sundays."

"Those dogs have guns," Pancho said in alarm. "How did they get out of that fence?"

"They have a tunnel to get out," said Goldie. "The dogs have a lot of speakers, too. Maybe you would be more interested in them."

Pancho looked at Rosy. "I guess I'm just not a joiner," he said.

Goldie shrugged, "it never hurts to listen, sometimes you learn something." With that she lifted her paw and signalled the two shepherds with their leaves of chow to join them. As the young dogs headed toward them Pancho felt sick. Sabo quietly moved to a barrel behind Rosy and checked her escape routes.

The dogs sat down and began tearing into their food. "Pancho, this is Hans and Kurt." The dogs nodded at their names, but kept chewing. Goldie ventured further. "Pancho has some questions about your kennel. Could you answer them for him?"

"Sure, what do you want to know?" The answer was direct, but not unfriendly.

"Well, I've heard you are unhappy at your kennel," he thought this was a tactful way to begin.

Kurt continued for him. "And you want to know why any dog would be unhappy locked up, over-crowded, too little to eat, cruel owners?" The dogs started laughing at their in-jokes.

"So why don't you leave?" asked Pancho.

"It's our kennel. We were born there. Those poodles weren't born there," Kurt began to froth at the mouth.

Hans snapped, "A few years ago everyone wanted shepherds. We worked as guards and police dogs and even pets. Demand was high and the breeders overbred. But electronic alarms really cut out the guard dog market and the pet market shifted mostly to ... cats." His eyes landed on Sabo and her fur bristled. "The owners of the kennel claim they're broke. They said they needed to restructure," mouthing the last word like it was covered with nails. "So we get shoved over to make room for some fancy little poodles. Well guess what, they aren't selling either!" Hans paused to swallow the rest of his plate and in a lively tone asked, "What's for dessert?"

"Pies, I think," said Rosy.

"Great," the dogs were looking at the line forming for dessert and wondering if they had answered enough questions.

"What happens if the owners go broke and go out of business?" Pancho asked.

"We don't know and we don't care!" flipped Hans.

"But really," Pancho said. "I mean, what happens to you?"

There was silence for a moment; even Goldie leaned in closer as Pancho continued. "Who do the owners owe the money to? Because they will own the kennel."

"Bankers," said Kurt.

"The corporation," said Rosy.

"What does a corporation look like?" said Hans, who did not remember ever seeing a corporation.

"It's hard to say," said Rosy, looking at Pancho for support.

"They're very tricky and always changing shapes, so it's very hard to tell what you're dealing with," the pig improvised.

"So how can you fight them?" Kurt asked. "You know we've got guns!"

Pancho bit his lower lip and shook his head. "I don't know." He looked at Goldie and Rosy and they shook their heads, too.

"We'll fight that corporation, no matter how big it is, won't we Kurt?" and Hans headed to the dessert table, but Kurt had lost his appetite.

Sabo started up a conversation with a rabbit named Fluff and began telling about the adventurous life of a forest protector. Soon a small group had gathered to hear her talk of bravery and tragedy. As she told the part about John Deer and how he died, most of the listeners were sure they had seen him when he visited their farm. They were a wonderful audience, laughing and crying at all the right parts. Sabo began to feel better for the telling.

After supper the animals cleared the food away and the goats and colts re-arranged the hay bales, clearing the center of the barn. At one end near the stables stood a platform. Pancho smiled as several animals with homemade instruments climbed onto the stage. "Are we going to have music?" he asked Rosy.

"Sure, and singing and dancing," she answered, to his delight. He had heard no real music for a long time, not counting the drums and coyotes at Cave Camp. There were, of course, the wash-tub and the wash-board. Also jugs to blow, bells to clang, many makeshift percussion instruments from barrels to pails, and several flutes made from pond reeds. Pancho was most impressed with the clever use of gourds: shakers and maracas, naturally, but also a carved out lute-like instrument from a single gourd, dried and strung with wire. When strummed it could be a guitar. When bowed (if you closed your eyes and pretended) it might be a fiddle!

The band grew and grew until almost all of the animals had crowded on stage. After quite a bit of shifting and shoving they were ready to go.

"They always start with the same song," Rosy leaned over to explain to the pig. "It saves arguments. They argue over the second number." She laughed. The orchestra started in screeches and scratches to play:

Old Margaret had a farm
E I E I O

It was the long version with every possible animal included with their own verse. Those who didn't have an instrument clapped or danced or stamped the ground. And just as Rosy predicted, after the final EIEIO, the arguments began over the second tune. "Old Grey Mare" won out with "Turkey in the Straw" next.

"This is great fun," Pancho said, turning to talk with Goldie. Suddenly his eyes were magnetized. There on the floor danced the most perfect, pink, plump sow he had ever seen. She had a chain of daisies around her neck and the cutest little snout; turned up and moist. It was love at first sight. Pancho reached back and recurled his tail, then with his most charming smile on his lips, he glided over to her side.

"How do you do?" Pancho bowed just a bit. "May I have this dance?" The sow looked around and then answered "Why not?"

Pancho felt that pigs could fly that night. The band played "It's Only Puppy Love," as he took her foot to lead her to the dance floor.

"I'm called Pancho," he said.

"Suzy," was her answer.

Pancho turned the name over in his mind. 'Suzy,' what a beautiful name for a beautiful creature. He stared into her little eyes as they swayed to music. He nibbled at her ear during the slow parts and felt the warmth of her body when they tangoed. This seemed the most magical night of his life. This must be the one sow in the world for him. When the band took a break they walked out to the barnyard for some air.

"Suzy," Pancho was almost speechless, "I've never felt like this before." His heart bared itself before her beauty. "I love you, I want to be with you forever."

Suzy stared at him blankly.

"I know it's very sudden," Pancho explained, "but when you know something's right..."

Suzy put her head down and kicked in the dirt with her foot.

"Have I upset you? I'm sorry Suzy, but please tell me you feel the same way." Pancho was on one knee holding her little foot between his large trotters.

Suzy removed her foot from his grasp. "Sorry, Pancho, you seem very nice, but..." she shrugged and the daisy chain slipped down on one shoulder. "I'm not into boars."

Pancho felt like he had been kicked in the stomach. "What do you mean, Suzy?"

"I don't date boars. I like sows." She turned to leave. "Nothing personal," she said over the daisy shoulder. "Nice to meet you." And she disappeared into the night.

Pancho stood in the darkness. He had always been one to control his emotions, but tonight he had let them control him, and they were not done yet. His heart ached, his head throbbed, his feet hurt and his eyes stung as they filled with tears. "This world is a mess, my life is pointless and I'm totally confused!" Pancho exclaimed to the moon. He sank down onto the ground and held his head in his forefeet. He prepared himself for a good cry, and felt he deserved one, when he started laughing, for no reason at all. It started as a giggle and progressed towards a chuckle. Soon he was rolling on the dusty barnyard, bent over in belly-laughs. Everything he thought of struck him as humorous. Dogs with guns, now that was truly funny. Corporations destroying the forest, hysterical. But especially a silly pig who took himself too seriously and thought he could change things. The laughter carried almost as well as the snoring, and soon Sabo, Goldie, Rosy and several others (including Bob the black sheep) had come to see what was so funny.

Goldie moved closer to the rolling pig and put a paw on his belly. "Pancho, are you okay?"

"What's so funny," Sabo asked.

"I am," Pancho snorted as he laughed. "I'm incredibly funny and so are you." With that he sat up against a fence post and giggled to himself.

"He's crazy," Bob pronounced.

"He is not!" Sabo loudly defended her pal. "Are you Pancho?" she added, a little less confidently.

"Oh yes, I definitely think so!" said the pig and started laughing so hard tears were running down his face. He turned to Goldie who had been holding herself back and then she no longer could. Giggles are usually contagious, especially pig giggles. Soon Rosy and Sabo had caught them too. Before long the kids and colts were tickling each other and the barnyard was turning into a free-for-all of laughter.

Bob was not amused. "Someone must have spiked the punch, maybe with loco weed," he mumbled to himself, and made some notes in a little book he carried with him. But everyone else had moved outside, instruments and all, to get in on the fun.

Pancho wore himself out with laughter and almost fell asleep in the yard, but Goldie led him to the guest stall in the barn. There he stretched out, and Sabo curled up, until morning.

11

By the time the pig opened his eyes the morning was mostly spent. The artificial darkness of the barn had allowed him to sleep through the breakfast call. He only awoke when he heard the mule raking the straw in the stables. Pancho noticed Sabo had left the little round nest she had slept in. He stood up, stretched his back and grunted a wake up yawn.

Jethro, an older grayish mule, poked his head around the wooden partition. "Oh, it's you, I didn't know anyone was in here," he said, partly to himself, and went on raking.

"I guess I overslept." Pancho said, rubbing his eyes, embarrassed.

"Well, you had quite a night, or so it seemed." Jethro leaned on the rake and chuckled. "What were you laughing at, anyway?"

The pig tried to recall his thoughts of the previous evening. "I guess sometimes you've just got to laugh or cry," he finally said. "Last night was laugh. But, you know, today I feel great. Much lighter!" Pancho felt glad to say it was true. He took a few deep breaths. "Yes, I've got to stop taking things so seriously." He smiled at the mule, who still stood leaning on the rake.

"Well, that's nice." Jethro slowly drawled and paused, still looking at Pancho. Finally he continued: "I'd like to clean this stall, if you don't mind."

"Oh, of course, sorry." Pancho moved out of the way as the mule began to rake the flattened straw bed he had just vacated. "Is this your job?" Pancho asked as he watched Jethro rake.

"I guess," the mule said, getting every last straw from the corners. "I'm the one who likes it clean, so it's something I do." He moved the hay into the big pile in the center of the room.

"And I'm good at it." He smiled at the bare stall floor and moved to the next.

Suddenly Pancho remembered his promise to water the corn. "I think I'll go check out the day. Nice meeting you."

The mule nodded as he raked, "same to you."

Pancho pushed open the big wooden door and put up a foot to shade his eyes. The sky was the color of cornflowers and the clouds looked like ... Poodles? He wondered where everyone was; he had never received a formal tour, and now set out giving himself one.

To the right of the barn were many smaller structures: chicken coops, rabbit hutches, goat sheds, pig pens, and some other little homemade houses Pancho could not identify. "That looks like Goldie's house." He looked at the typical doghouse of wood with an arched door. In front and on the sides flowers climbed to the roof. Then he looked closer at the other homes. Each was planted, painted and decorated to suit its inhabitants. Pancho felt drawn to the pig's house and noticed how carefully it was designed. A shed offered protection from the elements; the troughs were carved and painted. The mud bath was large and soft-looking, confined to one section of the pen, with its edge defined by smooth grey stones. On the other side were hay bales and sweet-smelling lavender had been sprinkled on the hard, swept-dirt floor.

Staring at the empty pen he thought of Suzy. "We could have been so happy here," he sighed. "But, alas, it wasn't meant to be!" Pancho walked around the barn toward a small ramshackle building. As he came nearer, he heard the sound of machinery clanking. The windows were covered and the door shut tight, but Pancho could sniff out who was inside.

"I smell wool, I bet it's Bob, the black sheep." Pancho stood for a minute deciding whether to knock. He had just decided to leave, not wanting to spoil his wonderful day with unpleasantness, when the old goat came racing toward him, head in ramming position and bleating loudly: "Now I've caught you! Sneaking around our shed! I knew you were a spy!"

The door began unlocking from inside and finally flew open. "What's going on, Gruff?" asked the sheep. "It's not your turn yet."

"I caught him spying and it is too my turn." It seemed they did not know what to fight about.

"This is one of your tricks, Gruff. Well, I'm not falling for it!" Bob started to shut the door but the goat got his hoof in first.

"It's my turn. It's noon. And he was snooping around here. Who knows what he saw!"

The attention shifted to the pig again. Both sheep and goat looked at him with squinty eyes. "What did you see?" Bob asked, ominously.

"Nothing!" Pancho couldn't believe these two. "The door was locked and blinds were closed. I only heard..." He wished he had not said that!

"What did you hear?" The goat leaned over the pig with threatening body language, but the smell was the real danger.

Pancho backed up. "I don't know. A machine. Maybe a pump."

"Ha!" Gruff and Bob exchanged a knowing glance. "You thought you heard a pump! Well, you certainly aren't a very good spy, are you? It's not a pump at all, it's a printing press."

Bob turned at Gruff in a rage. "Why did you tell him we have a printing press? He thought it was a pump. He would go back to his camp and tell that we have a pump and they would have false information, but now he knows. We'll have to kill him."

"You kill him," said the goat. "It's my turn, so let me in." He was pushing on the door but the black wool ball pushed just as hard to keep him out.

"It's not time yet. You came five minutes early and we wasted time on this pig. I get five more minutes."

While they seemed occupied Pancho took the opportunity to slip away. He ran to the far side of the barn, through a grove of oaks to a driveway leading up to twin stone pillars. Pancho checked to see if anyone followed, and when he saw it was safe he leaned up against a wrought-iron gate between the pillars, catching his breath. Looking up he saw, in metal above the gate, the Circle H.

"This must be the front entrance," he noted. It looked quite unkept compared to the areas he had visited so far. Weeds were growing around the gate, indicating it had not opened for some time. A padlock and chain locked the metal crossbeams of the gate. Pancho could see a sign on the stone pillar. He squeezed his belly under the gate to get a better look. It read:

FARM AUCTION
LAND, EQUIPMENT, LIVESTOCK
SAT. JUNE 10, 8 AM
EVERYTHING MUST GO

Pancho read it three times. He did not know when June 10 was, having no need for dates in the forest, but he thought it would be soon. "I wonder if the animals know about this. Some can read, I know." Pancho's lighter, less serious side now started to melt away. He squeezed back to the farm side and took off looking for the others. The pig trotted down the driveway and past an old yellow farm house that must have been Margaret's, he deduced. He continued through the back yard and past a well-tended herb garden until he could see the farm land below.

Many of the animals were taking a noon break and snacking right off the vines. Pancho had missed breakfast and felt his stomach tug in the direction of the corn cobs, but his head kept him looking for a familiar face. And there stood Rosy with her new buddy Sabo sitting down near the potatoes.

"Pancho! Well, it's about time! Do you feel better today?" Rosy asked in her comforting tone.

"Ah, yes, and no," Pancho answered. "I mean, I did feel great, but..." he sat down next to the cow and cat, "did you know about the auction?"

The cow looked confused. Pancho continued: "there's a sign about it posted on the front pillar. The farm and everything on it, including the animals, is going on the block on June 10th. What's today's date?"

Rosy sighed and shook her head so hard the bell around her neck rang. "I'm not very surprised, I guess, I knew it was too good to last."

"What is the date?" Pancho looked from cow to cat in desperation.

"I don't know. Yesterday was Sunday, today is Monday." Sabo said, "I think it's this week." She was counting on her paws. "It must be this Saturday."

"I think we need a meeting," said Rosy in a serious tone. "Might as well!"

"Yes!" Pancho's blood-pressure rose. "Not a minute to lose."
Rosy shook her head hard and the bell clanged loudly. Animals stopped their work and play and they quieted to hear the announcement. "Meeting at the pond, right now." Rosy's voice carried better than Pancho would have expected. "Pass the word!"

Soon the animals were chirping and clucking, bleating and neighing the message till the whole farm was on its way to the pond. Even Bob and Gruff were arguing their way towards the meeting.

They saw Pancho, who smiled and waved as he stood by Rosy. She cautioned them all: "Not now!" and they obeyed. Goldie came slower than the others since she was caring for the chicks and had to herd her little fuzzy flock down the hill to the pond and not lose any along the way. Pancho grabbed an ear of corn on his way to the pond and sat munching seriously as the meeting came to order.

Rosy asked, "whose turn is it to run the meeting?" This caused a bit of confusion before a fat goose wadded up to the rock serving as a podium.

"I get to be time keeper," cried a brown lamb who had won the einy meiny miney mo game.

Pancho looked at Rosy, "this is supposed to be serious."

"I know, it is, but we always let a young one keep time."

Rosy rang the bell and the goose tapped a stick on the rock. "Okay, let's begin with a song!" She honked, obviously proud to be in charge. Paws and hooves went up from the crowd and titles were shouted out.

Pancho rolled his eyes and pleaded to Rosy, who shrugged and said, "one song, what could it hurt?" She joined the others in an oddly morbid choice: "There Was an Old Woman Who Swallowed a Fly." It had become a big favorite since it had been revised to mention all the types of animal in attendance.

Without musical accompaniment the song sounded a bit flat, sharp, and non-rhythmic, but when they reached the last line — "There was an old woman who swallowed a horse, she died of course" — the whole meadow burst into applause. Pancho decided it was not so inappropriate after all.

While the animals started lobbying for the next song, Rosy whispered something to the goose who raised her eyebrows at

Pancho and tapped her stick. "It seems that the pig has something to say," she announced unceremoniously, and a groan arose from the crowd.

At center stage Pancho suddenly had stage fright. But he spurted out, "I'm just visiting here and don't know you well, but I was looking around the farm today..."

"Spying!" screamed Gruff from the far back.

"No, I was just looking..."

The goose had to tap her stick so hard on the rock that it snapped to settle the mumbling animals. "The pig has the floor!" the goose announced, handing the stick to Pancho. "And the talking stick."

Attention was immediately directed to the flustered Pancho, so he began again. "There is a sign on the stone pillar that says there is to be a farm auction here. The sign says they will sell land, equipment and livestock, and that means you, Saturday June 10th at 8 A.M."

There was silence. You could not even hear breathing. The very pond water lay still. "We think that June 10th is this Saturday." He took a deep breath, then realized that was all he had to say. He handed the stick back to the goose.

The poor goose did not know how to proceed and stood silently holding the stick as the news sunk into the animals.

"Time!" announced the lamb, who enjoyed her chance to help, and it did snap the goose from her reverie. "Yes, time is of the essence," she said, not quite sure what that meant, but it sounded official. Then a wooly black hoof waved in the air.

"Yes, Bob."

"I want the pig to show me the sign," Bob said slowly and seriously.

"I want to see it too," Gruff was not going to be left out.

All the animals wanted to see for themselves and Pancho walked with them to the front gate.

"It's true we never go up here," said the goose. "It may have been there a long time."

Rosy nodded solemnly. Not all the animals could squeeze under the gate and of those who could, not all could read. But enough saw and enough read to see that it was true.

Finally, Goldie spoke. "I don't know what to do, but maybe we can each think about this as we finish our chores, and then have a meeting after dinner in the barn."

Others seemed to think that was a good idea and went back to work immediately. Pancho thought they worked harder than before, maybe out of frustration. After watering the corn as he had promised, and helping to pick pears, which he always enjoyed doing, he wandered towards the barn. On the way Gruff and Bob intercepted him. "Oh great, now what," thought Pancho.

The goat approached. "You had better not be a spy," he warned.

Bob interrupted. "We know all about you and that farm of yours," he said. "Your own comrades accuse you of treason, you were run out!" He paused. "But I know they lie about many things, and we don't like what's going on up there," again he paused and Gruff broke in.

"There seems to be a sign, but who put it there? You saw it first. Don't you find that suspicious? We're keeping an eye on you!" And he quivered so hard his little beard shook.

"Okay, keep your eye on me," Pancho said, frustrated. "I'm not a spy. I just don't want you to lose this wonderful farm to humans!" And with that he trotted into the barn, leaving the sheep and goat talking in low tones.

Jethro arranged a bouquet of sweetpeas in an old crock. Pancho noticed the barn smelled better than any barn he had been in. "You certainly keep this place clean," he complimented the mule, who seemed pleased.

"It helps that most of the animals sleep outside in their own homes when the weather is nice. But in the rainy season, well, it's a different story." Jethro smiled for a second and then fell serious again. "So, Pancho, what are we going to do about this auction thing?"

Pancho sat on a hay bale. He felt old and tired and out of ideas. Jethro handed him some hot tea in an old tin mug. "It's camomile, it calms the nerves."

"Thanks, I can use it." Pancho took a sip. The mule dusted some cobwebs from the rafters, then sat next to the pig.

"You've had some experience in this kind of..." the mule searched for the right term, "situation. How did your farm handle it?"

Pancho breathed the steam from the tea cup and sighed. "We fought," he said somberly.

"And you won," Jethro reminded him.

"Yes, we won and we lost, too," the pig recalled the rebellion. "It's a big decision. I'm sick of violence, but sometimes..." he let it rest.

The mule got himself some tea and refilled the pig's half-empty cup. "Maybe there's another way," said Jethro optimistically.

"Let's hope so." Pancho patted the mule's shoulder as they sat in silence, sipping their tea. When they were finished Pancho helped set-up the barn for the night's important meeting. The mule put the bales in a circle and Pancho found an old door and some brown butcher paper, which he tacked up "for plans," he explained to Jethro. He found a yellow pencil which just needed a little sharpening and a pen with no cap. Even though this was not really his farm and it was a serious occasion, Pancho found himself humming a tune as he worked. He really liked planning meetings.

"Are you hungry, Pancho?" Jethro asked when they finished.

"Of course," Pancho looked around. "Where's dinner?"

"Well, we don't always eat together, different folks like different foods," the mule gestured to his trough. "My favorite is oats, you're welcome to join me, but you might prefer to go to the garden and get what you like."

"I think I'll do that," Pancho replied. He liked oats, but really loved the fresh corn he sampled at lunch and maybe wanted a few apples for desert. He trotted out to the farmland as the sun got low behind the hilltop. Pancho headed straight for the corn, which had grown quite high for early in June, he thought, selecting the largest ears he could find.

"Hello, Pancho," the voice stabbed him like a dagger.

"Hello, Suzy," he stuttered, stumbling and dropping his corn. As he scrambled to pick the ears up, Suzy put down her basket to help.

"Hey, I'm sorry we got our signals crossed last night."

"That's okay, no big deal."

"Friends?" She extended her right foot.

"Sure, friends," Pancho reached out and shook trotters, but avoided her eyes.

"Hey, want to come for dinner? I'm cooking."

Boy, Suzy did know the way to a pig's heart. "Sure, why not." Pancho had been lonely for some pig company. Together they gathered vegetables for stew and some fruit for afterwards.

"How many pigs are there on this farm?"

"Three," Suzy replied, "all sows."

"No boars?"

"Only you," she teased.

Pancho proceeded with caution. "Why only sows?"

"Well, my dad was the only boar, but he died last year," she said sadly.

"I'm so sorry," said Pancho and decided he had asked enough questions as they approached the pen.

"Mom, this is Pancho. I invited him to eat with us."

"Welcome to our pen." The large spotted sow smiled at Pancho. "I was hoping you'd stop by." She ushered him over to the mud bath and, following the age-old custom of pig etiquette, Pancho nosed his way in.

"Ah, this is wonderful, it's been so long since I've had a real wallow." He felt the soft mud caress his body. "Won't you be joining me?" he asked the sow.

"Just got out, myself," Suzy's mom answered.

"And I'm getting dinner right now. Please make yourself at home." Suzy said as she husked corn busily. As Pancho rolled around in the sticky bath the old sow sat patiently by and watched.

Pancho opened polite conversation: "Suzy told me about your husband. I'm very sorry, mam."

"Please call me Martha," she smiled at the formality. "Yes, we miss George very much. You know he was a great admirer of your farm, we both were, in the beginning." Her eyes went far away as she reminisced. "When we were young, we talked of going there, joining your farm, before all the problems." She looked back at her muddy house guest. "You fellows sure gave pigs a bad name."

Pancho suddenly felt defensive. It seemed unfair to be judged from the outside. His face flushed red, but he held his tongue until his temper cooled. Martha could see his anger. "I knew the intentions were good, but that's what power does," she shrugged it off, "and the other animals are as much to blame. They handed over the responsibility, so you took it."

Pancho sank into the mud until only his snout showed. In the cool darkness his mind whirled. "Everyone thinks it was fun to make all the decisions and shoulder all the problems. I worried all the time about the welfare of that farm. I had no family, no life of my own." He wiggled deeper into the mud. "Not until I was run off did I finally have a moment to think my own thoughts. It was probably the luckiest day of my life."

There in the mud Pancho finally let go of his old farm. At the bottom of the wallow he dropped his plans, his fears, his guilt and all the weight of his former comrades' expectations. "I still care," he whispered to himself, "but don't have the answers for everyone. I'm not sure I even have my own answers." Then he slowly climbed out of the mud bath. After rolling in the dust to dry off he felt like a new pig. No one ever knew how much he left in the mud that day.

"Dinner," Suzy called over in his direction. Martha was setting the trough for four. Pancho looked around for the other sow. "Sally's late again," Suzy said, shaking her pretty head. "she's a school teacher and sometimes she stays late to help her students with their reading."

Pancho carefully phrased his question. "Is Sally your ... friend?"

Suzy breezed right past his innuendo. "No, she's my sister."

"Twins," Martha said proudly.

"Oh really," Pancho did not know what to make of this and thought discretion and caution were his best guides, so he changed the subject. "This looks wonderful, Suzy, but shouldn't we wait for..."

"I'm here, I'm here, I'm sorry I made you wait." Sally bustled in, kissed Martha, hugged Suzy, and extended her foot to Pancho. "How do you do?"

She had the same sweet snout as Suzy. He meant it when he said, "My name is Pancho. Very nice to meet you."

With Suzy on one side and Sally on the other, Pancho could hardly eat, but managed anyway. Pigs don't chat much at dinner, they take their food quite seriously, but they always finish quickly, so there's plenty of time for conversation afterwards.

"A delicious meal!"

"Yes, Suzy, very good."

Suzy grinned as she passed out apples and Sally cleaned the trough. Martha sat next to Pancho and said in soft tones, "I hope my discussing your farm earlier didn't bring up bad memories. It's been an interest of ours for a long time. We've learned a lot from watching your farm."

Pancho was intrigued by the last bit. "What have you learned?"

"Well, the power thing, as we were talking about before. That it sort of takes two to tango: no one can take your power if you're not willing to give it."

Martha paused to think and Pancho jumped in. "So how do you stop someone from giving over his or her power to another," he wondered aloud. "And how do you stop someone from taking it?"

Martha laughed at the question. "Well, you don't stop it at all, they do." She paused to think of an example. "Would you follow my orders, just because I say to?"

"No," Pancho answered quickly.

"And would you expect me to follow your orders? Would you even want me to?"

"No way," Pancho said, fresh from his mud bath revelation.

"Why not," Martha waited for the boar's answer with a knowing grin.

"Because I've learned..."

"Exactly! You've learned and what you've learned can be taught. I saw that as I raised my piglets." She gestured to the two lovely creatures giggling in the kitchen area.

"What exactly did you teach them?" Pancho was still a little unclear on what he had learned.

"The joys of self-reliance," she announced. "But I didn't teach them, they taught me."

"So it's natural?" Pancho was skeptical of this new way of looking at things.

"Yes, all of us are born with the ability and inclination toward self-reliance and responsibility. Too bad so many of us get those things taught out of us at a young age."

"So we're taught to surrender our power!" Pancho struggled over this.

"I'm not saying it's always intentional," Martha explained. "Still, someone stands to gain."

"Mom, are you boring Pancho with all your theories?" Sally and Suzy bounded to the rescue, but Pancho replied that he was very interested in this topic.

"But we can't be late for the meeting." Sally was right. The sun dropped low on the horizon; they could see others moving in the direction of the barn.

Pancho followed behind the sows as they walked to the meeting. While the others took their places in the hay-bale circle he stood at the back, looking for Sabo. She had been talking to some rabbits and came when he waved to her. Pancho and Sabo felt they should not speak at the meeting unless asked, since they were only visitors.

When all seats were filled (almost a hundred animals were present by Sabo's count) the meeting began. The goose continued her duties as conductor. She had, however, found herself a new stick and tapped it on the drawing board Pancho had set up. They did not even discuss singing this time.

The goose started simply, "We all know the situation. Does anyone want to talk?"

Looking around the barn for who would start, Pancho worried that no one would.

Finally, Jethro stated, "As I see it, we have two choices, we let them sell us and the farm, or we fight." Then he sat down.

The animals started a murmur which grew to a roar. A fat red hen stood on the hay bale. "Do we have consensus that we won't let the farm go without a fight?"

The goose said, "Show of support," and all the animals raised a paw, hoof, or wing. "Passed!" cried the goose.

She picked up the pencil and wrote on the paper: "#1 We will not let the farm go without a fight."

Pancho leaned down to whisper in Sabo's ear, "This is the fastest meeting I've ever been to. Don't they even need to discuss it?"

"Now," said Madam Goose, "how shall we fight?"

Goldie stood up and said, "I think we must not use violence of any kind."

"I agree," said Rosy.

"It won't work." It was Bob standing now, and Pancho thought that would mean a long argument.

Sally stood up and faced the group. "You might be right, Bob, but it's very important to try every peaceful way before we use violence."

Heads nodded around the circle and Bob shrugged. "Okay, but I still don't think it will work," he said.

Pancho was amazed at how fast Bob gave in to the group, thinking, "Perhaps he's lost many times before. Well, at least he stood up."

Responding to a strong scent behind them, the pig and cat suddenly turned around. There stood Hans and Kurt from the kennel. "Just here to watch the meeting," Kurt whispered to Pancho. "We heard it was important."

Pancho nodded. The goose asked for "approval for all non-violent means to be tried first" and again they consented unanimously. She wrote #2 on the paper.

The meeting continued in this smooth, agreeable way. The animals decided to sit down and block the gate, not letting anyone pass. They would also spread the word about their situation to their neighbors, hoping for support. Committees were formed and Pancho volunteered to help with the flyers, much to the annoyance of Bob and Gruff, who had enough trouble working with each other, let alone with Pancho. But generally everyone seemed happy, even excited.

Two adorable lambs came to the center of the circle. They had written new words for the animals favorite song:

All the animals shared the farm, EIEIO.

It was a big hit; the whole meeting sang it through three times. After that they never used the old words, everyone liked the new ones so much better.

Kurt and Hans left disappointed. "There will be violence, all right," Kurt said, "but the animals will be the victims. As usual."

Pancho and Sabo sat in the corner and shared their thoughts. The reason the meeting went so smoothly and agreeably, the reason the animals were so happy and optimistic, was inexperience. But soon they would have some experience. The pig and cat grasped paw and foot. Pancho looked at Sabo and she said, "I really hope this works."

12

Just before the sun rose, Pancho heard the cock crow. "I won't miss breakfast today!" he told himself. He stretched and looked around for Sabo cat, but she had gone. "Maybe I should start sleeping outside again, like Cave Camp."

Pancho picked his way through the hay bales towards the pinkish light streaming through he cracks of the barn door. Oversleeping seemed like laziness and therefore a character flaw; something he judged harshly in others and felt guilty about himself. A gentle nudge on the doors sent them gliding silently open to reveal the new day. Photographers call it magic hour, when shadows are long and the sun wears rose colored glasses.

Pancho's feet soaked wet with dew as he shuffled towards the meadow. "Where is everybody." He hated being left out. "What can they be doing at dawn?" He came to the corral fence and hopped through a broken rung. "Everything is kept up on this farm but the fences," he noted to himself. On his old farm that was always the first thing fixed. "If those dogs had chased me a day later, that escape hole would have been mended." He loved these convoluted thoughts. "I wouldn't be here today."

Pancho turned this over in his mind and smiled at the irony: it would have been his own order to plug the hole in the fence that would have prevented his own escape. Just then he reached the top of the small knoll and looked down into the meadow. "What in the world is going on down there?" The pig scratched his ear with puzzlement.

At first glance, it appeared to be a flock of sheep being chased around the meadow. First they would run one way, then they would stop. Suddenly, as if one organism, they would run in the opposite direction. Oddly, nothing gave chase. Odder still, when he noticed it: the flock consisted not only of sheep, but of cows and goats, pigs and mules, chickens and, in fact, everyone on the farm. Pancho spotted Goldie right near the center of the crowd. "Now that's something," he shook his head, "sheep herding a dog."

The retriever caught his eye and wagged her tail "good morning" and the pig waived back. Pancho sat on the grassy slope watching the stop and go, twists and turns of the running animals as if he sat in a box seat at the ballet. The choreography was every bit as impressive. Gracefully and powerfully they danced around the pond. A pause, then a sudden dash to the left, revealed a small black member of the corps who missed her cue racing to catch up. "Sabo," Pancho blinked, but the mass of racing creatures engulfed her in an ever-tightening circle. Smaller and smaller, the circle contracted as the running slowed to a walk and then a stop. The animals laughed and clapped as the crowd dispersed.

Pancho noticed another unexpected face, Emma, the wild turkey. She climbed the hill with Goldie, a little out of breath. Pancho trotted down to greet them.

"Good morning!" Pancho slipped the last few feet on the dewy grass and ended up with a very dramatic entrance as he joined the dog and turkey.

"That looks like fun, maybe we should try that too?" laughed the turkey. Goldie grinned her famous grin, then suddenly, on some invisible cue, they both slipped down the wet hill on their backsides, giggling all the way.

Pancho walked carefully down the slippery slope. He was not sure whether he was being made fun of or not. Whatever had gotten into everyone? Had they forgotten the important problems discussed at last night's meeting? He sat on a dry rock near the pond and slowly Emma and Goldie made their way to him. Most of the others had gone off, to breakfast, perhaps. The turkey chicks joined their mother, pecking near the water's edge as the adults talked.

"What was all that about?" Pancho gestured with a leg encompassing the whole meadow.

"Morning exercises," Goldie said, shaking herself to remove the dampness from her coat. "Here they come!" the dog and turkey looked up and Pancho followed their eyes.

The yellowing rays backlit what appeared to be a ferocious cloud traveling towards them, too fast and solid to be mere vapor. The swarm passed over them, then took a wide circling turn. Pancho had seen flocks of birds, or course. Their precision had always been an inspiration, from a military standpoint, but never had he seen a flock like this. Overhead, in aerodynamic acrobatics of heart-stopping beauty, flew every type of bird from the hawk to the hummingbird. Connected to each other as if by invisible threads, they moved as one, spinning, tumbling, divebombing, soaring and gliding.

"Why?" was all the pig could muster.

"Why not?" Emma sighed. "I wish I were young enough to join them."

"Go ahead, get up there," nudged Goldie. "I'll watch the chicks."

"Why not?" The turkey smiled and took a running start, spreading her wings. It took her some circling to catch up, but Pancho could see the moment Emma joined the formation, just as a skater grabs the outreached hand in a game of crack the whip. One minute Emma flew solo, then suddenly she became part of the group. Pancho turned to Goldie, his eyes full of wonder. "I've seen birds fly before, why is this so much more beautiful?"

"I think it's the variety," said the dog. "Have you ever seen a Christmas tree?"

Pancho shook his head, confused.

"We dogs get invited in to human homes more often than pigs," she acknowledged. "The best and most beautiful Christmas trees always have the most variety, all different kinds of ornaments that you wouldn't think would look good together, but somehow when it's all on the same tree, it's amazing. Once we visited someone who had a white tree and it had only red balls," Goldie shrugged. "Speaking as a dog, I've always liked red balls, but somehow it just wasn't as exciting."

Pancho half listened, focussed on the birds. "I could watch this all day. I wish I could fly." He watched the flock split into two groups and begin circling in opposite directions. "How do they know how to do that? When to do it? Who goes where?"

"It's the flocking instinct, or herd mentality," Goldie said, matter of factly.

"Herd mentality," Pancho repeated with disdain. Pigs did not herd together; that kind of activity was for lower animals. Pancho had always thought of himself as an individual, a leader even. So now, perhaps, he agreed that a leader might not be the most desirable thing to be, but at least he must think for himself, stand on his own four feet, be his own pig. The idea of being an anonymous cog in the wheel of some vast machine he was not driving, well, it frightened him. If Pancho hated one thing, and hated it because he feared it, it was not being in control, at least of himself. He wouldn't give up that control to anyone.

But, strangely enough, taking control of others did not bother him. "Because I can be trusted," he thought. "Others, well, who knows where they might be headed, and I could be dragged along into some ... dangerous situation." Pancho stopped watching birds and rolled a pebble in the mud with his foot. He looked at Goldie with squinted eyes. "It that what you were doing in the meadow this morning? Trying to become a herd?"

He punctuated his final word by kicking the pebble into the pond, where it plopped to the mud below, sending continuing circles out to the very edges of the pond. Goldie watched the circles dissipate until the water lay calm and still again. Then, picking up a large stone in her mouth, she flung it into the center of the pond. It fell with a big splash and set off a ripple of several inches growing in all directions until the entire pond had felt the power of the stone. The animals watched in silence as the pond regained its composure.

Goldie chose a tiny pebble and carried it to the far corner of the pond. She let it drop from her mouth into the shallow water. Tiny circles formed where the pebble dropped, spreading in a delicately etched line to the furthest corner of the pond. The dog turned and smiled at Pancho. "This is what we are trying to be," she said.

Pancho grinned back. "Pebbles?"

"No," said Goldie, "the pond!" She gave the pig a nudge with her head, pushing him into the water. Pancho laughed as the golden retriever jumped in after him.

They swam around the pond as the birds tumbled overhead. On the bank of the pond the turkey chicks chirped and tried to follow their babysitters into the water.

"Can turkeys swim?" asked Goldie.

"Well, ducks sure can," said Pancho. "We can help them if they get in over their heads." So the dog and pig helped the little turkeys into the shallow water at the edge of the pond. As youngsters do, they loved splashing each other with water. They were chirping so loud they awakened some ducklings who were napping in the nearby cattails. The ducklings swam over to join the fun as Pancho and Goldie climbed out of the pond to supervise from the bank. The game had turned into a sort of splash-tag; the baby birds were having a grand time.

"I guess turkeys can swim," Pancho said, turning to the dog. "But I still don't understand. You want to be a pond?"

"I don't know how to explain it," Goldie sighed. "Why not just come and try it tomorrow morning."

"No way, it's too scary." Pancho shuddered. "The whole idea gives me the creeps."

"Scary," the dog opened her brown eyes wide and rolled them in disbelief. "It's fun. That's really why we do it. Like a game, and good exercise. The rest is just an interesting side-effect."

The ducklings and chicks had moved into deeper water where they were hidden by some reeds. Like a good sitter Goldie moved to a better vantage point. She looked skyward to check on the birds, but they were nowhere to be seen. "Emma, come on," said the dog. "Today's a busy day."

Pancho remembered his postering duty and also his stomach. "And we haven't even had breakfast yet!"

"I don't eat breakfast," said the dog. "Just one meal a day, but you go ahead."

"Well, just a little something," said Pancho. "I'll bring back some corn for the chicks," and he took off over the hilly part of the meadow, the shortcut to the cornfield. He came back in no time, carrying several ears of sweet corn. Goldie still played lifeguard. The ducklings made little figure eights in the center of the pond. Pancho saw that the ducks were better swimmers than the turkey chicks. "Must be the webbed feet," he thought as he husked the corn and waved the golden ears above his head to call the youngsters to breakfast.

They raced out of the water, stripped the ears clean in minutes, then went back to the pond. Still no mother Emma.

Pancho sat with an anxious Goldie. "Usually I wouldn't mind," she said, "but I'm on the barricade committee and they will need my help."

"Go ahead," Pancho urged her. "I can watch the chicks and Emma will be back soon, I'm sure." Pancho knew that his fellow committee members were not at all missing his input. However, he anxiously wanted a peek at the printing press.

"I can tell you've never been a parent," said the dog. "Emma left her chicks with me and I must stay with them no matter how long that takes. She's counting on me."

"Of course," Pancho nodded. They watched the swimming in silence for a few minutes, then Goldie interrupted.

"Juanita and Carlos," she said suddenly. "We should let them know about the auction. They will want to be here. And we need them."

Pancho agreed. "Maybe a bird could go, if they could find Cave Camp."

"That would be fastest." Goldie gazed the northern sky. "Well, it's about time."

Spiraling toward them in a fancy corkscrew formation, the birds circled the meadow and began landing on the far side of the pond. All except Emma, who swooped down right next to the golden retriever.

"Sorry," the turkey smiled gently, "but it was just so exhilarating."

"It's okay, but really, I have to go." Goldie trotted off, up the hill to the barn. "Bye, see you soon," she barked over her shoulder and disappeared behind a hedge.

"That was amazing," Pancho said to Emma, who was still trying to catch her breath. "I didn't think turkeys could fly."

Emma stopped panting and turned to look him in the eye. "What did you say?" she slowly asked the pig.

"I didn't think, I mean I've always heard that turkeys can't fly." Pancho sensed slippery ground.

"You've always heard? Heard from who?" Emma had her bill almost touching his snout.

Pancho slowly and softly stammered, "Well, everybody says they can't."

"Everybody? Maybe everybody repeats this slander, but only a few stand to profit by spreading this mind control."

Pancho started backing up. Emma's feathers were really ruffled. "What are these?" She extended her wings and tensed them to display every feather.

"Wings," Pancho gulped.

"And what are wings for?"

"To fly. Yes, of course." Pancho searched for words. "I guess what they say is that turkeys can't fly very far, just a few feet."

"That's ridiculous." Emma had puffed up to twice her normal size. "It's the same as when they tell pigs that they can't see in the dark, when you know as well as I that pigs have exceptional night vision. They just don't want the pigs to get any ideas about escaping in the night, because it's the farmers who can't see in the dark. And the farmers can't fly either. But these farmers," she had calmed a bit now, her voice more disgusted than angry, "these farmers make up lies and tell everyone turkeys can't fly and the young chicks hear it and lose their confidence." She turned on Pancho again, "Can you imagine how much confidence it takes even to attempt to fly? It takes amazing bravery and strength and self-confidence to leap from a tree, trusting only in your wings and in the air."

Pancho nodded in accord. He couldn't fathom jumping from a tree and expecting to fly.

"But these farmers, first they told the chickens, 'You can't fly. Better stay in the hen house,' and slowly the chickens believed them. Then the turkeys, and their young chicks were afraid and they believed the farmers' lies. They never flew, and then they told the lie to their own chicks, telling the farmers' lies for them. Farm turkeys never even try to fly, but wild turkeys do it all the time. My chicks will never hear the farmers' terrible slanders. They will grow up strong and confident and they will do whatever they want to do." Emma snorted as she finished her lecture and looked around. "By the way, where are the chicks?"

"Swimming," said Pancho.

"Swimming! In water?" Emma raced to the pond's edge, clearing the reeds that blocked her view.

"Yes, in the pond with the ducks." Pancho hurried down to join the worried mother. "I hope it was okay to let them. I didn't know if turkeys could swim, but I see they are quite good at it."

Emma watched as her chicks played chase with the ducklings. They waved to their mother on the shore and Emma gave a hesitant wave back. Turkey and pig stood and watched the youngsters playing in the warm June morning. Pancho saw Emma wipe her damp eyes with the back of her flight feather. "Emma, what's wrong," Pancho asked.

"Nothing," she said. "I just never knew turkeys could swim." She smiled a proud mom smile.

"Look, all the other birds are gone." Pancho surveyed the meadow. "I was going to ask someone to fly to Cave Camp and tell Juanita and Carlos about the auction."

"I'll go," Emma offered. "I haven't seen Judi since the chicks were born, and Mac and Red ... I really miss those guys."

Pancho thought for a secret camp everybody seemed to know an awful lot about it. Except, hopefully, the humans.

"You can watch the chicks, can't you?" Emma began to do her pre-flight stretches.

"Me!" Pancho mumbled. "I'm supposed to do something. A poster and flyers. And water the corn."

"Two hours max." Emma signalled her chicks to the shore. "I'll be back by lunch." The mother turkey now addressed her three wet fluff balls. "I want you to stay with Pancho until I get back. Do what he says and stay close to him, no matter what."

She directed the last phrase to the largest of the three, if you could call any of them large. Pancho had already noticed that particular chick was more adventurous than the others.

"Keep an eye on Orville. Wilber and Amelia are no trouble at all. Be good. I'll be back soon." With that Emma began her running takeoff. With minimal flapping she lifted her legs and soon disappeared into the tree tops.

The pig surveyed his charges. The little ones were looking him over, too. Pancho thought to himself, "if you want their respect, you must never show fear. I must act like I'm in charge and have a plan." But it was too late. The chicks knew they had a novice babysitter and exchanged their knowing glances. "Okay," said Pancho in a condescending tone, "let's go water the corn."

He turned to lead the way to the garden, but after a few steps he heard the splashing of water and quacking of ducklings. The chicks were back in the pond.

* * *

At the barn the preparations for Saturday were underway. Goldie, Jethro, Rosy and several other large animals had started to build barricades and lookout points. As they were a little unclear on the concept, the structures had taken on an aesthetic, artistic quality. The builders behaved like architects, arguing whether or not to put a stair here or window there.

Quite the opposite at the printing shed: it was all business. The press had many type-styles, but few letters of any one kind or size. This did not seem to bother the sheep and goat as they fought over the text of the flyer, always selecting the smallest letters they had so that longer, more complex sentences could be spelled out. They set aside the largest letters of all the fonts for the headline, which would be decided last.

Some animals had walked next door to the dairy where the Sacred Cow was giving non-violence training.

Chickens, ducks, lambs and other youngsters gathered to stockpile food under the direction of Suzy and Sally. They had turned it into a school project; Sally thought it made a good educational experience.

Sabo and her rabbit friends gathered chains and pieces of rope. Meanwhile Pancho sat and watched the turkey chicks swimming in the pond. Time seemed to crawl for a pig with nothing to do, so Pancho walked the perimeter of the pond, examining the flora and fauna, always keeping half on eye on his charges. The irises were just beginning their bloom with violet and white flags swaying on top of green poles. Clumps of cat-o-nine tails and pampas grass fought for space between the rocks.

Pancho parted some reeds at water's edge to get a better look at a lavender waterlily and found himself staring into the angry eyes of a large mallard. Papa duck was sitting on a clutch of eggs and watching the ducklings from his secret nest.

"I beg your pardon," said Pancho, as startled as the duck. "I wondered who was looking after those ducklings." He was not always the best at small talk. "I'm in charge of those chicks."

"Poults," said the duck.

"I'm sorry, what did you say?" From the duck's angry tone Pancho was not sure if he were being insulted or not.

"Poults," the yellow bill formed the word as clearly as possible. "Not chicks, poults."

"Really?" Pancho raced through his memory. "I've never heard them called poults before."

"Well, that's what they are and what they ought to be called," the duck said adamantly.

"Fine, poults it is!" Pancho shrugged. The two animals sat in silence for a few minutes, which seemed like hours.

"And they're not supposed to be swimming." The duck seemed almost disgusted.

"And why not?" The whole tone of the conversation surprised Pancho, who began to feel a little defensive of the ... poults. "Emma thinks it's okay."

"Emma's crazy. Emma thinks she can fly?"

"Emma can fly." Pancho was getting red in the face.

"Well, she can't swim. Turkeys can't swim and poults can't swim." The duck rested his case.

Pancho could not believe his ears. "But look," he pointed to the splashing poults in the middle of the pond. "They are swimming."

The mallard shut his eyes. "But they shouldn't be." And he shook his head in dismay.

Pancho did not know how to counter this reasoning, or persistence, so they sat for a few more moments of tense silence.

"Shhh," hissed the mallard, spraying Pancho in the face with emphasis.

"I didn't make a sound," the pig whispered back, wiping his snout with his muddy forepaw.

"Well, don't, just listen." They both closed their eyes for focus and yes, above the waterplay of the youngsters could be heard mumbled voices and muffled chuckles: strangers near the water's edge.

The duck quacked twice and the ducklings snapped to, abandoning their play to swim straight to papa. The poults followed instinctively; soon all were huddled in the rushes.

"Go see who they are," ordered the duck.

"Me?" Pancho stammered.

"I'm just a little busy," the duck quacked sarcastically and motioned to the eggs and ducklings.

"You poults stay here," said Pancho.

Sensing danger, all the young birds crowded together behind the nest.

Pancho took a deep breath and headed out to check on the voices. He tried his best to move silently through the mud and rocks, not so much to surprise the strangers but because he could just imagine the mallard's sharp ears listening for his every misstep. As he picked his way in the direction of the voices he could hear more distinctly the words of the strangers.

Pancho paused and cocked his head. Were they discussing music? It hardly seemed the sort of thing you talk about if you're out stalking helpless ducklings. Still, one can't be too careful. The pig continued his reconnaissance of the area, rounding the bend and standing on tip-toe to peek over a boulder.

There they sat, eating stolen apples and paying not the least attention to the pond or its swimmers.

"Rats!" Pancho mumbled a little too loudly. Four multi-colored heads turned his way. Pancho grinned self-consciously and came from behind the boulder. All four strangers got up and raced towards the pig. Pancho began to back up until he noticed their outstretched paws.

"Hello, hello. Beautiful place you have here." The speaker had originally been a white rat, but seemed to have gotten into some blue dye, which took quite brightly on white fur. Only his eyes were their original pink.

"How do you do?" said Pancho, reaching cautiously to touch paws with the blue rat. Pancho tried to smile, but found his eyes were drawn to a tag punched in the rat's translucent ear. His face went into a sort of grimace.

The rat tapped the tag and said, "Dioxin, that's my name."

Pancho noticed the name stamped on the metal ear tag. The blue paw waved in the direction of a black and white splotched rat with shaved bald spots. "This is Nick."

Pancho turned his head sideways to read the tag. "For Nicotine," he ventured.

"Yeah, that's me," answered the splotchy rodent. Pancho saw Nick was much younger than his mangy appearance would indicate.

"I'm Ben." The green-headed rat extended his paw to the pig, who did not respond, trying as he was to read the ear tag. "They put it on backwards," Ben said with a shrug and turned around so Pancho could see.

"Benzine?" What odd names, Pancho thought.

Behind the others stood a small bright pink rat. Pancho noticed that although the fur was all pink, the tail was multicolored like a rainbow. She didn't seem anxious to introduce herself, so Pancho walked over and read her tag. "Saccharine!" he stated. "That's a very sweet name."

Pancho thought his words clever, but the pink rat must have heard that line before. She stared at the pig with a look somewhere between disgust and boredom.

Pancho turned back to the others. "I'm Pancho and this isn't really my farm, I'm just a visitor."

"Oh," said Dioxin. Pancho sensed a drop in the friendliness level.

"Well, we're a band, the Free Radicals, maybe you've heard of us?"

"I don't think so," said the pig. He felt his approval rating drop again.

"We are very well known in the city," Saccharine said, her voice high-pitched and scratchy.

"I hope she's not the singer," thought Pancho, saying nothing.

"Anyway we're on tour," explained Ben. "Do they have a barn on this farm?"

Pancho nodded.

"Maybe we can play a gig or two?"

Pancho looked at the rats. He knew the cranky mallard would not appreciate his eggs and ducklings being exposed to this dangerous element. And he also remembered his promise to Emma.

"The barn's up there," he indicated the general direction casually. "Everyone is very busy today..." He caught himself. Maybe these city rats were spies or police agents. Now he was thinking like the old goat and sheep. Perhaps he shouldn't allow them unattended to snoop around the barn, and how would it seem if he had been the one to send them and they turned out to be spies?

Then Pancho hit upon an idea. "Are those your instruments?" he asked, looking at the odd shaped bundles lying nearby.

"They sure are!" Nick brightened up.

"I wonder," asked Pancho in a sweetly innocent voice, "could you play a song for me? I love good music!"

The rats did not have to be asked twice. They happily began setting up. Dioxin and Ben had guitars, (Pancho was not sure, but he thought Ben had a bass) Nick had a sax and Saccharine had a drum set. Though the drum set was rat-sized it took her a while to set it up. In no time the eager guitarists were ready and stood holding cords.

"Where do we plug in?" they asked a puzzled Pancho.

The pig looked around the meadow and shrugged. "We don't have electricity," he said.

"What?" The rats were shocked. "Everybody has electricity."

Dioxin patted Ben on the shoulder as his squinted red eyes searched the meadow and orchard for an outlet. "There!" The blue rat turned the others' heads to a tall post which Pancho had never noticed before. At the top were wires. Ben and Dioxin raced to the pole, carrying long bundles of electric cord across one shoulder like mountaineers. Ben ran right up the pole as only a rat can. He tapped into the lines and tossed the wires down to Dioxin. In minutes they were tuning up.

Just as Pancho had hoped, the sounds of the electric guitars, sax and drums echoed across the whole farm, and possibly the whole countryside. Soon the farm residents stopped their projects and followed the sounds to the pond-side music hall. Even the ducklings and poults swam out a bit to see what was going on.

Dioxin took over. "Welcome everyone," he began his patter, as if the farm animals were the guests, and he their host. "We are the Free Radicals," he said to a wild drumroll from Saccharine. The animals stared quietly. "We are laboratory rats who escaped to the sewers of the city. For our first number we would like to do a song we wrote about our escape. It's called 'Trapped Like a Rat.'"

That was the last intelligible word Pancho heard. The amplifier was cranked to 11, the drums banged and the sax wailed like a bear caught in a trap. The singers screamed (it seemed that all the band members sang at some point or another) but understanding their words was impossible. Pancho would not call this music, but looking around at the audience he saw them smiling, nodding their heads with the beat and tapping hooves.

Sabo sided over to Pancho and asked the obvious question, "What's going on?"

"Travelling band," he shouted in her ear and noticed himself swaying a bit to the tune.

The turkey poults spotted Pancho up near the front. They decided it was completely proper for them to be with their babysitter at a time like this. They left the pond and the ducklings and scooted between the legs of cows and goats to get next to, actually in front of, Pancho.

It seemed that the longer the band played (and the first song went on quite a while) the more the younger animals pushed to the front. The older animals graciously stepped back. Pancho backed up to make room for some kids who were kicking up their heels too near to his face. At the same time he tried to keep an eye on the young turkeys. They were shaking their tail feathers in front of the speakers.

Pancho backed right into Sally, the plump pink school teacher. Sally was doing much the same thing as Pancho, keeping her eyes on her students while moving back to protect her eardrums.

"Isn't this great!" she shouted. "Just what we needed!"

Pancho nodded and smiled, although he had no idea what she meant. Sally started dancing; Pancho watched. She was every bit the pig her sister Suzy was, maybe more so because she seemed even a little plumper. Pancho was wary, he did not want to make a fool of himself again, but still, a dance would not hurt. He offered a foot to lead her to an open spot of meadow. Sally smiled and took the offer, dancing all the way to higher ground. There they could still view the crowd, but had more room to dance. They danced in a friendly, playful way, bumping rears and rubbing snouts.

The pigs both laughed when the song abruptly ended. The crowd went wild with applause and animal calls of all kinds. The rats took bows happily and reintroduced themselves for the benefit of their new fans. Pancho's eyes scanned the meadow, looking for his little charges, when he saw something unexpected. From the angle they were at the pigs could see far into the orchard and way back, deep into the peaches. Pancho recognized Hans, the shepherd from the kennel next door.

He probably came to check out the music, thought Pancho, but who was that with him, snuggling and cuddling? It looked like a sheep, but Pancho doubted that. "Sally, who is that with Hans?"

Pancho pointed in the direction of the peach trees, but Sally did not even look. "Probably Monique," she said and turned to Pancho. "Are you shocked to see a shepherd and a poodle in love?"

"Well, let's say I'm surprised to see that shepherd and any poodle in love or even friends," Pancho said. "I thought Hans and his buddies hated poodles."

"They've been sneaking over here for weeks now to get some time together. Poor Monique, her family doesn't approve of Hans either." Sally sighed. "Everybody makes problems where there aren't any, and then overlooks the big mess right under their noses."

The rats cranked up again, so talk became impossible. There was nothing to do but dance. Pancho and Sally trusted that their youngsters were in no danger, so they could concentrate on each other. After dancing to three more songs, which all sounded pretty much like the first, they sat down in the grass to watch.

All the farm animals focussed on the band. Even Hans and Monique had begun to dance, Pancho noticed as he scanned the scene. But wait, who were the animals by the power pole? Pancho squinted to see. Bob the black sheep and Gruff the old goat stood with their backs to the band, staring up at the electrical wires.

13

Emma's arrival at Cave Camp caused quite a stir. The flight had not been long, but the morning's aerobatics had tired her. When she landed it took a long while for her to catch her breath.

The forest protectors had decided to lay low since their last sabotage. Breakfast had become a leisurely activity. They were just finishing their acorn crepes when Emma made her entrance.

"Look, it's Emma," squealed a silvery squirrel as the turkey swooped in to the breakfast circle.

"Emma, what's the matter?"

"Where are your chicks?"

"Is everything okay?"

Emma huffed and puffed as she held up her wing to stop their questions, but they could not wait.

"Are they cutting the trees?"

"Did the humans find out about us?"

"Is there a fire?"

"Carlos and Juanita," Emma gasped.

The llamas were not in the circle around Emma, but a young bunny scampered off to the hillside where they grazed. Emma sat on a log; a squirrel brought her some water to drink. By the time the llamas galloped into camp the turkey had caught her wind and become her usual talkative self.

"It's not such an emergency," she tried to explain to the animals, "but it is serious."

"Ahhh." The crowd listened.

"It's the farm, your farm," she said to the llamas, who nodded for her to continue. "There is going to be an auction, Saturday, this Saturday, and everything goes, even the animals."

"No!" clamored a chorus of disbelief.

"The animals can just come here," said a deer. "They don't have to be sold."

"That's very kind," said Juanita, "but it's our land and we will fight for it."

"Yes," Carlos jumped in, "we must fight! They don't care so much about the animals. They can always breed more. It's the land they are after and we won't let them have it."

"Just as you are fighting for your forest home, we must fight for our farm." Juanita's eyes teared up as she spoke.

The animals fell quiet for a few minutes, then Mischief the raccoon spoke. "Okay, let's go. You helped us protect the forest, we'll help you protect your farm!" A cheer of approval from the hearts of all the animals echoed through the camp.

Judi noticed a look of uneasiness on the llamas' faces. "Before we all go down to the farm, perhaps it would be smartest if Juanita and Carlos went home and send word when we are needed." A grumble of disappointment rattled the animals' ranks. "That way we maintain the element of surprise," she added.

"Ooooh," the animals understood.

"That would be best," Juanita agreed. She knew not everyone on the farm would welcome wild animals in their midst, despite their best intentions. "It's very important for us to know you are here to help if we need you!"

"Very important," Carlos added.

Emma cleared her throat. "What about the rabbits?" she said in a low voice to the llamas, tipping her head in the direction of Hamilton and Blackstone.

Juanita and Carlos exchanged glances. Blackstone and Hamilton were not their favorite fellow-animals, but Emma was right: they were smart and might be the most helpful animals right now. Also, the farm animals were not likely to fear rabbits, not even wild ones.

"Yes, if they will come it would be good," Carlos said.

Carlos felt the little claws and weight of the monkey on his back. Bonkers had become best friends with Carlos. He was not about to be left behind on this adventure. He climbed Carlos's neck and whispered in his ear, "if those flea-bitten rabbits go, I go too." And Carlos nodded, yes.

The llamas sprang to action, getting ready to go home. They put on their packs, loaded up the rabbits and monkey, and started down the trail within the hour.

Emma stayed to chat a bit. Turkeys are known to gobble-up gossip and Judi had lots to tell. With elaboration from squirrels and raccoons, Judi told Emma about the last forest action and about the hidden human friends. Emma's eyes were ready to pop.

"Humans. Well, I never thought I'd see you folks protecting humans," she said in awe.

"They aren't all the same," explained Judi. "Just like all bears aren't the same, or all turkeys."

Emma chewed on this for a while. "If they aren't all evil, how can you tell who's the enemy?"

"It's hard to tell." Judi sounded dismayed. "I hope we didn't make a terrible mistake drugging those guards, maybe they weren't really bad, I mean maybe they would have joined us if we had just talked to them first."

Emma shook her head and several raccoons joined her in the motion. "I don't think so Judi," said the turkey. "Men with guns, men who guard clearcut machinery, it would take a lot of talking to make them join a rag-tag group of animals, no offense."

Judi sighed. "Then I'll be doing a lot of talking."

Emma liked to keep an open mind. "Humans, hmm," she mused. "I've never talked to one, always avoided them."

"Me too, smart plan," Mischief chimed in.

"These were my first," Judi said, "but probably not my last. They are different from us, of course, but ..." they looked at each other... "we're all pretty different."

It's true, Emma thought, for years she had lived only with turkeys. That was how she had been brought up, but now she had friends among all like-minded animals. Why not humans as well? "I think I'll have to go look at these human forest protectors," she clucked, "and maybe even have a talk."

"Quoth the raven can give you aerial directions," Judi told her. "You never know, they might be able to help with the farm problem."

"Oh, I don't think we want humans involved." Emma hugged Judi goodbye. "See you soon, I hope," and the turkey walked over to old Quoth to get a flight plan.

"How long are we going to help out those stupid humans?" Mischief asked aloud. "Talk about potential spies."

Judi did not answer, so he continued: "First they kill Rascal and the little buck..."

"That was an accident," the squirrel named Mac jumped in.

"So they want us to believe," Mischief said mysteriously. "This could be an elaborate plot. First they gain our trust ..."

"Mischief," Judi interrupted him in a sharp tone, "this doesn't sound like you. Where did you get this stuff?"

"Well, Blackstone and Hamilton said ..." The masked eyes searched around for support, but found none.

Judi jumped in. "You were there, Mischief, I wasn't. Blackstone and Hamilton weren't there either, not right at the scene. You tell me, was it an accident?" She looked into his beady eyes.

The raccoon sat down on a log and covered his eyes with his paws. "It was terrible," he cried.

"I know," said Judi, moving over to stroke his soft back. "But was it an accident?"

"Yes," he sobbed, "a terrible, terrible accident."

Emma circled overhead, calling goodbye to the forest protectors, who waved back. Even Mischief lifted his damp face to watch her fly off. Everything looks different from the air, and Emma always marvelled at the way distance put things in perspective. The higher she flew the tinier Cave Camp looked and the more she could get the bigger picture. She could see the forest stretching below her; the trees looked like moss on rocks. This was the way to truly understand the horror of clearcuts. From the ground, it's true, you can't see the forest for the trees sometimes.

From the sky Emma could see the ravaged hillsides, brown and dead, of the corporate lands to the north. Beyond them lay the concrete monoliths of the city. To a wild turkey this view was horrible, so she closed her eyes and turned to the right. When she opened her eyes again she saw the horse ranch that bordered the city. It looked green and pleasant from this distance, so she flew lower for closer inspection.

The grass looked like velvet and the neat white fences crossed and crisscrossed the property, dividing it into tiny sections. Emma sailed past the white and green shuttered home of the owners.

Over the manicured gardens she flew and down to the stables, long buildings with red roofs and white doors every few feet. Out of the top of every door hung a horse's head.

The turkey looked around the stables for signs of danger; seeing none, she took a leisurely swoop down the aisle between the stables turning every horse's attention her way. There was instant commotion as the horses stomped and whinnied with excitement. "They sure must be bored to be so easily amused," chuckled the bird as she circled around for another pass, this time at top speed, just to give them a thrill. The audience went wild, kicking at their doors, neighing, and shaking their manes to rattle their halters.

Emma landed on the cupola of one roof, too high to be seen from the horses' vantage point. She listened until the stables got suddenly quiet again. Then she noticed why. A human with a whip in hand walked towards the stables.

The man was small, with a limping gait, and although any horse there could easily trample him, they cowered in silence. Emma stayed hidden as the man searched for the cause of the upset. He cracked his whip a few times and said some words Emma did not understand, but by his tone she could guess the meaning. All was quiet now, no horse made any sound. Even their breathing seemed to have stopped.

The man spoke in a kinder tone. "What's the matter, Corvette?" Emma snuck down to peek over the roof and saw the whip-man stroke the brown nose of Corvette. Soon all the other noses wanted petting, so the man walked down the line bestowing attention on some, sugar on others, and a carrot or two towards the end. Then off he went toward the barn.

Emma noticed that not every horse got a pat; one horse did not even stick his head out in hopes of one. But now that the man had left, that horse stuck his head out of his cubicle and looked straight at Emma as she perched on the roof.

"What are you trying to do," he called, grinning and showing his huge yellow teeth, "get us in trouble?" He laughed a crazy horse laugh that made Emma step back from the rain gutter.

"You're the one who always gets us in trouble," snapped Corvette. "Behave yourself."

"We don't want him to come back, do we," said a giant palomino, shaking her blond mane. "Stop that laughing."

But the horse wouldn't stop. Once the talking started, Emma got bolder and slid down from the roof. She walked over to the stall of the laughing horse. "Maybe he'll talk to me," she thought, then said aloud: "Quit that laughing, or I'll just fly on." Emma looked at the shiny black horse and at the strange word painted over the door of his stall. "Edsel," she squawked, "what does that mean?" She hoped this would open up a conversation.

The black horse stopped his laughing and answered with disinterest. "It's a car that gives its owners a lot of trouble," he said simply. "It's also my name."

Emma looked down the row of horse heads and saw above each one a name unintelligible to her. "Mercedes, Rolls, Beamer, Volvo, Porsche," she read aloud, slowly.

"Car names," said Edsel. "Isn't it too clever," he sneered. "You know, people name their cars after horses. Pinto, Colt, Mustang..."

Emma shook her head. "I don't know anything about cars," she muttered.

"Here he goes," snorted Corvette, and she pulled her head into her stall.

"Please don't get him started," pleaded Mercedes, who seemed to wish her stall was located further away from Edsel's.

"I'm talking to the turkey, not to you," he said, the black eyes twinkling with mischief. "If you're not interested, don't listen."

Emma knew that option did not apply to her. She perched herself on a bale of hay and hoped the lesson would be brief.

"When cars were invented they were going to be the salvation of the horse." Heads all along the row pulled into the shadows. "No longer would horses have to do man's hard labor, provide his transportation, plow his fields. Horses everywhere saw a new era of leisure and freedom for their colts. But it didn't turn out that way. Horses became obsolete, no longer needed. The only way we can survive is by becoming highly educated and highly specialized, and then only a few of us are needed. If you are the very fastest or most beautiful or can jump the highest, then you can live locked in these tiny cells trying your hardest to make the most money for the owner." Edsel paused and seemed lost in thought.

"What do you specialize in?" Emma asked. The whole concept seemed odd to the wild turkey.

"Dressage." Noticing the blank stare on the bird's face, the horse explained: "Following directions, doing whatever I'm told without hesitation."

Snickering erupted from the nearby stalls; obviously they were listening.

"They laugh because, well, I snapped. One day I just couldn't stand to follow one more stupid, pointless command. So right in the middle of a very big event I stopped. The rider tried to make me conform. She kicked me, she whipped me, so I threw her off." Edsel announced this last part proudly and looked the turkey right in the eye.

"Good for you!" cheered Emma. "Then did you kick her or whip her?"

All the horses gasped as they poked out their heads to get a look at this horrible bird. Even Edsel seemed shocked. "No, of course not, she's fine, not even hurt." This also seemed like a point of pride to him.

"But you won't act repentant, that's the problem," Corvette scolded from across the way. "They will forgive you and give you another chance, but no, you won't even kiss up to the grooms and get petted."

"And you know what happens to stallions who won't behave..." Mercedes sneered and all heads turned to look at a chestnut head which disappeared into a door marked Fiat.

"Another troublesome car?" thought Emma.

"They'd better not try and geld me," declared Edsel, "or someone will get kicked!"

"And then they'll 'put you down'" reminded Corvette. "Bam, one bullet to the head."

Emma couldn't understand. "Why don't you leave? Why are you here, any of you, but especially you, Edsel?"

The black horse sighed. "But where would I go, what would I do? Dressage is all I know."

"I'd say it's time to learn something else." Emma hopped off the bale and walked down the cement path between the stable rows. She looked at the horses and noticed how clean and shiny their coats were; some were wearing fancy blankets and had braided manes with ribbons. All were well fed and cared for; their tiny stalls had fresh hay. "It won't be this easy out there," she cautioned. "You'll never be as safe and comfortable, but you will be free. You probably can't eat fancy oats every day, but what have you really got to lose?"

Edsel looked at the ground. He tried to imagine giving up all that he had worked for. He remembered the applause and awards; lumps of sugar and praise from the owner. There had been a time when that seemed very important to him. If he behaved well and repented he could be there again.

All eyes fixed on Edsel as he weighed his future. No horse had left of its own free will since anyone could remember.

But the silence of thought was shattered by a high-pitched voice. "Come on, Edsel, let's go!" Everyone turned to the voice of a tiny pony who was not locked in a stall. Brown and white shaggy hair covered her body and her mane hung in her face, covering one eye.

"Oh, Jeep, don't be ridiculous, you can't go anywhere." Corvette's voice condescended.

"I can go anywhere I want," said Jeep, "and Edsel can, too."

"You're too young," said Mercedes in a motherly tone.

"Yes, I'm young enough to still remember Chincoteague Island," Jeep said, turning to Edsel. "I mean it, let's go."

The black stallion looked at the pony. Then he looked at the other horses locked in their stalls. Finally his gaze settled on Emma. "Why not," he said, smiling.

Jeep kicked up her heels in delight. She had planned an escape for a long time. "We should wait until night to make our escape, and then in the woods we can sleep and hide in the day and travel at night. You're smart and strong and I know what plants are good to eat. We'll make a good team."

"Follow the river downstream," said Emma.

"Quiet," shushed Corvette, "he's coming back."

Emma saw the limping man, hobbling toward them, carrying a rope bridle. "I'm out of here," Emma said to Edsel as her wings started flapping. "Remember, downstream." The turkey lifted off into the air above the stables, making circles long enough to see the man put the bridle on little Jeep and lead her off toward the main house.

14

At times like this Emma felt lucky to have wings. "Free as a bird," she said to herself as the horse ranch shrunk down to miniature again. Catching an updraft, she played in the gusty spring air, struggling with her conscience. "I know I should head back to the farm, but..." the turkey breathed the scent of wanderlust. "I so rarely get the chance to go exploring and the chicks are fine with Pancho, I'm sure." Emma remembered this morning's swimming lesson and smiled. "Who knows what they'll learn by the time I get back."

With that thought she gave herself permission to play hooky. The terrain below had turned to brown shingle roofs interlaced with asphalt streets for as far as she could see. There was very little greenery, and even fewer trees. "Some kind of clearcut?" mused the turkey as she flew faster to pass the desolate sight.

She headed toward an emerald-green oasis just ahead. It looked park-like once it lay beneath her, with flowering trees, green lawns, and the chatter of birds. "Of course," Emma nodded. "This is the kind of place birds would live." We're too smart to be trapped in a drab and lifeless landscape." She circled down for a landing on the lawn next to a cement birdbath with a fountain in the center. Emma looked around at the manicured estate and even she was impressed. "This is a bird paradise" she exclaimed to herself as she walked over a little bridge spanning a fish pond. In front of her, lining the walkway, shaded by an arbor of trees, stood a row of perches. On each one sat a beautiful bird. Emma had never seen such brightly colored plumes. For a moment she hesitated, looking at her own subdued feathers.

"What nonsense," she thought, snapping out of her reverie. "These birds don't care what I look like. It's what's inside that counts." But she did try to spread out her tail to make a good impression as she approached the nearest perch.

"Hello," Emma addressed a large blue macaw. "What a lovely day it is."

The macaw sat perfectly still as though no one had spoken.

"My name is Emma," the turkey tried again. "You have a beautiful home here."

The blue bird continued staring straight ahead, but with a casual flick of her foot she knocked a half dozen sunflower seeds from her food dish to the ground in front of Emma. The turkey looked at the seeds in confusion and then back at the macaw above her. "Perhaps she thinks I'm begging," thought Emma, "and she doesn't want to embarrass me by bringing up my unfortunate condition." She knew she looked far too plump to appear to be starving.

"I'm not hungry, thanks anyway." Emma tried to make the best of the gesture. "I'm expected at home for lunch," she added cheerfully as she tried to make eye-contact with the bird on the perch. The macaw closed her eyes and pivoted on her metal rod, displaying her tail feathers to the turkey's face.

Emma took the hint and moved on. But as she approached each bird turned its back to her before she could even speak. "What's the matter with all of you?" the turkey asked in a loud voice. "Are you afraid to talk? Have you been threatened?" Emma stared at the row of multi-colored tails, but none of them moved.

"You don't understand," the voice came from a barn wren who stood pecking fallen seeds from under a metal ring where a red macaw with yellow wings perched. The wren had grayish plumage, as do most wrens, but she had gathered the colored feathers dropped by the macaws and stuck them in amongst her own. Emma thought the wren looked silly, but shut her beak to listen as the wren explained: "the reason they won't talk to us is because they're exotic." The grey bird managed to add a tone of grandure to the last word.

"What does exotic mean?" Emma asked.

"It means worth a lot of money," the wren winked knowingly at the turkey. "The green one over there is worth plenty, and the blue one you were trying to talk to, she's worth even more. But this red one..." the wren lowered her voice and gestured for Emma to lean closer. "The Big Red, she's worth the most!"

"Why?" the turkey asked, cocking her head to size up the macaws. "Why is the red one worth the most?"

"Because she's the most exotic." The wren seemed to think it was self-evident, but Emma was still confused.

"So is that why you wear the colored feathers from these birds?" the turkey asked. "To be exotic?"

"I'll never really be exotic," the wren admitted sadly. "Do you know what I'm worth? Nothing." She continued gathering fallen feathers.

Emma watched the wren for a minute, then said, "I think you have it wrong. You are a perfect wren, and wrens are very important birds. You have a lovely voice, and I bet you can fly faster than even Big Red over there."

"She can't fly at all. None of them can. They all have their wings clipped," the wren stated. "But they don't need to fly. Everything they need is brought to them. What a life."

"What a life indeed!" Emma snorted. "I would never give up my wings no matter how much I was worth."

The wren looked at her sympathetically. "You're probably worth about the same as me. Nothing. Except maybe at Thanksgiving."

"Well, I'm worth a lot to me and to my chicks," Emma said and fluffed her feathers defiantly. "These birds may be exotic, but they seem like prisoners to me."

"You're right!" came a raspy voice from behind them. Emma turned and for the first time noticed a caged macaw apart from the rest of the birds.

"You are talking to us! That must mean you're not very exotic." Emma waddled over to the caged bird.

"No, not very exotic," she said through a smile. This macaw was mostly white and peach colored, but the feathers on her neck were plucked out. She had sad eyes with a hint of mischief in them. Emma smiled back.

"Why are you in a cage?" Emma hated cages. "What happened to your feathers?"

"I pulled them out," the caged bird laughed. "That way I'm not worth much. I also bite. That's why I'm in the cage."

Emma's eyes grew wide. "Shall I let you out?" The turkey fumbled with the latch.

"No, I'm not ready," said the prisoner. "I must stay until my wings grow back. If I keep biting and plucking my feathers they will keep me here, but I'll be safe and fed. When my wing feathers are grown, I'll escape and fly away to my home."

The turkey looked at the poor plucked bird. "I hope it works out like you said."

"Sometimes you have to sacrifice for your freedom," the bird said sadly, pulling a few more feathers from her raw-looking neck.

The wren quickly gathered the freshly plucked plumes and added them to the mixture on her belly.

"Don't those feathers fall off when you fly?" Emma asked the wren, who seemed to be having a bit of trouble getting the new peach-colored down to stay where she wanted it.

"Oh, yes, but I don't fly anymore," the wren answered. "None of the well-bred birds do. In fact, the best bred turkeys don't fly either, I would think you'd know that."

Emma did know, and she knew why. "Those turkeys you call 'well-bred' are raised for their meat!" She snorted at the wren and then, in a rush of recognition, turned to the caged macaw. "Are they breeding macaws for meat?" she asked in alarm.

"Not exactly," the prisoner answered. "They don't eat us, but it's meat all the same."

Emma could not understand the bald macaw's reply and was about to ask her what she meant when the glass doors at the far end of the pathway flew open. A human started fluttering in their direction. The wren grabbed the turkey's leg and pulled her into the shrubbery. They hid behind a tree that had been clipped into the shape of a bunny. Emma peeked out between the ears.

She saw a woman draped in soft, multi-colored fabric. There were ribbons streaming from her hair and bright paint on her eyes and lips. The woman carried a bowl of fruit and began passing out pieces to the grateful macaws.

"Hello, hello, hello," said the blue macaw who had ignored Emma.

"Hello, Athena," cooed the woman as she petted the bird. Athena took some grapes from the fruit bowl.

"Pretty lady," screamed the green bird. "Pretty Lady!" The woman seemed pleased.

"Pretty Venus," she petted the green macaw and handed her a peach.

"Aphrodite wants an orange," squawked the Big Red bird.

The woman floated over to her perch. "What does Aphrodite say?" the woman asked in baby talk.

"Pretty please," begged the red macaw and the woman held out the orange.

"Can you give a kiss?" the woman taunted, holding the fruit out of reach. The red macaw bent over and kissed the woman's cheek with her beak, then quickly snatched the orange.

The woman bent down to talk to the white and peach caged macaw. The colorful skirts settled in a pool around her and she put her face very near to the bars. "How is little Diana today?" her condescending baby voice asked. "Does Diana want a plum?"

The plucked macaw moved to the back of her cell.

The woman held a plum out to show the bird. "Come, Diana, see the pretty plum."

The bird ignored the fruit and the woman's pleading.

Then the woman opened the door of Diana's cage and attempted to pet her. The powerful beak of the macaw clamped down on the woman's finger, tearing the soft white flesh.

The woman jumped up screaming as the red blood added another color to her skirts. She gave the cage a kick before running in tears through the glass doors.

The cage lay on it's side, but the door hung open. The imprisoned macaw shrugged, then stepped outside.

"Can't argue with fate," she grinned at Emma, who crept out from behind the bunny bush.

"Are you going to escape?" the turkey asked as she watched the macaw test her wings.

"I'm going to try," Diana answered. Probably can't go far, but I can get out of here."

Emma waved good luck as the clipped macaw barely cleared the outer hedge. "That's what I call an exotic bird," she said to the wren. But the wren was not listening. She had crawled into the empty cage and shut the door.

Emma shook her head and walked slowly over the fish pond bridge to the clearing before taking off. Then she let the wind into her unclipped wings and rose into the sky. Looking down at the gardens from such a height made Emma wonder how such a lovely place could be a trap and prison. "But most of those captives are willing," she thought, "they traded freedom for comfort or safety or beauty." She did a couple of aerodynamic rolls to celebrate her wings and turned westward.

Soaring over long, low warehouses and erector-set factories, Emma only half noticed the mill for paper and the electrical plant. Finally, something below did catch her eye: a huge collection of cages filled with every species of prisoner. Concrete cells housed the fierce and the meek. Metal bars and chain fences kept the wild ones in. She had heard of this place, the zoo, but it looked even more terrible than she had imagined.

Emma turned away, circling to the east. Her heart pounded in her chest. Part of her wanted to go back and see, the rest of her wanted to pretend the zoo did not exist. "I won't land," she decided, "I'll just have a quick look and be on my way." The turkey turned again toward the zoo complex. Flying low over elephants, giraffes, and hippos; animals of legend to turkeys. She saw legs chained to posts and walls barring escape. In the monkey house Bonker's friends and relatives peered through the bars, dreaming of freedom. The tigers paced back and forth in frustration, and even the great eagle was trapped in a small space, unable to spread his wings. That was enough for Emma. On this beautiful day she did not want to see others suffering.

She took to the sky and winded eastward, following a flock of sea gulls. "They must be going to a beautiful place," she mused, "not a prison or a zoo." The gulls led her over a small hill. On the other side, hidden from view, the gulls landed in a pit dug into the ground and filled with garbage. Emma held her breath to avoid the smell of rotting garbage as she watched the gulls squabbling and fighting over bits of food they found in the trash. The turkey perched carefully on the back of an old sofa. She surveyed the dump with a critical eye. This was the cast-off pile of human civilization, and along with the material discards (old appliances, tires, disposable diapers, and much more) Emma saw the social discards. Rats swarmed over the piles, gathering what they could before mangy dogs with protruding ribs and hollow eyes snatched up rotting bits of carrion. The gulls competed with other scavenger birds in squawking battles over the gold mine of waste. The turkey jumped in surprise as out of the torn cushion of her sofa crawled a feral cat and her six hungry kittens.

The mother cat bared her teeth and gestured with a claw-filled paw at the large turkey looming above her family.

"I didn't mean to frighten you," a startled Emma explained. "I won't harm you!"

The cat looked her over and did not seem to like what she saw. "Get out of here," she hissed, and Emma obliged by moving to the protruding leg of an upturned coffee table. Her eyes followed the feline family as they filed out of the sofa cushion and scattered themselves amongst the garbage. The mother cat positioned herself at a safe distance and kept her eyes glued to the turkey, making Emma feel uncomfortable.

"So you live here?" The large bird asked, not intimidated by this scrawny orange cat. Instead she was curious.

"You have a problem with that?" the cat snapped back defiantly.

"Yes, don't you?" Emma continued.

"No," the cat replied. "I was born here, I've always lived here."

"Do you like it?" the turkey paused. "It looks like the perfect place to leave."

"And where would we go?" The cat threw her paws up in the air. "There's no place for us. At least here we have scraps to eat and an old sofa to sleep in."

The wary mother seemed to be relaxing a bit around the turkey. She started to dig at the trash near her nose and soon produced a partially eaten hot dog, which she chewed at hungrily. Emma said nothing as she watched the cat eat. One of the kittens tumbled over and the mother surrendered the rest of the hot dog to her little one. "It's not a good place for the kittens," she admitted to Emma. "I worry about their safety and their future. But what can I do?"

"I don't know," Emma admitted. Looking at the kitten, she asked, "What would you like to be when you grow up?"

The kitten purred. "I'm going to be a mother, just like you," and she turned to give her mother a lick.

"Yes, sweetie, you can be a mother and what else?" the older cat prodded.

The kitten puzzled over the question. "I don't know, just like you, Mom."

The mother cat looked at Emma and said, in a fearful tone, "We really should get out of here, but how? And to where?" She searched the turkey's face for an answer.

Emma shrugged. "My chicks and I travel around. We do a little of this and a little of that. It's a good life for a turkey, but for a cat, I don't know." She shook her head.

The two mothers sat and mused. "It's hard to leave the only home you've ever known," the cat complained. "My mother told me her mother lived in the city, but that was a long time ago, when humans cared about cats. It was a better time."

"Perhaps you can make things better here," the turkey said, hopefully, but as she looked around at the piles of trash it seemed doubtful. "Or perhaps once you leave, you'll find it's not so hard."

"Sometimes I can't think of anything I'd miss," the cat stated. "But could we make it in the wild, out on our own?"

"Many do and many don't," Emma said, philosophically. "How about a farm? I have friends on a farm and you might go there. It's not great timing, though. They are having a big problem with the corporation."

"That's an idea! There's always jobs for cats on a farm, so I've heard." The cat's ears perked up at this thought.

"It's a great place, only animals, no humans at all. Just hope they can keep it from the bankers." Emma elaborated. "If you go into the woods and follow the river downstream you can't miss it."

"It's a nice idea. Maybe we'll go someday." The cat went back to pawing in the piles. "Can't go right now, though, I'm so busy and a trip like that takes so much planning." She shrugged. "Travelling with six kittens!"

Emma nodded. Perhaps it was not the answer for all animals. Still, she felt sorry for the kittens growing up with so little hope. "Well, I need to keep moving," she took leave of the cat.

"See you later," the mother cat mewed over her shoulder as she continued her food search.

"I doubt that," thought Emma, pushing off from the table leg and flapping furiously to gain altitude. She had to fight for airspace with the swirling gulls until she was over the forest once again.

"I had better go see those humans and then head back to the chicks," Emma thought as she peered down at the trees, looking for landmarks.

15

L et's see, Quoth said left at the dead tree, south of the rock that looks like a quail..." Emma circled lazily over the same acre of forest, trying to make some sense of the raven's directions. She squinted at a nearby rock and tried to see a quail. "No, it can't be that one, it's definitely not part of the pheasant family. More like a turtle, I think." Then she noticed two dead trees up ahead.

She sighed and flew over to the grey trunks poking their bald heads through the greenery. Perching lightly on a broken branch to test if it would hold the weight of a not-so-thin-anymore turkey, she said aloud and with a bit of despair: "Left? How can I know what left is?"

"That's heavy, really deep," said a voice within the tree.

"Excuse me?" Emma looked around and watched a sleepy looking spotted owl stick his head out of a hole in the trunk.

"It's like everything's related, you know," the owl yawned. "Like just when you think you know what left is, you turn around and it's right!"

"I'm lost," said Emma, trying to bring the conversation back to reality.

"I hear you," said the owl. "I totally feel the same way."

Emma took a breath and tried again. "Do you know where I can find a rock that looks like a quail?"

The owl perked up and opened his big round eyes as his pupils dilated wildly. "Wait, wait, don't tell me. I can guess this ... rock like a quail?"

He rotated his head completely around, to Emma's amazement, then answered quickly, "To get to the other side. No, no, that's not it."

"It's not a riddle," Emma gave it one more try. "I'm looking for humans hiding in a cave, have you seen them?"

"Why, yes I have," said the owl proudly. "I'm the lookout to protect them from danger. I'll show you where they are."

"You're the look-out?" Emma asked, surprised. "Why do you care about humans?"

"But these guys are really cool." The owl fluffed up, ready to take off. "They really helped me out and it's the least I can do to be a look-out. Let's go."

Emma followed the owl down through the trees to the foot of a hill. There a few bushes looking slightly out of place marked the opening to a small cave. The birds rolled the bushes aside and peered in. It was a bear den, used for winter hibernation. Even thought it was spring the smell lingered and was mingled with humans-who-need-a-bath scent so strong that Emma withdrew her head to get some fresh air.

"Not here," announced the owl with a shrug.

"Obviously not." Emma got ready to head back to the farm, but she mentioned, "you know, as the look-out, it is part of your job to know where the humans are."

"It is?" The owl only half listened.

"And really, I don't think you should have brought me here, either. I could be a spy for the corporation or something," Emma explained to the preening bird who looked up at her in alarm.

"Are you a spy?" The eyes dilated again.

"No, I'm not," Emma smiled.

"Well, then it's okay," said the owl.

"But you see, if I were a spy I would not tell you the truth, because I would want you to bring me here," she explained slowly.

The owl sat silent, puzzling. "So, maybe you are a spy?"

Emma looked at the little bundle of white and brown feathers. No wonder this creature was on the verge of extinction. "I'm not a spy," she said firmly.

"But that's what you would say if you were a spy," the owl mumbled. Emma rolled her eyes.

Just then, through the woods, bounded the humans, laughing and teasing, yet keeping their voices low. They approached the cave and stopped in silence to see the bushes rolled away. The owl stepped out of the cave and the humans breathed easy again.

"Horace, what are you doing here?" one of the men asked the owl.

"Well, I just brought this turkey to see you, but be careful, she might be a spy!"

"I'm not a spy," repeated Emma as she flapped her way from behind a bush. "I'm Emma," she said. As she looked at the humans her beak dropped open. The humans had no clothes on.

"If she might be a spy, why did you bring her here?" The man questioned the owl as the turkey walked slowly around the humans, staring rudely at their nude bodies. The other men and the woman began to drape their wet clothes over the low hanging branches. Emma noticed their hair and bodies were dripping water in puddles where they stood.

The owl stammered out his excuse. "Well, I didn't know she was a spy 'till we got here. That's when she told me."

"I'm not!" Emma turned to the man to explain. He bent down to look at her and his wet red beard and long curly hair dripped water on her feet. Emma cocked her head and looked him over. "He looks like Goldie after a swim," she thought. But she was so stunned by his nakedness that she forgot what she wanted to say. "I'm sorry to stare," she started, "but I've never seen a human without clothes before." And she looked at the four shaggy dripping creatures shaking their heads to dry their hair, just like any other animal would. "You look better this way," she announced, "and I did not come to spy, just to talk."

"Emma, did you say?" The man smiled at her. "My name's Redwood, and this is River and Rocky, and over there is Rainbow." He indicated the woman last and she waved from a bush where she arranged her damp socks.

Odd names, thought Emma, horses named for cars, humans named for nature. "I was just up at Cave Camp and Judi suggested I visit you," Emma began clumsily.

Redwood sat on a rock to talk. The others scattered themselves in patches of sunlight to listen and dry. "We're sensitive to the spy issue because we believe there is a spy or two in Cave Camp." He had cut to a serious point, dispensing with the usual small talk.

Emma was skeptical. How would they know what was happening at Cave Camp. And why trust the word of humans over animals? Still, he had aroused her curiosity and she could not resist asking, "Who?" Even Horace moved in closer to hear the answer.

Rainbow broke in: "We don't know for sure. Don't make it sound like we have evidence or something," she warned Redwood.

"But we do want to get word to someone of trust at Cave Camp," River reminded her, "to be careful."

"Everyone at Cave Camp is trustworthy," Emma said defensively, "but I guess animals come and go and ..." she stopped speaking aloud, but finished her sentence mentally, "I don't really know all of them very well."

"It's not anybody whose been around a long time like Judi or Red or Mac," Redwood continued, "but about a year ago we began to hear things." He looked at Emma, who had hung her head in dismay.

"We want to get word to someone because they are helping us and we're on the same side, you know," said Rocky.

"But who?" Emma raised her head and shook her waddle, "who is the spy."

"Whoever it is can read and write very well," said Redwood, "and they are trusted by Judi and the others."

"But we don't know Cave Camp," offered Rainbow, "so we don't know names."

"Who are they spying for?" Horace asked innocently.

Emma and humans answered in unison, "the corporation."

"Oh, yes," the owl nodded. "The corporation."

Emma sat in silent thought, running animals through her mind to think of one who could read and write.

"What did you come to talk about?" Rocky asked the quiet bird.

"Nothing really, I just never talked to a human before, and never saw one without clothes." Emma smiled. "You look much more like regular animals this way," she said, rubbing his bare leg with her wing. "Could use some more fur or feathers or something," she joked.

"Especially in the winter." Rainbow pretended to shiver. "I wish I had a down comforter like you do."

Emma narrowed her eyes and said to herself: "I'm sure it was just a thoughtless remark, but I would not be surprised if she does have such a barbaric item at her home."

"Are you a forest protector?" River asked.

"I like to think of myself as one," Emma remarked. "I'm wild, you know, and I live here so I have a real stake in what happens." She paused and turned to River. "What's in it for you?"

"The wilderness is important to everything on the planet, whether you live here or not, wild or not." The young man felt defensive; he knew he wasn't truly wild like the turkey.

"True, true, that's the right answer," she gobbled, walking around the human like a sergeant doing inspection. "But what about jobs? I thought you humans were all worried about that job stuff, and the corporation, well, they have the jobs!"

"The corporation could care less about jobs, they only care about money, about profits, and power," River said with indignation.

"Face it, River, you care even less about jobs than the corporation does!" Rocky said, laughing.

"Okay, so a job as a wage slave is not my idea of a life, but I don't mind working for something I care about, like the forests and oceans and freedom from oppression."

"Oppression?" Emma squawked. "What do you humans know of oppression?"

"I know, you animals are more oppressed, but we humans are oppressed, too," River whined. "Most of us, anyway. Just a few humans have all the money and power. The rest of us are given the choice of doing what they say, or starving, or being put in prison."

"There are humans held in the zoo?" queried Emma.

"Prison is like a zoo, for sure," River told her, "and the humans inside are treated as badly as animals. Well, almost. So we came to live in the forest where we could still breathe free. But pretty soon the forest will be gone, there will be no place to escape the corporation."

"We're free right now," added Redwood, "but if the corporation catches up with us, they'll pin the killing of the guards on us, and that means the death penalty."

Everyone was silent.

Emma thought before she spoke. Perhaps these young humans could be trusted. Maybe they could even help. "Something is starting," Emma began. "The animals of the farms and forests are restless."

"Really, is there going to be a revolt? I mean, more than just the forest protectors?" Rainbow opened her brown eyes very wide and Emma could see her own reflection in them.

"I hope so, I think so," but Emma did not want to say too much. "I'll keep you informed if I can."

"I hope it's not too violent," Rainbow whispered.

"Me too," Emma lowered her tone, "but the corporation isn't going to wake-up one morning and decide that they've been unfair and selfish and just roll over and die. They have a lot at stake and they will kill if they have to, just to keep control."

"That's right, the corporation itself is violent and shows no remorse," River complained. "Why must we always be law abiding and tiptoe around so as not to upset them?"

"Because they have the guns!" Emma said. "Well, most of the guns."

"Might makes right," River shook his head in disgust.

"What is that old saying?" Redwood wondered aloud. "Discretion is sometimes the better part of valor."

"What's that supposed to mean?" River questioned. "That I'm over-zealous?"

"No, but it would be wonderful to find the least violent path to freedom, don't you agree?" Redwood finally got a nod of agreement from his young friend.

Emma nodded, too. "We can try to be non-violent, we can plan the best we know, but we must be realistic. Look at what happened at the last forest action. It's important to set the best goals, but the bank and government and corporation will all fight to the death..." her voice trailed off.

They all looked at the ground, lost in private thoughts. It was the turkey who broke the silence. "So those are your feet?" She laughed. "Really strange looking!" She walked over to River and put her talon next to his foot, then shook her head. "Strange," she said, "Those claws aren't much good, are they?"

The humans laughed and admitted that no, the toenails were not as helpful in everyday life as one might hope.

"You know, some humans might think your feet are strange looking," Rainbow said with a smile as she gazed at the reptilian skin on Emma's leg.

"I suppose they might," admitted the bird. Then she noticed the position of the sun in the sky. "I really have forgotten the time," she exclaimed. "I'm expected somewhere. It's been interesting to meet you. I'll try to keep you informed."

"Nice to meet you, as well," said Redwood, as usual speaking for them all. "Think about the spy thing."

"Oh, yes!" Emma remembered. "The spy thing."

The turkey walked over and shook the sleeping owl. "Goodbye!" she said to the drowsy Horace. "Some lookout!"

She flapped once more her tiring wings and lifted skyward.

16

The Free Radicals wound down their set as the llamas arrived at a gallop. The farm turned its attention from the rats to Carlos and Juanita, and especially to Bonkers, who was already a celebrity for his driving ability. Blackstone and Hamilton were of less interest, so Pancho was able to make his way through the crowd to say hello to the rabbits.

"That was a quick trip!" said Pancho as he touched paws with the Cave Camp lawyers. "Why did you decide to come?"

Hamilton held his stomach and Blackstone lay in the grass panting. The rabbits looked at each other and shook their mangy heads. "Emma's idea, I believe," said Hamilton. "What a terrifying way to travel!"

"And where is Emma?" The pig suddenly realized he had missed most of the day's action by chick sitting.

"Last saw her at Chez Nuts eating acorn crepes," Blackstone sighed and closed his eyes.

Pancho gathered the poults and made his way back to Sally. She had her youngsters together and started to return with them to the garden. Pancho appealed to her to take the young turkeys with her, but she refused the responsibility.

"May we come with you, then?" Pancho asked hopefully. "Who knows when Emma will return."

Sally smiled her agreement and the pigs set off with the youngsters to gather food from the garden to store in preparation for the upcoming emergency.

Bonkers found Sabo and gave the cat a big hug, which set her purring. Sabo introduced the monkey to the other animals, and after prying him away from the pink rat's drumset, they set off to explore the farm. It was always fun to see a place with Bonkers; he viewed everything in his own special way. The rats tagged along for the tour and added their own unique observations.

The llamas headed for the barn with Goldie and Rosy to look at the resolutions of the previous night, and to think about how they could best help in this crisis.

Soon all the animals had returned to their tasks, leaving the rabbits alone in the meadow to recover from their bouncy trip. But as soon as they were alone, Blackstone and Hamilton seemed to revive and began exploring the electric instruments. So it appeared to Bob, who was slowly making his way back to his shed from the power pole.

The black sheep stopped and watched the rabbits from behind a bush of blueberries. After some plugging and unplugging, the rabbits took off toward the barn and Bob moved cautiously toward the electric guitars to see what they had done. Always suspicious, but not up on electrical band equipment, the old sheep poked his nose around the speakers and amps. These black boxes looked ominous and the guitars looked strange, but when he followed the electric cord only one small briefcase was plugged in. Bombs are known to reside in briefcases, so Bob did not dare open this one. He did read the printing on the outside. "Motorolla Cellular," he mouthed, but the words had no meaning to him. "Where is that old goat when you need him?"

Bob sat down near the instruments to think about the briefcase, when Emma began to circle low over the meadow, looking for Pancho and the poults. Seeing only the black sheep, she landed near him and asked if he had seen her chicks.

"I don't keep track of other animal's offspring," Bob snapped.

"I can't imagine why you're not asked to babysit, Bob!" Emma replied as she began to walk around the band set-up. "What is this stuff."

"Get away from there," the black ram scolded in a voice that made Emma jump. "I think it's a bomb!"

"Don't be ridiculous. You're always so paranoid," said the turkey, but she stepped back anyway. "It looks like some musical instruments," she said, cocking her head, "doesn't it? And some boxes or baskets." She waved a wing at the drumset.

Bob took a deep breath and released it slowly. Then, in his most condescending voice, he began to explain the rat band and what the rabbits did.

"I know what you're thinking, Emma, that I'm always suspicious of newcomers, but they were actually behaving very strangely." The sheep seemed so sincere that Emma almost confided in him what she was really thinking, about what the humans had told her of spies in Cave Camp. But she thought better of it. Bob would jump to conclusions and poor Blackstone and Hamilton would be accused, and probably falsely.

Emma waddled over and looked at the briefcase. "Let's unplug it," she said, "and look inside."

Bob nodded in solemn agreement, walked over and pulled the plug from the case. They tried to open it, but the latch was locked. The turkey and sheep pondered the briefcase and were about to force the latch when it started to ring. Was it an alarm? Or perhaps a bomb warning? The turkey flapped back but Bob, in a moment of bravery, grabbed the case and flung it into the middle of the pond. It sank making large concentric circles that splashed at the bank. The sheep and turkey covered their ears and waited, but there was no explosion. Bob grabbed the cord and yanked it from the pole.

"Electricity is evil," he said, "I always knew it." He marched off toward the printing shed.

Emma set off to find her family. She headed toward the garden, where it would be most likely to find a pig, she thought. Hopping over the hill so fast they almost knocked her down, came the rabbits. They raced to the instruments and searched among the cords. Emma watched as they discovered the torn cord and searched for the briefcase without success. Hamilton held a small black something the size of a potato, but square. He looked at the something, shook his head, and tossed it into the pond before he and Blackstone started back to the barn.

Emma decided to take a chance. "Something wrong?" she said sweetly. "Perhaps I can help."

The rabbits paused and stammered a bit. "Why, no, Emma, everything is fine. Pancho has your poults in the garden," Hamilton said.

"Lovely farm," Blackstone added, and they hopped off.

"That was the most suspicious of all," thought the worried mother as she hurried to the garden. "I will keep my beak shut and my eyes open for now," she vowed. Emma ran with her outstretched wings toward her chicks, who were only half as glad to see her as Pancho was.

With a hug from Sally, Pancho headed toward the print shed and his poster committee. As he neared the little crooked building he heard the hushed voices of sheep and goat in deep and secret discussion. Pancho paused to listen for a moment, but, fearful of being accused of espionage, he raised his foot and rapped loudly on the door with his pig knuckles.

After a second or two the door opened a crack and the goat stuck his beard out the opening.

"What do you want?" he bleated at Pancho.

"I'm on your committee. I'm here to help," the pig explained to the beard.

The door slammed shut and Pancho could hear arguing inside. Finally the door opened again, this time wide enough for Pancho to get through.

"We decided it was easier to keep an eye on you this way, come on in," was his welcome.

Pancho had to let his eyes adjust from the bright daylight to the dim lantern light of the print shop. The windows were blocked with what looked like paper from the outside, but which Pancho now saw were old political posters. Dust filled the room; the press was ancient. Everywhere crumpled papers and random letters lay about. Still, Pancho loved the smell of ink. He was eager to start.

"Here," Bob shoved a damp flyer under his snout. "This is it, we just need a headline."

Pancho looked at the piece of propaganda the sheep handed him. The top of the paper was blank, but a third down the page, in the tiniest print possible, using dozens of different type styles, began a long description of the farm, its history, its current situation, the world situation, the personal philosophy of the old goat and also Bob's beliefs (which were similar, but you could not tell from the flyer, because they emphasized their differences). Pancho considered himself an intellectual, but he was not exactly sure of the meaning of several words. He completely lost track of the point of the flyer after the third paragraph. Still, it looked impressive. If they could just come up with the right headline, perhaps it would do the trick.

They had several ideas: Anarcho-Syndicalism Now; All Power to the Imagination; Back to the Pleistocene; Subvert the Corporate Conspiracy; and Defend Animals' Rights.

They argued about each one, the goat being for the ones the sheep was against. It was evident to Pancho that there would be no consensus, but they moved in the direction of running several together: Subvert the Corporate Paradigm through Imaginative Anarcho-Syndicalism.

Sally interrupted them by banging on the door.

"I hope you haven't finished the flyers yet," she squealed, "because the rats have a great idea: a free concert and dance party tomorrow night. Animals will come from all around and we can tell them about the auction and ask for their support. This is going to be such fun!" She smiled at Pancho, who felt his heart hop in his chest. Then she was gone.

"Fun. This isn't about fun," fumed Gruff.

But the headline, after another hour's arguing, finally said: "SUBVERT THE CORPORATE CONSPIRACY THROUGH A FREE CONCERT AND DANCE PARTY," spelled out using the largest letters of each type style. Then in the next size smaller: "Wednesday night at the Circle A Farm." No one noticed the typographical error until after all the flyers were printed, and by then it was too late to correct it.

All the animals were impressed and pleased with the posters.

"And what does the Circle-H stand for anyway?" Bob asked defensively.

"Humans," shouted Gruff, "and Circle-A stands for ..."

"Apples," Pancho shouted, and all the animals cheered.

Only Goldie shook her head. "The H was for Hansen," she said. "It was Margaret's name."

But she was alone in her nostalgia. Within minutes Bonkers grabbed a mallet and climbed the front gate. He beat at the top of the wrought iron H until the vertical bars were touching inside the circle to look like a circle-A.

The animals gathered at the gate to watch Bonkers work. The monkey brought a smile to all their faces and the new symbol lifted their hearts.

Pancho walked over to the retriever at the edge of the crowd. "A new name is good, it will bring us together. A new identity," the pig told her. She smiled her tired smile and went back to her work on the barricade.

Rosy decided her brand was out of date. Sabo got a brush and paint and did some touch up work on her. Soon a line of young animals waited for Sabo to paint a Circle-A on their hindquarters.

Pancho noticed the rats had already influenced many of the youngsters, who had painted themselves in a vibrant array of colors. The lambs and kids took the dye particularly well. Others, who had darker fur, had adopted the ear tags, to the raised eyebrows of their elders.

Preparations for Saturday's anticipated conflict had slowed, but energy picked up for the free concert. A new batch of volunteer roadies set up the barn for the following night. Jethro tried to make suggestions, but was overruled by energetic groupies who had some new ideas for the decor. Suzy and Sally gathered supplies for the barn decorations, but the mule and sows were asked to wait outside until the rats and their new fans had finished.

"Just leave the paint and stuff at the door," chirped Orville, Emma's son, "and don't peek inside. We want to surprise everyone with the new club."

Jethro shook his head. "I hope there's a clean-up committee," he said to the pigs.

Sally laughed. "Oh, I'm sure we'll be invited to help with that. Still, it's really great to see them so involved and excited."

"It makes me feel old," Jethro sighed.

"It makes me feel young!" said Sally.

"Are you sure that's what's making you feel young?" Suzy tickled her sister.

"I don't know what you're talking about," Sally giggled as she waddled off waving her curly tail to the others.

"I think she likes Pancho," Suzy whispered to the mule. "I hope he likes her too."

Jethro loved knowing a secret.

Luckily the poults were totally involved with decorating the barn; Emma had her wings filled with rabbits. She did not want to falsely accuse them, but her conversation with the humans had put her on alert. After that mysterious briefcase now resting at the bottom of the pond, well... "I'll just stick next to Hamilton and Blackstone at all times. That way they won't be able to do any spying, if that's what they are trying to do," she decided.

Emma stuck to the rabbits like glue. Eventually the rabbits became suspicious and irritated.

"I did not know you were so interested in patent law," Blackstone asked the turkey skeptically. "Do you have an invention or idea you want to protect."

"Well," stumbled Emma, "I don't really have an invention yet, but I'm thinking about inventing something in the future." She was having trouble keeping the rabbits' attention and had run out of subjects. "Tell me, Hamilton, what is the gross national product of Brazil?" She had noticed Hamilton gazing off toward the barn. "I never can remember."

"Emma, where are those delightful little balls of fluff that usually keep you so busy?" Hamilton smiled at the turkey and rolled his eyes at Blackstone. Then the rabbits locked thoughts, as conspirators can, and saw their means of escape. In unison they said, "Emma, it's been magic, but gotta go!" They hopped off in opposite directions.

The turkey was flustered; what to do? She started running in one direction, then stopped and ran in the other, not knowing which rabbit to follow. Finally she sat down. Emma had cornered the rabbits hours ago, and had exhausted herself with chatter. Now they were suspicious of her and would avoid her. "Even if they are innocent," the turkey admitted to herself, "I'm sure they are sick of me. I need help." And she flapped her way over the barricade.

Goldie worked alone, piling up pieces of wood and shrubbery to create a false hedge row. The design was supposed to hide the animals so the bank humans and police would not know the size of the resistance force.

Emma's squawk broke Goldie's concentration. "Goldie, get Rosy and meet me at the printing shed."

The dog nodded. She could tell from the turkey's demeanor that it was a serious matter.

Emma flew to the shed and rapped at the door. Inside the old goat, the black sheep and the white pig bundled their fliers for a sunset air-drop by the tumbling pigeons.

"Who is it?" The door opened a crack and the goat-beard stuck out.

"It's Emma. Bob, are you in there?"

The black sheep emerged and, of course, so did the other two, just as Goldie and Rosy trotted over.

"Look at my new brand!" the cow said, sticking her rump in Emma's face.

"Very nice, Rosy, but this is important," the turkey began. "I talked to some humans today," there was a gasp from the printers, but Emma continued. "The humans who are being hidden by the forest protectors." Pancho leaned in to hear better since the turkey had grown horse from so much talking.

"They weren't wearing any clothes."

"Really!"

"What did they look like?" Bob's eyes narrowed to a slit trying to imagine such a sight.

"Better, a little better. Not much hair or fur. Kind of like..." Emma looked at the animals, then pointed a wing at Poncho ... "him. Their skin I mean."

The others all laughed and Pancho blushed. "Thanks a lot. I look like a human!" He turned to go back into the shed.

"I did not mean that, come back, Pancho." Emma coaxed and the pig drew nearer. "Anyway, they did look more like animals, you know, so it was easier to talk to them." The others nodded. "But what I wanted to tell you is this: the humans said there is a spy, or maybe spies, in Cave Camp. They don't know who, but the leaks started about a year ago and the spies can read and write well."

"Most of us can read and write," said Pancho, feeling defensive. "At least a little."

"But that's not all," Emma looked at Bob, who was about to burst. "Tell them, Bob."

The sheep was so glad to have an audience who would believe him this time, he launched into a very dramatic presentation of the scene at the pond. He even had Emma to corroborate.

"I've watched the rabbits all afternoon, but they gave me the slip," added Emma.

"We'll do it," said the goat, nodding to Bob.

"Be nice, you two, remember they are invited guests," Goldie said. "If Pancho and Rosy help it will be less suspicious."

"Like a tag team," Rosy mooed.

"Emma, you show me where the case is. We must have proof." Goldie grinned. "They don't call me a retriever for nothing."

The turkey and the dog set out for the pond. The others went looking for the rabbits.

Hamilton and Blackstone were not hard to find, they sat outside the barn talking with some other animals about the plans for Saturday. Pancho felt anger, but told himself they were innocent until proof was brought against them. Here they sat doing just what they had been asked here to do: give advice about the situation with the banks.

"It doesn't matter what they know," he whispered to Bob, "as long as we don't let them leak it."

The sheep nodded yes, but it felt like no.

"I don't know if you should resist on Saturday," advised Hamilton.

"Definitely not," chimed in Blackstone. "It would be better to let them think they have won, then surprise them later with a revolt."

The animals were confused.

"But we decided not to let them take the farm, we would be peaceful but we must resist," Jethro recited slowly.

"Do you have any idea what you're up against?" Hamilton put on his condescending tone. "The bank is huge, but the corporation, well, the corporation is too powerful to challenge." He shook his head and several fleas dropped off his ear and landed on the dirt before them. "You will be crushed like bugs," and with that he lifted his large hind foot and came down with such force on the fleas that they were probably driven to China.

"They will have guns, they have the police," Blackstone explained. "You see, ultimately the police are there to protect the corporation, don't get confused about that."

"The dogs next door have guns," a goose said optimistically.

"I wouldn't count on the dogs to protect you," Hamilton laughed. "They can't even protect themselves."

Pancho listened to the rabbits talk. Everything they said about the power of the bank and corporation were true. Perhaps it was hopeless to try to fight something as big and powerful as the corporation. Pancho could see the change in the animals as they listened to the rabbits. They became unsure and fearful, but maybe that was reality.

"We could do a surprise attack," said a pacing bantam rooster, "at dawn!"

Blackstone sighed and then began slowly in a hushed but urgent voice: "Listen, you are in way over your heads. When the corporation attacks you, they are everyone. The police, the media, even the government and the bank. But when you attack the corporation they are no one. They hide behind piles of paper and they can't be found."

"If the corporation wants this farm, they will take it," Hamilton continued. "If they have to kill all of you to do it, they will, and the media will put a spin on it and the government will justify it, the banks will finance it, and everyone else will ignore your pleas for help, because, after all, it isn't them."

The animals felt stunned. They looked at the rabbits, at each other, at the ground, but no one spoke. The barn rattled with the party preparations and the happy young voices of the decorating committee inside. Pancho looked down at the flyer he had in his forefoot. Suddenly he felt naive. Things had changed since the old days of revolt. One farm could no longer fight something as big as the corporation. Even if they won on Saturday, by Monday they would be defeated.

The animals began to drift back to their tasks, heads lowered, lost in thought. Soon the rabbits were left with Bob, Pancho, Rosy and Gruff. To break the uncomfortable silence, Pancho spoke.

"What about the forest protectors?" he asked. "They fight the corporation."

"Sure, they fight, but do they win?" Blackstone replied. "One step forward, two steps back."

"If they started to win, they would be crushed," answered Hamilton. "I mean we, we would be crushed."

"It must be difficult for you to fight for a cause you find so hopeless," Rosy added in her sweetest voice. Bob bit his tongue and looked toward the pond, wondering about the evidence.

The day grew dark and the muddy bottom of the pond made the search for the black briefcase difficult. Goldie dove over and over until she nosed into it, and then with one last dive grabbed it firmly and hauled it ashore. Emma and Goldie examined the case with suspicion before forcing the lock with a stick.

"It's a telephone," the dog announced. "I've never seen one in a case before, but that's what it is, I'm sure."

"I'm glad it's not a bomb," said Emma. "Is this evidence of spying?"

The dog traced her memories of telephones. "They are for talking to friends," she remembered. "Still, you could be friends with spies."

"What is this, written here, very small?" Emma pointed to several little white labels that marked buttons. The water had begun to peal them off, but Goldie could still read them, even though she did not know what they meant.

"FBI, CIA, Corp. Head., Mom," she pronounced slowly. "Gruff might know, or Pancho."

"I'll get them," Emma exclaimed as she started off.

"Act casual," cautioned Goldie.

"Always," she answered.

Her less than graceful landing at the barnyard drew everyone's attention. The rabbits groaned at the thought of her continuing conversation, but instead Emma walked slowly behind the rabbits and began jerking her head to the side, first to the black sheep and then to the pig. It took several jerks for her meaning to communicate to the others. With lame excuses they drifted down the hill, first Bob, then Pancho and Emma, leaving Rosy and the anxious goat to guard the rabbits.

"A very odd bird," smirked Blackstone.

"Perhaps she's had a little too much Wild Turkey," Hamilton quipped and they chortled together.

Bob and Pancho examined the phone buttons, then exchanged knowing looks.

"Well, FBI and CIA," the sheep began, "are government anti-animal organizations. FBI stands for Farm Bureau of Investigation. CIA stands for Committee to Infiltrate Animals."

Pancho nodded. "Spy central."

The dog and turkey looked alarmed.

"Corp. Head probably means corporate headquarters," the pig added. "But Mom... what could that be?"

They all puzzled for a while, then Goldie suggested timidly, "Maybe it's their mother, do you think?"

With a shrug, the others agreed it could be a mom of someone.

"At any rate, the other labels are very significant," said Bob.

"Very significant," agreed Pancho.

"Is this enough proof?" the turkey asked. "Should we throw them off the farm?"

"It's enough proof for me!" Bob declared.

"But they know too much to let them go."

"There must be a trial," Goldie said, and Pancho agreed. "But we can wait until after Saturday, then even if we let them go it will be too late for them to ruin our plan."

Up the hill, the animals marched carrying the still-dripping phone case. Bob laid the case before the rabbits, who feigned innocence.

"Never saw it before," said Hamilton.

"I take the fifth," Blackstone snipped.

Rosy rang her bell and soon all the animals converged in the barnyard. They all inspected the phone. Bob told his story, Emma told hers, and Pancho and Goldie filled in what they knew.

"This is not a trial, we will have a real trial later, but we need to protect our secret plan," Goldie explained to the animals.

"Secret plan!" exclaimed Blackstone. "What are all these flyers about? Your concert will be packed with spies of all sorts."

"Amateurs," sniffed Hamilton.

"CIA scum," shouted Carlos, from the back of the crowd. The animals parted to let him through. No one had ever heard such words from the soft-spoken llama. "To think I brought you here myself, on my back. In my country we know what to do with spies."

"No," Rosy blocked his path, "they will have a trial." She looked at Carlos. "A fair trial. But until then we must find somewhere to keep them where they can't be spying on us."

"We've got a place."

Everyone turned to see who had growled from the rear. There stood Hans and Kurt.

"Yeah, let us take them. We'll watch them real closely," Hans barked.

"Well, they are professional guard dogs," Suzy said, "Why not?"

"Okay with me," Goldie said. "Okay?" she asked the assembly.

Nods and shouts affirmed the idea. The rabbits looked shaken: they had assumed they could talk their way out of the predicament. Even so they did not give up.

"You can't do that. What about our rights?" Blackstone declared.

"We refuse to go to the kennel," Hamilton threatened.

"You don't get a choice," said Bob, very happy to be dealing with actual spies.

"You're lucky we believe in real democracy or you'd be dead already," added Gruff, shaking his beard in their faces.

"Don't hurt them," Goldie cautioned Hans and Kurt.

"We wouldn't think of it," said Kurt as he grabbed Blackstone roughly by the ear.

"As gently as my own grandmother," Hans said, carrying off Hamilton to the tunnel. The dogs shoved the rabbits into the tunnel and disappeared from sight.

17

On Wednesday morning the day broke clear and pink. Pancho saw the dawn that morning since he had slept outside with the other animals; the barn was closed in preparation for the night's big event. The night air-drop had been successful and the posters were causing quite a stir in the neighboring areas. The farm got up early and, as usual, most animals headed toward the meadow for the morning exercises.

"Oh, why not," thought Pancho. "I can try something new and I could use some exercise," as he trotted to the pond with the others.

"Stand right here," Goldie beckoned and Pancho slipped into the herd between the dog and Jethro.

"What do I do?" the pig asked but before he got an answer he was knocked to the ground by the sheep behind him. The animals ran off to the right, leaving Pancho behind, scrambling to catch up.

Goldie ushered him back into the group. "Try to focus on the others around you," she said. "Don't worry about where you're going, be sensitive to others around you and when they are about to move."

Pancho tried, with a little more success this time. He focussed on Goldie and ran forward and stopped when she did. When the herd moved to the other side, however, Pancho missed the cue and his hesitation caused a ten-animal pile-up. Everyone laughed and picked each other up from the dewy grass.

"You have to be aware of everyone, not just one or two animals," Sabo told him as she moved into the furry mob and disappeared.

"This is harder than it looks," Pancho thought, but tried again. Each time he got better at feeling a part of the group. "It's very interesting, makes you feel strangely powerful, even mighty." He was surprised since he had always feared that groups took power away from an animal. "We are really a force to be reckoned with."

Pancho felt exuberant at the end of the run. He sat by the pond to catch his breath. A frisky white sheep with a black face came over to join the pig. "You did great for your first time," the white sheep congratulated Pancho. "Isadora is my name," she smiled. "I already know yours, but you're calling yourself Pancho now, aren't you?"

The pig dropped his jaw. He looked the sheep over very carefully, but he had to admit, most sheep looked alike to him. Pancho did not recognize her.

"I'm sure you don't remember me. I was little more than a lamp when I escaped our old farm." Isadora continued. "I got out before things got really bad, luckily."

Pancho could hardly believe it. A sheep from his old farm! But she talked about escaping. Was it so terrible for the other animals that they planned escapes? And were the pigs so insensitive to their plight that they did not even notice when animals were gone? In this case, Pancho assumed the answer to be yes.

"So you came here?" he asked rhetorically.

"And so did you!" the sheep smiled. "I always thought you were as bad as the other pigs, until you came here. It seems like you're changing."

Boy, that one stung. Pancho hardly knew how to respond. "I've learned a lot. Still learning." He waved a paw at the meadow they had just left. "You sheep are natural experts in whatever it is we were practicing down there." Pancho could not bring himself to say "herding."

"I think of it as empathy," Isadora said, "the ability to feel the feelings of another. Did you notice that the word sheep is the same for one sheep or many sheep? That's because we feel for each other: an injury to one is an injury to all."

Pancho nodded and the sheep continued. "Many pigs would be afraid of empathy because they see it as diminishing their individuality, when really it's just adding to, not taking away. Like falling in love."

Isadora winked at Pancho. "That's what makes you so different from those other pigs on the old farm." Since Pancho did not speak, Isadora decided to take her leave.

"I've got to get going. I'm late for my shooting lesson," the sheep stated.

"Shooting lesson?" Pancho spoke now. "I thought there were no guns on this farm."

"I'm going to the kennel. Kurt is teaching me to use a rifle." Isadora laughed. "You never know when that kind of knowledge will come in handy." She added, "See you tomorrow morning."

"Nice meeting you at last," the pig said. "I'll be here tomorrow." He watched the sheep trot towards the kennel. "That is one sheep who is an individual," he thought, "and what about Bob the black sheep." Pancho chuckled to himself. "He certainly doesn't run with the herd, so to speak."

Pancho sat and surveyed the farm. The rats strung new electric cords to the barn. Food preparations began for the party. Off in the orchard, near the peach trees, Hans and the poodle Monique rolled in the grass. Pancho found his thoughts drifting to a certain plump schoolteacher with a soft moist snout.

"I hope she doesn't already have a date for the party," he thought as he headed toward the pig pen. Sally was getting ready to start her class in the little corral near the barn, but she had stopped to talk to Goldie and Sabo.

"We're going to visit the Sacred Cow," Goldie said. "She's too old to come to the party tonight, but I want her to know what's going on." Pancho nodded and Goldie asked "would you like to come meet her?"

"Sure, I'd like that," Pancho answered. "I just wanted to ask Sally something." Sabo and Goldie stood and waited while Pancho looked at Sally. "Alone, if you wouldn't mind."

"Oh, alone," hissed Sabo and smiled at the dog as they took a few steps backward. Sabo strained to listen.

Pancho mumbled something and Sally smiled and nodded. Sabo was sure she heard the word 'date'. The pig turned back to wave at Sally before joining the dog and cat. He looked very pleased with himself.

"A date, Pancho?" the cat purred.

"And what's wrong with that?" the pig snorted. "She's a wonderful intelligent sow."

"Leave him alone, it's cute," said Goldie, using a word Pancho had never heard used to describe himself or his activities.

They crossed the fence between dairy and farm, carefully picking their way through a meadow mined with cow pies. In a white barn at the far end a tiny brown and white cow lay on a bed of straw. She was so thin her bones protruded on her back and her big brown eyes seemed sunken in her soft face. She smiled at the approaching animals.

"No Rosy?" she asked the retriever. When Goldie shook her head the cow sighed, "Rosy is my daughter, but she rarely comes to visit anymore."

"She's doing fine," Goldie said. "This is Sabo, and this is Pancho, newcomers to the farm."

"You've come at an important time," the cow said in greeting.

"That's what we came to talk with you about," Goldie continued, and told of the problems and the spies. "What do you think, Mother cow?"

The cow waited in thought, then answered, mooing softly, "A time to be born, a time to die, a time to chew cud and a time to stampede."

"Stampede!" Pancho said in surprise. "Can that work?"

"It's unstoppable," the old cow replied. "But a true stampede requires full participation, total dedication, and all animals running together in unity."

"But it will take so much planning to co-ordinate all the different groups," Pancho pleaded.

The cow shook her head slowly. "It requires no planning, planning will ruin it. Does a forest fire require a plan? No, only a match."

"But what about spies," Pancho demanded. "They could be all around us."

"Spies, spies, spies. You all worry too much about spies." The cow seemed tired out by so much explaining. "No number of spies can stop a stampede."

"It's true," replied Pancho. "If we have no plan, what good is a spy?"

Goldie had been thinking too. "Mother Cow, you have always taught non-violence. But this stampede, isn't it violent? Won't animals get hurt?"

"Animals get hurt every day, life is dangerous. An animal can get hurt plowing a field, or jumping a fence or climbing a hill. Yet these are not violent acts. But if you do not stampede, the corporation will come and may slaughter you, even if you cooperate. The stampede does not intend violence, and will be most successful if no animal is hurt. Therefore, it may be dangerous, but it is not violent."

Pancho thought this over. For him the question of violence or non-violence was second to whether the stampede would work. "But what if we gave a stampede and nobody came?" he half-joked. "How can we be sure all the animals will join in? I know we have the numbers, if we can just get everyone to commit themselves to the Great Stampede, we could overcome the corporation and establish a new type of government." Pancho raised his fist in the air to punctuate this declaration.

The Sacred Cow looked him over as she chewed a bit of cud. "What kind of government did you plan to establish?" she asked.

"Oh, you know, a kinder, gentler..." Pancho looked to Goldie and Sabo for support, but they both stood silently. "I don't know, a better government," he said, "one where all animals are equal."

"Didn't we try that before?" Sabo reminded him gently.

"I think it might be wise to skip the new government. We've all had plenty of old government," the cow said in a tired moo. "I know I have. And to answer your question, you can't be sure they will join in, but it doesn't matter." Pancho looked puzzled by the cows words. "If the animals don't move as one, if it isn't a spontaneous consensus decision, it's not a Great Stampede."

Pancho began to pace around the barn. What could he do? Something must be done! He must do something.

The cow read his mind. "Little pig, relax, you are not in charge. You may help sow the seeds, you may help water them, and if you are lucky you may have some bread. But you are not the baker."

"What are you talking about?" The pig's voice was a little too loud. "I want to be the baker!" Pancho felt a bit silly, so he added, "Maybe I could be one of the bakers?"

The cow chewed on. Pancho paced a bit more, then stopped and confronted the cow eye to eye. "Why do you get to pick the baker?" The brown eyes gazed unblinking. Pancho paced more.

Goldie held back a smile. She had seen the Sacred Cow at work before, but she always found it amusing. Sabo rolled her eyes at Pancho, but still he paced. He stopped once more in front of the aged cow.

"Okay," he snorted, "who is the baker? I'll help him," he caught himself, "or her, however I can. I will devote myself to the baker!" He begged the cow, "Who is it?"

"How should I know?" answered the cow.

Pancho threw his paws in the air. "Then what are we talking about?"

"I have no idea," said the cow, and she chewed some more.

Pancho narrowed his eyes and paced another lap. He retraced the conversation in his mind. "You said I was not the baker," he demanded.

"Are you?" the cow asked. "What would you bake?"

Pancho was stumped. He had gotten a little unsure of what they were talking about. "Bread?" He thought he had heard that mentioned.

"What kind?" the cow questioned.

"I don't know, it depends on the kind of grain," Pancho answered carefully. Then, thinking his answer seemed weak, he added, "Whole wheat! I would bake whole wheat bread." He smiled triumphantly.

"And what if the grain was rye?"

"Well, then probably rye bread." He began feeling unsure.

"Now suppose the seeds were not grain at all, perhaps they grew pumpkins?"

"Pie!" Pancho felt sure that answer was right.

"And maybe no seeds sprouted and nothing grew," the cow posed to the pig. "What would you bake?"

"Nothing?" Pancho puzzled. "Is that right?"

"Of course it's right," the cow said, "there would be nothing to bake and no need of a baker." She sat silent again. So did Pancho. He re-ran the baker thing again in his brain.

"So what you're saying is: it's too soon to have a baker, but perhaps later I can be the baker?"

Sabo broke in. "What is the big deal about being the baker?" she asked Pancho. "Why do you care so much who gets to be the baker?"

"She made it sound important," he whined, pointing at the cow, "and she indicated I wasn't good enough to be the baker," he sulked.

"No she did not," said the cat. "I heard it all, and you just assumed that. All the Sacred Cow meant was sow some seeds, see if anything grows, and don't try to bake bread before you even sow the seed." The cat turned to the cow. "Right?"

The old brown head nodded.

"And, also, don't try to control everything and everybody. Some seeds don't even need a baker!" announced the cat.

"What a wise little cat," whispered the Sacred Cow, and she turned to Pancho. "Sow some seeds, water them if you like, but this time fate is the baker."

And with that the Sacred Cow turned her back to the animals, signalling the end of the visit.

The pig and dog began to leave, but Sabo ran over to the tired old cow and whispered in her ear, "May I come and see you again?"

"I would like that," said the cow, smiling.

The farm bustled all day with excited activity. Bonkers had wiggled himself an invite to sit in with the Free Radicals on a few numbers. He noisily converted scrap metal into a steel drum. Others made a bonfire circle, piling it high with old wood and brush. Several dogs had come over to help with the fire building, a particular favorite of theirs. The tower of flammables reached almost as high as the barn.

"Where did they get all that stuff," Pancho wondered loudly.

Goldie walked slowly around the pile, eyeing it suspiciously, then, with a sudden growl, she took off at a run. Pancho followed to the front gate where Goldie looked at her demolished barricade.

"I can't believe they tore it down," she lamented.

"I guess it was so well disguised that they couldn't tell it was a barricade." Pancho tried to put an upbeat spin on the situation. "We can build it again tomorrow."

"Out of what?" Goldie walked to her dog house and lay down inside.

"Maybe we won't need a barricade," Pancho thought, "not if we have a stampede."

Sabo had been so impressed with the Sacred Cow that she searched out Rosy, who was picking apples in the orchard.

"I met your mother, the Sacred Cow," said the cat in awe.

Rosy said nothing and kept on with her gathering, putting yellow, green and red apples all together in a big bushel basket.

"She asked about you, Rosy," Sabo continued. "You should go see her."

"She's alright, isn't she?" Rosy asked. "Not sick or dying?"

"No, I don't think so," the cat reflected, "but she is old, of course."

"Still full of her sanctimonious manure?" the cow snorted and rang her bell. "I really can't take her holier-than-thou act. It drives me nuts."

Sabo was surprised. "She seemed very wise to me, I liked her."

"Then you visit her," Rosy said as she picked up the apples and headed for the picnic tables set out by the barn.

"I'm going to," yelled Sabo after her. Then she climbed the golden delicious tree to think. She never had seen Rosy so irritable.

Eventually Goldie took a walk in the orchard, checking for any fallen limbs that might be useful in rebuilding the barricade. Unfortunately there were none, since she had gathered them all only yesterday. Sabo leapt down from the apple tree and chased after her.

"I don't understand why Rosy is so angry at her mother," said the cat. "They're really a lot alike."

"That's probably why," said the dog. "Like Bob and Gruff, always arguing, splitting hairs, it seems to me."

"But why is Rosy here instead of at the dairy?"

"Rosy was always running away when she was a calf, jumping the fence and coming over here. The life at the dairy is regimented and strict, a time for this and a time for that. The Sacred Cow had to keep fetching Rosy whenever she escaped." Goldie chuckled. "Some animals just can't be trained, in fact we have a whole farm of non-conformists, in case you haven't noticed. One day when the humans were branding animals with the Circle H, Rosy jumped in line. She probably did not know how painful it would be. But the brand kept her mother from dragging her home anymore. Cats and dogs are lucky, we don't get tagged or branded. A collar is bad enough."

Sabo nodded. No collar had ever lasted more than an hour on her.

"But Mother Cow was a rebel in her day," Goldie added. "There are tales of great protests for animal causes, victories and tragedies. She was young and thought she could change the world. I felt that way once, but like the old cow, I began to look inward to find meaning in the world we have." Her voice trailed off softly.

"So Rosy wants her mother to be that young rebel?" Sabo asked.

"I don't know what Rosy wants, she's no spring chicken herself," Goldie mused. "There's room for many ways in this world even within the same animal. My goodness, now I sound like the Sacred Cow."

Sabo agreed.

Hans and Kurt were rolling a heavy log toward the bonfire. "Hey, pig, give us a foot!" they yelled.

Pancho got between them and pushed on the big section of pine with his front legs. Pushing was still quite difficult, so after a few minutes they decided it made a fine bench right where it stood.

"Those rabbits are going nuts over there," said Hans. "They really want us to let them go."

"I'm sure they do," said Pancho.

"They keep telling us that the kennel is going to be attacked and they don't want to be there when it happens," Kurt scoffed. "How could they know anything about the kennel?"

"They just want to scare us, it's a trick, isn't it?" asked Kurt.

"You're probably right," said Pancho, reassuringly. "But after all, they are spies. Who knows what information they may have. Why would the kennel be attacked?"

"The rabbits say because we have guns and the government doesn't want anybody to have guns but themselves," said Kurt, "and that's certainly true."

"We have the right to have guns, but the government says we don't need them." Hans was foaming at the mouth. "If they attack us to take them away, doesn't that prove that we do need them?"

Pancho was puzzled. He did not like the thought of dogs with guns, but they had a point.

"I have no idea whether or not the kennel will be attacked, but we know the rabbits are liars and there is no advantage to letting them free," the pig reasoned. The dogs nodded thoughtfully.

"I bet those pinko poodles have been complaining to the government about us shepherds," Kurt growled. "Oh yes, the government is always ready to protect those foreign French poodles. What about the rights of red-blooded native born German shepherds?"

Emma had been listening from her perch on a nearby fence post. The conversation had gotten too lively for her to keep quiet.

"The day the government listens to poodles is the day I listen to the government," the turkey squawked into the fire circle. "There is no way the government will attack anything on the orders of poodles, or shepherds or pigs or turkeys. If the government attacks it is for one reason and to support one thing."

They all stood in silence as if in a classroom. Pancho felt as if he should raise his paw before meekly offering, "the corporation?"

"Of course, the corporation. They own the government and the media and most everything else they can get their hands on." Emma puffed up her chest. "And talking about immigrants, we turkeys are indigenous, unlike you johnny-come-lately dogs."

"See, I told you it wasn't the poodles' fault," Hans said directly to Kurt.

"Poodle-lover!" Kurt snapped back, but walked off mumbling, "corporation, conspiracy, jack-booted government thugs..."

"Listen," Emma put a wing on Hans's shoulder, "we can't keep fighting each other. We must stick together and fight the real enemy."

"Divide and conquer, that's their plan," Pancho agreed. "Instead of always seeing our differences we must find our common ground."

"But we are different," Hans said, exasperated.

"Of course we are, but that's not a problem," Emma told him. "It's our biggest advantage."

"Monique said her grandfather was in the French underground," Hans recounted. "She says poodles are brave fighters. We can use every dog we can get if the corporation attacks." Then Hans turned towards the kennel. "I'm going to see those rabbits. We have ways of making them talk," and off he ran.

As the sun set food was set out on the picnic table and on a nearby makeshift buffet. The youngsters circled the food, hoping for an early handout, and Pancho thought of joining them. Then he noticed his own muddy feet. "Perhaps a quick dip in the pond before I go meet Sally," he decided and headed down to the meadow.

Several others had the same idea and soon the pig swam with goats, cows, sheep, geese, dogs, ducks and a monkey. Only Sabo stayed on shore, preferring to lick herself clean. Goldie and Pancho climbed out of the water near Sabo's rock, but she did not seem to notice them, frozen as she was, staring into the distance.

"What is it?" Pancho tried to see in the dimming light.

"Who are they," Sabo asked with a hiss. Walking along the stream toward the pond was the biggest, blackest horse she had ever seen, and beside him pranced a tiny pony with her mane in her eyes.

"Probably here for the concert," Goldie exclaimed and hurried down to meet them.

The horses stood still as the dog approached, still dripping wet.

"Welcome to the Circle-A. Make yourselves at home." Goldie smiled her finest smile. "The concert's up at the barn. You're the first ones here, but the food is ready."

The big horse stood his ground and looked around the meadow, finally resting his gaze on the golden retriever.

"We left the horse ranch near the city. On the advice of a turkey we followed the river," he explained to the dog.

"That would be Emma," Goldie grinned. "She's up at the barn."

"See, it's okay, Edsel," said the pony, tossing her mane to get a better look at the dog. "Did you say the food was ready?"

Goldie nodded and pointed her paw barnward. The pony took off with skips and leaps and Edsel followed with a more stately gait. Goldie would have gone with them, but she noticed more visitors coming over the fence at the back of the orchard. Pancho and Sabo saw them too and took off at a trot to greet them. It was Judi and Mischief and all the squirrels. Behind them followed Red and the other bears and raccoons, deer and all the animals from Cave Camp. The pig and cat had a happy reunion with the forest protectors, introduced them to Goldie, and showed them the farm.

The residents of the Circle A were prepared for these wild visitors, but their arrival still caused much excitement. The kids dared each other to touch a bear and the hens made sure the raccoons had so much food on their plates they couldn't possibly eat another bite when they were finished.

The dairy cows had arrived and dogs were pouring through the tunnel, and not just shepherds, but poodles, too.

Pancho had met up with Sally. They filled their plates and sat with Judi, whom Sally had longed to meet.

"I teach my students about the forest protectors," Sally told the bear. "You are a hero to them."

Judi smiled. "I hope someday they will come and help, we need all the animals we can get."

Pancho watched a strange group of cats who just arrived at the party. They wore dark glasses and smoked cigarettes and some had claws painted bright colors. They stood apart and looked bored. Sally leaned over and whispered in his ear, "Artists."

"Really?" Pancho expressed surprise.

"Well, maybe not really," Judi laughed, "but they think they are. Or poets, maybe."

The cats would carefully chose some tidbit from the buffet, taste it and act as though it were poisonous. Then they would go get another bit. Pancho thought they looked very thin and very unhappy.

"Where do they live?" the pig asked his date.

"Most of them are born in the suburbs," Sally answered, "but end up living in lofts and basements." She had read that somewhere.

"Oh," Pancho did not understand. "But they don't work for the corporation, do they?"

"They try not to, but sometimes they end up part of the propaganda machine." Judi added, "But not these cats. It's obvious they're still starving."

Loud static and feedback began to draw the true music lovers to the barn. The art cats were among the first to enter the newly decorated nightclub. Pancho could tell it met with their approval because they took off their glasses and almost smiled.

The rats and their helpers had truly transformed the old barn. Electricity made possible colored lights strung on the rafters and spotlights on the stage. The hay had been swept away to reveal a wide plank floor perfect for dancing. Tables and chairs (boxes and crates) were set up cabaret-style. The musicians had brought their own mirror ball and the tiny glimmers spinning through the dark made even an old barn look magical. One hand-painted banner announced the band, Free Radicals, and another the cause, Circle-A Forever.

Pancho and Sally took a side table toward the back, remembering the volume level. The rats tuned up and Bonkers joined Saccharin at the rear with his new steel drum. Young animals scurried around plugging cords and moving mikes as the barn filled to overflowing.

Dioxin took the mike and his blue fur shone in the spotlight. "Welcome to Club Circle-A." A huge roar of excitement and much stomping of hooves followed. "We are the Free Radicals, plus we have a monkey on our backs." Bonkers waved his mallet from the rear of the stage to the cheering crowd. "We'd like to start with the farm's favorite song," and with that the band struck-up a deafening and almost unrecognizable rendition of "All the animals owned the farm, EIEIO."

It sounded to Pancho very much like the next song and the one after that, but no one cared as they danced on the old barn floor with all their neighbors and friends. The dance floor got so crowded that the animals could hardly move and the club became steamy hot. Sally and Pancho decided to step outside for some air and found they were not original in that idea. In fact many of the larger animals and ones with heavy fur had moved the party outside.

"You can hear the band just as well out here," said Judi, signalling to the pigs to join her. "And it's nearer the food."

Some animals danced in the barnyard and others gathered to talk.

Kurt and another shepherd tried to light the bonfire. They lit match after match, and still it would not catch.

Pancho said, "Isn't it amazing how there is a huge pile of very flammable wood, and someone trying to light it, yet it won't catch fire."

Judi nodded. "Yet a single match tossed carelessly in the woods sometimes starts an inferno."

The dogs now poured gasoline on the pile. They stood back, tossed a match, and watched as it exploded in flames.

"Well, that's one way," Pancho said as they took seats around the bonfire.

Emma and the horses, Edsel and Jeep, moved towards the blaze. Emma leaned over to Judi and gobbled, "Well, what do you think of those rabbits?"

Judi looked surprised.

"I forgot to tell you," Pancho said.

"Let me!" squawked the turkey. She proceeded to recount the tale of intrigue and spies. The squirrels, of course, were interested and moved closer, as did the horses and others who had not heard this before.

But Pancho's mind wandered and so did his eyes, until he noticed some listeners on the far side of the bonfire. In the flickering light it was hard to tell who they were or even what they were. The pig got up and slowly walked to the other side of the fire for a better view. He sauntered casually so as not to be noticed, all the while his eyes fixed on the strangers. Suddenly from behind someone grabbed him and put a hoof over his mouth. That close to his nose Pancho had no doubt who it was: the old goat Gruff and with him Bob, the black sheep.

"Shhh.." they said in unison as the goat released the pig and pointed in the direction of the strange figures now lit by the firelight.

"Humans!" Pancho choked as the self-appointed security guards slapped their hooves over his mouth again. When they all calmed down Pancho whispered, "We have them completely and utterly outnumbered."

"Go get a bear," said Gruff.

Pancho slipped over to where Red had stretched himself out for a nap after too much food and dance. Whispering in his ear, the pig revived the bear to his feisty self and delivered him to the waiting goat and sheep. Together the animals, bear in front approached the humans.

"Hey," growled Red, inarticulate but fearsome. The humans jumped and turned around quickly to face the bear. The terror in their eyes melted quickly.

"Oh, Red, it's you," said a bearded man.

"It's okay." Red turned to the security force. "It's those guys from the forest, remember, Pancho."

Pancho remembered. "What are they doing here?" he asked in an angry tone.

The humans held up the flyers to show their interrogators.

"Free concert," said Rocky, "everyone come," he read from the paper.

By this time Judi, Emma and the others had crowded around them. Judi stood close to Pancho. She could feel him quiver in anger. "The enemy of my enemy..." she whispered, and Pancho sighed.

Then Emma spoke. "I've got an idea, why don't you guys take off those clothes!"

"I beg your pardon," said Rainbow, blushing in the firelight. "We hardly know you."

"Besides, it's cold," said Redwood.

"So stand by the fire, or better still, go in the barn, it's really hot in there," the turkey said.

"Okay, I think I get it," said River as he pulled off his shirt. "Sort of a solidarity thing."

"Let's just say it puts an unnecessary wall between us," the turkey replied.

The humans shrugged, stripped off their clothing, and stood naked in front of the bonfire. Pancho, Bob, Gruff and other curious and wary animals looked them over closely.

"They look better, don't they?" asked Emma.

"I wouldn't say that, but they do look like real animals," Bob said.

"Real ugly animals," Gruff added.

"I do not look like that," Pancho snapped at Emma, remembering her earlier remark.

"My mistake. Now, can they go in and dance?"

The mumbling of the security goat was taken for a yes. While the other humans went into "Club Circle-A" Redwood stayed outside to hear more about the rabbits.

Jeep was young and in a party mood. She skipped inside to kick up her heels on the dance floor. Sally took Pancho's foot and led him in under the spinning mirror ball. Sabo danced right next to them, her partner a real cool tom cat with orange tabby stripes and just a stub of a tail. Pancho felt a bit protective of the little black cat and decided to keep an eye on this artsy character. But soon he was lost again in Sally's tiny eyes. This music was not the most romantic, but somehow the mood in the barn was. Monique and Hans hung in the corner, locked in an embrace only thinly disguised as dancing. Suzy and her girlfriend from the petting zoo were, well, petting. Old couples and new smiled and cuddled and then the spell broke, the music stopped.

"The band's going to take a little break," the blue rat announced, "but don't go away, someone from the farm would like to speak."

The animals looked around to find the speaker. First the mike was handed to Goldie, who passed it to Rosy. The cow gave it to Jethro, who gave it back to her. Rosy reluctantly took the stage. She thanked the crowd for coming and praised the band.

"We at Circle-A farm are facing a corporate take over," she continued. "I know many of you have the same problems where you live and work," there rose a mumble of agreement. "A takeover will mean we will lose control of the farm and with that of our own lives." Rosy's long pause highlighted the silence in the room and Jethro could see her crying. He stepped onstage and took the mike from the sobbing cow.

"It was decided by the animals at Circle-A that we will not let them take the farm," the mule continued for Rosy. "We will fight the takeover however possible, but we hope it can be non-violent." Jethro stopped as he looked out at the barn full of animals and realized he was talking on stage. Fright washed over him and he thrust the mike at the golden retriever.

Goldie hopped onto the platform and finished the speech. "We are asking for your support in our fight against the corporate grab and we offer our support for you in this common struggle." Heads were nodding around the barn and conversations began among the audience animals. Goldie could see the Free Radicals chowing down on the free food through the open barn door, so she opened up the discussion.

"Would anyone from off the farm like to speak?" Of course, the dogs went first.

"Our kennel is under attack by the government," a graying shepherd announced. "First there was a conspiracy to take our jobs, replacing guard dogs with new-fangled alarm systems. Those of us who were domestic dogs began to lose those jobs to imported breeds." He glared at a group of fluffy poodles near the stage. "We have gathered guns and armed ourselves. We plan to fight the government and its corporate master to the last dog." The German shepherd turned neatly and marched off stage.

Monique had held her tongue long enough. She leapt on stage to defend the poodles. "Let's face it, there are no jobs for dogs anymore. Sometimes they want us poodles because we are smaller and cost less to feed," her soft accent hid her anger. "They say we are easier to train and don't shed. But we know as soon as they can find a machine to replace us they will." She glanced at Hans who stood beside her. "The corporation wants us to hate each other and fight each other. That keeps us too busy to fight them."

Hans stepped up, "If we joined together we would be twice as strong. We need to focus on the real enemy." Hans looked at the old shepherd, who hung his head in thought.

Edsel moved to the front of the room, his shiny coat sparkled with the mirror ball. "The horse ranch has similar problems. We horses have been pretty much replaced by cars. A few of us compete for highly skilled jobs, but most of us are turned out to pasture." The room nodded in recognition and the horse continued. "The corporation tries to brainwash us with sports, to make us believe that horse races and jumping and all the other games are actually important in some way. The horses at the ranch are more concerned with who wins the Kentucky Derby than with who wins the race for President."

Mac the squirrel from Cave Camp picked up the mike next. The tiny animal sat on the speaker to be seen. "It really doesn't matter who wins for president anyway, they're all the same. Just like at camp when we offer a choice for dinner: acorn stew or acorn porridge. They're both the same."

Mischief leaned over to Judi and whispered, "I thought so," and the bear stifled a giggle.

Mac concluded, "It makes everyone feel good to think they have a choice, but elections are just the Corporation serving up the same nuts and calling them by different names."

Judi took the stage from Mac. "The forest has been under corporate siege for decades. The loss of the wild lands affects every animal on earth, and yet so few put energy into their defense. Time is growing short. This must be a top priority for all of us, or none of the other problems will even matter." With that Judi carried the mike to River.

The young man stood before the skeptical animals. He was not really prepared to speak. "Well, my human friends and I agree with what Judi just said," he blurted out. "In fact, everyone made important points. I want you to know there are many humans who share your feelings. Of course, there are those who don't." He looked around helplessly and was rescued by Rainbow.

"I want to know," she asked, "what can we do?"

Pancho was now ready to burst. He had to get the floor. He wiggled his way through the crowd and reached for the mike. But he was not the only one wanting to express himself. From the left came the goat and from the right, the black sheep. The surprised Rainbow jumped back just in time to avoid being the epicenter of the collision. The microphone flew into the air to be caught in the claws of the quick thinking Emma. The turkey sailed onto the stage and picked up the discussion without missing a beat, much to the disappointment of Bob, Gruff, and Pancho.

"The first thing we need to do is put aside our differences, as individuals and as groups. Sure, dogs don't always think the same way as horses. Chickens don't have the same goals as raccoons, as a rule. But we all have one thing in common here: a great big corporate, banking, media, government, miliary, environmental disaster that affects us all and keeps us from getting what we want as individuals."

Emma paused to take a breath and immediately paws and hooves were grasping for the mike. "No," squawked the turkey, waving the microphone in the air, "this is the ultimate talking stick and I still have it." Then in a more civilized tone she asked, "Can we all agree on this one thing: the corporation is our common enemy?"

The crowd went wild. "I take that as a yes," she announced. "I'm done!" With that Emma tossed the mike to the grasping crowd and Pancho caught it smugly.

"I just want to mention one idea. I heard it today from the Sacred Cow." A gasp of respect escaped from many mouths, and Pancho continued. "We can all agree on the problem, but as the human asked, what can we do? I suggest we consider having a stampede."

"That crazy old cow," Rosy did not bother with the mike. "Why didn't she suggest having an earthquake or tornado?" the cow snorted. "You can't just have a stampede like you have a party."

Everyone laughed. Pancho handed the mike to the returning rats, much to Gruff and Bob's dismay, and the music cranked up again.

Pancho did not feel like dancing just then, so Sally and he took a stroll outside. The June moon was almost full and reflected in the pond and the water troughs. Young animals chased around the bonfire as older ones continued in serious discussion. It seemed not everyone was so quick to dismiss the stampede as a vehicle for change. Little Jeep was telling about the running of the wild ponies on Chincoteague and the deer remembered running in groups from hunters. The dairy cows were certain if Mother cow had suggested it there must be some merit to the idea.

Pancho and Sally talked of many things that night. Neither of them had first hand stampede experience and so they stuck to more intimate topics, strolling together watching the fire burn.

Bob was disappointed he did not get to the mike earlier, but he found a small group of dogs who seemed somewhat interested in his lecture on the history of the animal rights movement. Gruff the goat added to the talk by interjecting facts about the revolution in Cat-alonia. It was unclear whether the dogs were listening or sleeping; at any rate, they were quiet.

Sabo catted around with her new pal and even tried to smoke a cigarette, but had a coughing fit when she inhaled. She noticed Rosy slip away from the barnyard and cross the fence to the dairy.

"Maybe I should follow," she thought, but decided to stay with the tabby.

Tex and Mex had a gathering of youngsters at their feet. Unable to compete musically with their old acoustic guitars, the coyotes more than compensated in the story-telling department. As the bonfire warmed their calloused paws, Mex helped Tex spin out this yarn:

"Tonight you're going to hear a wild and woolly tail. There are many, many tails about the Woollies because the Woollies all love to tell tails. They also love to sing songs and dance the night away. But they also do some serious organizing full of hell raising and sabotage."

"Let's stay and hear this," Sally said. "I love Woolly tails." Pancho agreed and they sat down to listen.

"Now the Woollies have been around for a long, long time. Some of you probably think that all Woollies are sheep, but that's not true at all. They started out as mostly sheep and goats, but soon all kinds of animals joined up, even a couple of trail-weary coyotes." Tex and Mex winked at each other. "Now some say bad things about the Woollies, but don't you believe it. They fought the hard fight in hard times and any scraps of dignity we animals have today, we have the Woollies to thank, in part."

Tex grinned at his eager young listeners. "Now in those times the corporations were running wild. They scooped up the little farms and made huge corporate farms. They blasted holes in the mountains looking for coal and gold. They cut down timber as fast as they could. You would think they were in some kind of race. Sound familiar? But in every case the animals got the short end of the stick. They had their land stolen, then they had to work for corporations that overworked and underpaid them.

"So in the fields and mines and timber camps the Woollies organized resistance, and their membership grew until the corporations started to really get worried. The Woollies talked all the time about the Great Stampede and they worked for a day when it would happen." The coyote sighed and seemed lost in thought.

Mex pushed him with his elbow and Tex resumed his tail. "Well, one very big industry at the time was weaving wool into cloth. Animals from all over the world were lured by trickery and brought to a big city, where they were used like slaves by the corporation to manufacture cloth. The animals came from different species and from different lands, so they spoke many different languages. This made things very confusing and extra-hard for the animals to work together for protection and justice.

"The daily ration of oats was small and the animals were always hungry. But the corporation saw that money could be saved by feeding the workers even less. The rations of oats got smaller and smaller. The starving animals became desperate. But what could they do? If an animal protested she was given no oats at all and would really starve. Finally some animals said 'Let's call in the Woollies!'

"Some Woollies arrived and helped tackle the first big problem. They formed a committee of cloth worker animals representing all species and languages. The animals began to talk together. 'What can we do, how can we win?' 'Should we attempt a Great Stampede?' 'We are too tired and weak from hunger, the time is not right!' 'But we must strike, it's our only chance.'

"The cloth-worker animals made a bold and careful plan and the Woollies helped make it work. For the Woollies had friends in low places, and those are the kind that count. The cloth workers called for a strike. The animals refused to work in the cloth factory.

"The corporation laughed to themselves. 'We have lots of money, we can wait them out. Soon they will be starving and will work for even fewer oats than we give them now.' But the corporation underestimated the resolve of the animals and the cleverness of their Woolly friends. The Woollies snuck food into the striking workers and took the young ones to stay on friendly farms where there was food and safety. And so the strike held.

"The corporation decided if they could just find out who the Woollies were they could get rid of them and the strike would end. But that was impossible because now all the animals had joined up and become Woollies. The corporation would have to get rid of them all and then there would be no workers for the cloth factory.

"The corporation began losing money and they couldn't stand that. They had to settle with the animals, all Woollies now, and agreed to double their ration of oats. This was a wonderful victory for the Woollies and for animals everywhere."

Tex stopped to take a drink from the bowl in front of him.

Pancho stood up and asked, "But the Great Stampede, didn't it happen?"

"No, no, the time was not right," Tex said. "I never can figure why the time is never right."

"So, what happened to the Woollies?" Pancho seemed more caught up in the tail than the youngsters.

"Well, this is just one of many, many Woolly tails, as I said before, and all of them are mostly true. So you can see how the government and the corporations really had a big interest in getting rid of Woollies. They set up the Farm Bureau of Investigation for the express purpose of hunting down Woollies and killing them."

"What!" Pancho exclaimed. "The FBI was set up just to kill the Woollies?"

"I said so, didn't I?" Tex said. "They hunted every animal suspected of Woolly activity and killed them or scared them so much they stopped complaining. But the FBI didn't get all the Woollies. They're still around today."

"But we have to be very careful what we do and how we do it," said Mex. "Don't worry, Woollies will be a part of the Great Stampede, when the time is right."

The band played on and on. Bonkers did a steel drum solo backed up by the llamas on maracas. He decided he liked music as much as driving trucks. The rats had run through their repertoire twice and now were jamming free form. More and more animals moved outside to the fire circle; as it got late, many fell asleep.

The dogs and dairy cows went home since home was close by, but everyone else spent the night at the Circle-A. The humans curled up very close to the fire as they were unused to the cold, and by the wee hours Goldie had to cover them up with their jackets, they were shivering so. "Very, very fragile and poorly designed, it's amazing they can survive," she thought. Some of the forest protectors slept in the barn, to try something new, and the art cats took to the orchard trees only after the sky was almost light.

It had been a wonderful night, but they awoke to a terrible morning.

18

Sleepy animals a took a moment to come to their senses after the crackle of rifles firing exploded the farm awake. From the kennel came the distant sounds of dogs yelping and barking as they fired back at their attackers.

Goldie was first to reach the tunnel where Monique pushed puppies through to the Circle-A as fast as they would go. Tiny fluffy poodles and floppy-eared shepherd pups tumbled into the meadow. Sally rushed over to usher them to safety.

Pancho watched the battle through the chain-link fence. Everywhere shepherds were down, lying in the dirt.

"The rabbits told the truth," the pig thought. "They knew about the raid in advance. And the shepherds were right too: the corporation is afraid of animals having guns."

The dogs were taking a terrible beating, but whenever a shepherd fell, a poodle picked up his weapon and joined the fight.

"Break the fence," Edsel whinnied. "Give them an escape route." The horse kicked and tore at the metal post. Bonkers arrived with tin snips and soon a large section gave way, joining the kennel to the farm. But the dogs stood their ground; outgunned by the military and their automatic weapons, they preferred to die in the fight.

The horrified spectators yelled at them to run. Goldie and Red began to drag the wounded to the farm where they could be cared for by Suzy, Jethro and others in the barn. Many of the farm animals hid in fear or stood frozen, not knowing what to do.

Pancho helped Sally herd the puppies to the pig pen, where Martha rolled them in the mud, "to disguise them as piglets," she said, hopefully.

Sabo could not stand the gunfire. The art cats clung to the branches of the orchard, but Sabo took off at her top speed for the safety of the dairy. She did not stop running until she reached the manger of the Sacred Cow. There, with her mother, Rosy looked very upset. The cat panted, out of breath, but the cows wanted to know what had happened outside.

Sabo reported, "The government is massacring the dogs." As the cat said this she noticed how weak the old cow looked. "Are you alright, Mother Cow?"

"Yes, my dear, I'm fine. I'm going to the pastures of plenty." The Sacred Cow smiled; Sabo could see tears in Rosy's eyes. The old cow continued, her voice so weak that Rosy and Sabo had to move very close. "A Great Stampede," she whispered, "all the animals running together, caring as much for each other as for themselves." She sighed. "It's a beautiful dream, and I believe when the time is right it will happen."

Sabo's eyes were open wide. "When will the time be right?" she pleaded.

"When the straw breaks the camel's back," the old cow whispered.

"What does it mean?" Sabo asked Rosy, who shook her head, unknowing.

"Mother Cow," the black cat said, rubbing against her muzzle, "Please don't leave us. We need you!"

"Little cat, sit very close. I have a story to tell you," the old cow replied. Sabo lay her head near the yellowed teeth and listened.

"There once was a cat who wanted to know how to be in the world. She went into the woods to ask the help of the oldest, wisest tree. 'Please, wise tree, show me my way,' the cat asked, but the tree stood silent. The cat sat at the root of the tree waiting for her answer. After a long time she noticed a crippled fox under a bush.

'I wonder how that fox survives, crippled and unable to hunt?' thought the cat.

Suddenly a tiger leapt into the clearing, right near the fox's bush. The tiger had a rabbit in his mouth and he ate it right in front of them. But he did not eat it all, he left a big piece of meat right near the bush. The tiger bounded back into the woods and the crippled fox crept out and ate the meat."

Sabo nodded. "I understand," she said.

"Do you?" said the cow, with a weak cough. "The story is not over."

"The cat looked up at the tree and said, 'Thank you, now I see the way. If I sit down here and wait like the fox, my needs will be met. It's a matter of believing.'

So the cat sat by the tree and waited day after day. Every day the tiger came and brought food for the crippled fox, but left nothing for the cat. She grew very hungry. Finally she said, 'Oh, wise tree, I don't understand. I sat here and waited, just like the fox, but no tiger came to feed me.'

The tree rustled her leaves and lowered a branch to whisper to the cat. 'Little cat, you are not a crippled fox, you are a tiger.'"

The old cow had trouble finishing that last sentence. She coughed a bit and Sabo petted her nose.

"Thank you, I think I understand," the cat said softly.

Sabo felt she should leave Rosy alone with her mother at these last moments. The cows of the dairy stood silent like statues, looking straight ahead. They knew that Mother cow was passing and for them this seemed even more significant than the slaughter at the kennel. As Sabo left the manger hundreds of soft brown eyes turned her way. The cat shook her head sadly and tiptoed back to the farm. The shooting had stopped and she needed to be with her friends at this terrible time.

The gunfight at the kennel ended almost too quickly. The defeated dogs were dead or wounded and the soldiers began poking through the kennel, making sure the destruction was complete. At the Circle-A all the animals hid in the barn, as well as the four naked humans. Very frightened, they tried to keep quiet. Jethro shut the barn door from the outside, then lay down blocking the entrance with his body.

Emma flew over the kennel, counting the fallen dogs and keeping an eye on the enemy. She looked for signs of rabbits, but saw none. "Perhaps the traitors have escaped," the turkey mused, "or were released by the government thugs." As she looked at the killing field she recognized many familiar dogs, among them lay Kurt, and next to him a small gray poodle, Monique's father.

One soldier had made his way to the torn fence and was almost in the Circle-A meadow. Goldie had stayed there for just this possibility. She had a good relationship with humans, and had never been mistreated by any. The golden retriever believed that her friendliness would bring out the good in the soldier. Perhaps she could distract him and make him remember that he liked dogs. At least she could try. It was all she could think of to stop the violence.

Emma watched in disgust as Goldie wagged her tail and wiggled over to the soldier. He spoke to her roughly, but did not shoot, as he continued his advance toward the Circle-A barn. Emma hated to see her canine pal degrade herself this way, but Goldie redoubled her efforts. The dog rubbed the soldier's legs with her copper back and tried to lick his hand. "If I could get him to pet me, I'm sure I could win him over," she thought. But still the soldier marched slowly to the barn, ignoring the pleading retriever.

Sabo saw the mule in front of the barn blocking the door, while from the meadow a military man dressed in green camouflage and carrying a gun approached it. Goldie was running around him, trying her best to keep him from advancing. Just then the cat watched Emma fly overhead and land on the barn roof. Sabo, deciding that was a good place to be, climbed to the roof to join Emma in this bird's eye view.

Inside the barn the animals planned a defense for when the barn door opened. Bears in front, the others crowded behind, they were ready. The youngest and the wounded stayed in the back. Hans lay with the wounded dogs, but he was merely nicked. Goldie had dragged him off the kennel grounds "by accident" she said, but Red told him otherwise. Monique felt very grateful for this one miracle among so much tragedy.

The human forest defenders had torn their clothes into strips to bandage the injured dogs. Now they were committed to their nudeness. The art cats stood to the rear of the crowd, unsure of what they had gotten into. But the rats were all revved up and wanted to fight. Judi had to keep reminding them to keep quiet for now.

Pancho, Bob and Gruff jockied for positions right behind the bears. Positions of honor, not of insanity. Yet all three wished they had stayed outside; the suspense was killing them. Bonkers found a good peep hole and reported everything to Carlos, who discussed it with his partner Juanita before she whispered it to the others. "One of them is coming. He has a gun. Goldie is slowing him down, but she can't stop him."

From the roof top the cat and the turkey watched the drama below. Sabo mumbled to herself in frustration.

"What did you say?" Emma asked.

"We must have a camel," the cat hissed. "Is a llama a kind of camel?"

"I don't think so," the turkey thought for a minute. "Maybe. But why do you need a camel?"

"To start the stampede." The cat got frantic as the soldier neared the barn full of animals. "The Sacred Cow said we must break a camel's back with straw or we won't be able to have a stampede, and we need a stampede." The cat grew wide-eyed.

"That cow is crazy!" the turkey snorted.

The soldier tired of the retriever's antics. He picked up a rock and threw it at her. Goldie feigned a game of fetch and ran back to the man with the rock in her mouth, but he would not play. It was too late anyway; he stood only feet from the barn.

Jethro looked the soldier in the eye as he lay blocking the door. They both knew the mule would not move willingly. Lifting the rifle and aiming it at Jethro's head the man shouted "Move!" but the mule lay still.

Goldie paced back and forth. Emma and Sabo almost fell off the roof in their attempts to see. Inside the barn everyone held their breath.

Then in the silence, they heard a tiny click as the man cocked the rifle. That little click threw a switch in Goldie's head. The retriever jumped at the soldier and sunk her teeth into his leg.

The man screamed, turned on the dog and fired. The power of the shot tossed Goldie across the dirt yard, slamming her body into a water trough. The soldier did not even glance her way as he stooped to examine his injured leg.

Sabo saw red. She did not think, she could not fear. Her eyes grew wild, her fur stood on end and she arched her back like a

Halloween cut-out. Off the roof she dove, all claws and teeth, onto the back of the stooping man. Like a miniature tiger, she bit and clawed at his face and eyes. The soldier dropped his gun to use both hands. He grabbed Sabo and threw her as hard as he could in the direction of Goldie's body, but the cat landed on her feet.

Jethro stood up. He felt a feeling unfamiliar, rising in him, flowing through him. He looked at Goldie's limp and bloodied body, then turned to the hated stranger. One good kick was all it took: the soldier hit the ground with a thud.

At this moment, wailing and lowing filled the farm, from the dairy next door. The Sacred Cow had died. Without the mule leaning against them, the barn doors swung open on their own. The animals stood in horror of the scene before them. Emma and Sabo wept next to the water trough, by Goldie's body. The soldier lay in a pool of blood which ran in little rivers downhill.

The eerie mooing from the dairy inspired the Circle-A animals to howl or squawk or bleat their own requiem. Jethro stood quivering violently, his eyes on the meadow beyond, unable to grasp what had just happened, what he had done. All he felt, all he knew was he had to run. With an explosion of energy he took off toward the meadow.

The dairy understood immediately; they were quivering too. The usually docile cows kicked down the fence and poured into the meadow surrounding Jethro as they ran.

The sheep felt the pull and almost trampled the bears in their rush downhill. The other animals, humans and all, tumbled into the meadow and joined the race.

Rosy stood by Goldie's body. She felt numb from the day's enormous pain. Sabo whispered to her and pointed to the running animals.

"Yes, it's started." Rosy took a deep breath. "Well, let's go."

The cat and cow joined the others in the meadow. All but the most badly wounded ran. Around the pond and through the orchard, around the meadow they ran in laps. But instead of getting tired they got energized. Every animal had his own reason for running, but the same goal. The raccoons ran for the forest and the shepherds for the kennel, but that did not matter. They ran for freedom. The birds had gathered in the sky above the meadow and followed the path of the galloping animals like a shadow. Emma flew in the center with her poults. Although still young, they must not miss this. They would always remember being part of the Great Stampede.

After a few laps, the runners noticed a change. It was subtle, but important; profound, actually. Some of the animals began to cry as they ran, others to crow or laugh. The raccoons still ran for the forest, but also for the dog kennel. The dairy cows ran for the death of their Mother, but also for the horses' ranch. Pancho ran for Goldie and the farm, but also for the humans, and he really couldn't explain why. They were one unit now: one giant animal bent on justice for all.

They burst open the gates of the Circle-A and filled the road, the animals stampeding below, the birds forming a canopy above. Pancho ran next to Sally and Rosy. Sabo darted bravely between the legs of larger animals to get near Judi, who ran despite her injuries, as did many others. This was too important.

A small group of soldiers hid behind a truck as the stampede passed the kennel gate. They were no fools. Every animal knows, and humans are no exception, that when there is a stampede you must join in or get out of the way. Try to stop it, and you will be crushed. After the animals stormed past and the dust had settled a lieutenant picked up the phone to deliver this warning: "The animals have gone wild and are stampeding toward the city. Stay in your homes to avoid danger. Request National Guard assistance." The lieutenant had not noticed the four naked humans in the herd, or if he did, he just considered them animals.

Cheering onlookers lined the street, ignoring the military warning. Some just waved but many joined the stampede.

"Run with us to trample the corporation!" Some thought it exciting and ran for adventure, others went because they had nothing to lose.

As the stampede passed the horse ranch, Edsel broke ranks. He galloped through the stables, kicking in doors. "Come with us, you have nothing to loose but your bridles!" and the thoroughbreds pranced into the street, joining their fellow freedom seekers.

At the zoo, the imprisoned animals fought their guards and helped each other escape to join in the stampede.

The ranks of the rebels grew like a snowball rolling downhill. Every place they passed held more animals who hated what the corporation had done to their lives and land, and who had the courage and love to risk everything to stop it.

With so many bodies the pace slowed down a bit, and Pancho caught his breath. He looked around at the unfamiliar surroundings: buildings blocking the sky; no grass or trees. "How could anyone not agree," he thought, "this is no way to live."

Now the rats took the lead, showing the way towards the corporate headquarters. The animals marched more than ran in the narrow streets. Their parade stretched out for blocks. Dioxin led the stampede down a side street ending abruptly with a tall, tall building in the shape of a pyramid. They had arrived at the corporate headquarters.

Pancho couldn't see over the horses, deer, and bears in front of him. Soon the news had passed from the birds overhead. The National Guard blocked the street in defense of the corporation.

Any animal could tell that this was a trap. No doubt the army had moved in at the rear as well. There was, quite literally, no turning back.

Facing guns, the stampede halted. Whispers swept the crowd. Only the birds could really get a good look at the situation. Emma flew to the front and could not believe her eyes. Coming out of the big glass doors of the tall, tall building were those mangy, flea-bitten spies dressing in navy-blue wool suits with striped ties.

Blackstone carried a black briefcase and Hamilton grabbed a microphone to address the crowd. Although most of the animals could not see the speaker, his voice was unmistakable.

"My friends," the slimy rabbit began, "I tried to warn you that this would not work, and now look what has happened. You've come all this way only to be staring down the barrel of a rifle." He shook his head and made a little ticking sound. "Luckily for you, no real damage has been done; corporate property is still unharmed and the corporation is willing to forgive this unfortunate outburst, allowing most of you to go your way in peace. We will, however, need to punish the agitators who started this stampede. The animals of the Circle-A, or rather H."

A roar from the crowd drowned out the next sentence, but Pancho could tell it was now Blackstone's turn at the mike. "The corporation is also willing to admit that your grievances may have some merit. Hamilton and I have been up in that boardroom for hours trying to convince the chairman and others. And what we have come up with is an agreement, and it's a very generous one on the part of the corporation." He opened the briefcase with a click and produced a thick and official looking folder. The rabbit waved the papers at the animals. "The corporation is willing to appoint a committee of animals to make suggestions. We want to discuss our problems and co-operate with each other as good community members."

All those listening to the rabbits' Public Relations message knew it for lies. Not just the animals and humans to whom the generous offer was tendered, but the soldiers, the corporate heads and especially the rabbits themselves. It was an old game and everyone had been playing it for too long.

"We can't give in," Pancho said to those around him, "but we are in a difficult spot."

"I came here to smash the corporation, and I for one intend to," Rosy said with resolve as she pushed her way through the crowd.

"But the guns!" Pancho cried. "They'll shoot you."

"I suppose they will," Rosy sighed and moved to the front of the stamped.

She climbed the steps to where the rabbits stood. The soldiers followed her ascent with weapons aimed. Rosy leaned down to speak into the mike. "I do not speak for all, only for myself. I do not accept this or any offer made by the evil corporation. I came here to destroy it, not to reform it."

The cow turned her eye to the soldiers. "I am going inside, you must kill me to stop me." Rosy walked slowly and proudly toward the glass doors.

"Ready, aim, fire!" The command was hollered. Yet the soldiers hesitated: no one wanted to shoot first, so no one fired.

"I repeat! Soldiers, ready, aim, fire!" this time the rifles answered, but the soldiers fired into the air, causing the birds to pull back their ranks.

The commander got red in the face. He could shoot the crazy cow himself, but he needed to assert control over his troops. What had gotten into them?

"Walk faster, Rosy!" Pancho chanted. "Get inside the doors!"

"I am giving you all one last chance before I court martial the entire division. Shoot the terrorist cow! Ready, aim, fire!"

The guns roared. Probably each soldier had hoped it would look like an accident. But the bullets that did not go into the air went into the commander's body. He collapsed like a bloody rag doll.

Rosy stopped her march. She checked both her sides to make sure she was not hit, then looked at the surprised soldiers.

"Shoot the cow!" screamed Hamilton to the guards. But they were in too much shock to hear him.

Finally one of them whispered some words of common sense: "Let's get out of here fast." They dropped their guns and scattered into the crowd.

Rosy found her tongue. "Come on," she hollered as the glass doors gave way to the cow's weight.

Pushing the suited rabbits aside, the animals stampeded up the steps and into the lobby of the corporation's lair. Up the stairways to the boardroom they stormed, following the smell of old, dirty money. Edsel asked for the privilege of kicking down the old-growth hardwood door. He let Jeep and some others help, much as the older kid lets the little ones have first crack at a pinata. Then with a couple of powerful kicks from his hind legs he splintered the door into beautiful, old-growth, kindling.

Cowering in the far corner near the wet bar, behind the mahogany desk, was a balding, paunchy, aging man in a suit, whimpering in fear.

The animals could not believe their eyes. Here they stood, face to face with their nemesis, the head of the corporation. Sally thought of a film she had seen where a tiny terrier pulls back a curtain and the terrible wizard looked just like this man: small and powerless compared with the minds, hearts and courage of the animal revolution.

"Are you sure you are the corporate president?" Judi said, walking over to give the man a sniff.

Backing up to the plate glass window, the man's voice quivered as he answered. "I'm afraid so." Even being sniffed by a small bear like Judi was a terrifying experience for someone so insulated from nature. "I'm also the C.E.O."

"This can't be him. This weak excuse for a human can't possibly have done all that damage: destroyed the environment, busted our unions, sent our jobs overseas, foreclosed on our farms, replaced us with machines. He can hardly keep from fainting," Rosy said, disgusted.

"He probably had help!" Bob cried, pushing into the boardroom.

"Of course he did," said Gruff. The two leaned close to the corporate president and applied their secret weapon: aroma therapy. "Name your accomplices," demanded the goat. "Who else was involved," Bob bleated.

"Everyone was involved! Of course I wasn't acting alone," the man cried, wanting to save his own skin. "What about the banks?"

Emma flapped her way into the room. "You own the bank. The bank is you."

"Well, what about the government? They certainly bear some blame," the man whimpered.

"Stop it, you know the buck stops here!" scolded the turkey. "You own the government. You pay for the election campaigns, you own the newspapers that determine the elections, you appoint the judges and hire the police. Maybe getting rid of you won't fix everything, but I say you're a very good place to start."

"Did you shoot the commander?" the president asked, feeling doomed. "Are you going to kill me?"

"The soldiers shot the general. I guess they got fed up with being bossed around," Rosy snorted. "And so are we. You will have a fair trial. I'm afraid you won't have a jury of your peers since you have no peers. I suppose a jury of your victims will have to do."

They marched the pale corporate president to the front of the building.

The rabbit lawyers were found hiding behind a planter to avoid the wrath of the revolutionaries. The corporate president waved the lawyers on and decided to defend himself, to everyone's relief. Since the mike was still set up, all the animals could hear the proceedings even when their lines of sight were obstructed.

The jury had won their seats in einy-meiny-miny-mo. Martha, Sally's mother, was jury head. The other eleven represented quite a cross-section: Corvette the chestnut horse, Mac the Nuts-To-You cook, Red from Cave Camp, Daisy, one of the dairy cows and an aunt of Rosy's, Monique from the kennel, Jethro the mule, Sabo as well as an art cat named Dali, Nicotine the splotchy rat, the human River and Horace the spotted owl, his well-meaning look-out.

The trial was speedy. Emma served as the judge. Bob and Gruff begged to be the ones to question the criminal and enumerate his crimes. The CEO denied nothing but the definition of the crime.

"I did nothing illegal," he declared. "It was all within the law."

The question of motive puzzled the animals most of all. Why would any creature or man be so evil?

"Money, I did it all for money and for power," he stated, "and that, also, is perfectly legal."

"So for money and power you destroyed the forest, threw helpless animals out of homes and jobs, thwarted the democratic process, started wars, conducted horrifying experiments on unsuspecting creatures..." Gruff spoke pacing back and forth in front of the little man, listing the corporate crimes.

"All legal!" the CEO stated bluntly.

"Legal because you made the laws!" Bob jumped in. "But that doesn't mean what you did was right!"

The sheep stomped the concrete. When quiet restored itself Bob announced, "The animals rest their case."

"Do you have anything further to say?" Emma asked the corporate president and CEO.

"I repeat that everything the corporation has done is legal. I remind the jury that they must uphold the law!" The balding head was sweating now.

"Oh, nonsense," Martha said, looking him in the eye. "We aren't interested in upholding the law, we're here to uphold justice!"

From the open-air courtroom arose a cheer of enthusiastic approval. The jury huddled together for a moment to come to their unanimous verdict. It presented no surprise.

"We, the jury of your victims, find you guilty as charged," Martha stated in a clear voice. "We suggest the following punishment: since money and power were your criminal motives, you will have no more of either of these. We will not lock you in prison where you will be a burden on the rest of us. Instead you will spend your life trying to clean up the mess you made."

"You can start by planting trees in the forest you destroyed," Red shouted, and the animals in the street roared their approval. Emma took the mike. "We came here to destroy the corporation. Also, it's wicked stepsisters, the bank and the government. And we came to free its prisoner, the press." The turkey looked at the exuberant sea of animal faces. "Does anyone have any suggestions?"

The animals puzzled quietly. It had been such a big problem for so long that a simple solution seemed inadequate. From the front of the crowd a lamb raised her hoof. Emma chuckled and waved her wing for the lamb to come take the mike.

"Can we just say: no more bullies?" The little lamb's high-pitched bleating caused the crowd to smile. The lamb blushed and hurried back to her mother.

"You know, that is the way to do it." It was that flea-bag rabbit Blackstone, climbing out from behind the speaker. He and his buddy Hamilton had taken off their business suits to appeal to the revolutionary animals.

"Just abolish all hierarchies and all coercion," Hamilton hopped in, "no interest, money, or bosses..."

Emma grabbed the mike back. "How about no lawyers and no spies!"

Pancho had a thought and moved forward. "No laws means no lawyers. No hierarchies, no bullies. The lamb is right."

"We could write this up for you right now," Hamilton volunteered. "Just so everything is legal."

"No thanks," Emma said, grabbing back the mike. "No more legal and illegal. How about fair and unfair, right and wrong? That's something we can all understand. We don't need to write it down."

The rabbits threw up their paws in despair. They knew they would soon be planting trees with the ex-C.E.O.

Martha spoke from the jury section. "Before we go, by a show of paws, shall the corporation, the government, and the bank all be abolished, and animals returned to their natural state of freedom? All in favor?"

All but one.

"All opposed?"

The C.E.O. and the lawyer rabbits raised their paws.

If you're wondering how this could be ... the rabbits, of course, voted twice.

19

Papa, can we go over to the kennel and play with the pups?" the round white piglet begged.

Pancho looked at the warm June sun to guess the hour before giving consent. "Check with your mother first and don't be gone long. Remember what today is!" He smiled at his small litter. "Aunt Judi and Aunt Sabo are coming."

"And the rats!" the three piglets squealed as they scrambled over to the pig pen. "Mom, can we go to see the pups just for a little while? We'll be back for the party; Hans and Monique are bringing the pups anyway. So can we go?"

Sally was busy fixing a fruit salad for the pot-luck. "Okay, but be back in time to clean up before the party." She kissed three snouts and got back to work on her apples.

The barn looked fabulous. This year's decorating committee had outdone themselves, and the food tables now numbered six.

"It seems each year we add another food table," Jethro chuckled.

"No complaints here!" Pancho answered as he helped the mule set the buffet.

"This is going to be the biggest bonfire ever!" Hans yelled over to the pig as he helped a grey poodle pile the dry limbs higher. "Well, at last! Here comes the band."

The shepherd spoke the truth. Up the hill from the meadow, dragging huge amounts of equipment, came the Free Radicals and their friends the art cats. "Look at all those heavy instruments!" Pancho kidded, "I guess it's one of the burdens of fame."

Dioxin gave the pig a hug. "A rat really knows he's arrived when he has a cat for a roadie."

"Sabo!" Pancho ran to embrace the feline, who set down the guitar case to free her arms. "How's communal life?"

"It's great, mostly. We're using that pyramid building for artists studios. You must come see," she purred. "How's family life?"

"Great, mostly," the pig answered. "Where's your tabby friend?"

"Coming. He's helping to carry the speaker."

Sabo pointed her paw as the biggest speaker Pancho had ever seen or imagined appeared over the hill. It took four cats to pull it with ropes. The pig shook his head in disbelief. Everything about this celebration kept getting bigger and better. Goldie would have loved this, he thought.

Emma and Judi arrived together, bringing wild berries from the forest. The squirrels, visiting with some dairy cows by the pond, and the other forest critters, had been convinced to tour the new school built by the kennel dogs. They had a right to be proud of it, the first one ever.

"Where are those humans? Late as usual," the turkey complained.

"They do live the furthest away," reminded Judi. "I keep meaning to go and see what they've done," the bear sighed.

"I went a few months ago," Emma said. "What a strange place, but they seem to like it. Too much indoors for me. But if you go into business with llamas, you have to live where it's cold. Makes better wool, Juanita says."

"Being snowed in for a month with that monkey: that would drive anybody Bonkers!" Pancho joked.

Bob trotted over and handed Judi a newspaper. "Careful, the ink's still wet," he cautioned as he gave one to the turkey, too. The masthead read: Circle-A Free Press/Editors: Pancho, Bob, Gruff.

Judi was about to say how professional it looked when the band struck an opening chord so loud no one could speak.

All they could do was dance.

THE END

Anarchist Fiction From
III Publishing

The Last Days of Christ the Vampire by J.G. Eccarius
ISBN 1-886625-01-8   192 pages, 5½ x 8½" $10.00
The book that broke the silence about the vampiric nature of Jesus Christ
and his fundamentalist zombies. Jesus has set his sights on converting some
teenagers in Providence, Rhode Island, but instead they resist and set out to
hunt him down before he can release his Apocalypse upon the world.
Arguably the best religious satire of the 20th century.

The Father, The Son, and The Walkperson by Michel Méry
ISBN 0-9622937-9-2   192 pages, 5½ x 8½" $10.00
A web of fractalled tales mixing science-fictionish absurdity with a quantum-
improbability perspective of our information-oriented, reality-denying
technoculture. By taking society and intellect as spectacle to new heights,
Méry prepares you to be dashed on the rocks of surreality below.

Virgintooth by Mark Ivanhoe
ISBN: 0-9622937-3-3   192 pages, 4.25 x 7" $7.00
Elizabeth has not exactly died: she has been made into a vampire. Now she
has not only all the problems she had when alive, but she must also get
along with the other vampires. At times terrifying, at times hysterically
funny, Virgintooth will horrify and delight you.

Geminga, Sword of the Shining Path by Melvin Litton
ISBN 0-9622937-4-1   5.5 x 8.5", 256 pages $9.95
In a world poised between a superstitious past and a surreal future of
bioengineering, virtual reality and artificial consciousness, Geminga surfs on
the winds of the present. This bird has been trained since infancy to
assassinate the enemies of Peru's Sendero Luminoso. Now she's come with
her best friend, Jimmy the Snake, to California Norte.

This'll Kill Ya by Harry Willson
ISBN 0-9622937-2-5   192 pages 4.25 x 7" $6.00
The anti-censorship mystery that will have you laughing out loud and
examining your own reactions to materials that surely should be censored.
Caution: If you believe that words can be used as weapons to harm people,
reading this book may be hazardous to your health.

A.D. by Saab Lofton
ISBN 0-9622937-8-4   5.5 x 8.5", 320 pages $12.00
The future seen through African-American eyes: after decades of anti-
utopian racist fascism in the 21st century, revolutionaries create a society
based on Libertarian Socialist Democracy. Even then, a menace from the
past threatens society. "The price of Liberty is Eternal Vigilance."

We Should Have Killed the King by J.G. Eccarius
ISBN 0-9622937-1-7   192 pages 4¼ x 7" $5.00
Jack Straw and hundreds of thousands of other English peasants rebelled against their overlords in 1381, killing nobles, lawyers and tax collectors. Ultimately they were crushed, but the spirit of rebellion was reborn in America in the punk/anarchist movement during the 1980's and Jack Straw was there. A stunning look at the underground in the USA.

Resurrection 2027 by J.G. Eccarius
ISBN 0-9622937-7-6   192 pages 4¼ x 7" $7.00
Ann Swanson remembers her life as a nurse before the Apocalypse, before she died of The Plague. Resurrected years later by the grace of Mary the Mother of God, she is called to work at the Temple of the Resurrection. A brave new look at religious mind control.

My Journey With Aristotle to the Anarchist Utopia
by Graham Purshase
ISBN 0-9622937-6-8   128 pages 4¼ x 7" $7.00
No government? No taxes? No police? Wouldn't that be anarchy? Tom, is bashed by the police until they leave him for dead. When Tom regains consciousness he finds himself a thousand years in the future where he encounters Aristotle, who leads him down to Bear City where humans live happily without government or bosses of any kind.

Vampires or Gods? by William Meyers [non-fiction]
ISBN 0-9622937-5-X   192 pages, 8.5 x 11" $15.00
Vampires living thousands of years, commanding legions of human worshippers? Yes! Every major ancient civilization was associated with an immortal claiming to be a god. Egypt had Osiris, who rose from the dead after his body was hacked to pieces. He reigned for 3000 years. Asia Minor had Cybele, whose followers fed her their blood. Greece had Dionysus and Hercules, Rome had Quirinus, and the list goes on.

Tatoos!

Anarchist Farm Temporary Tatoos. Apply as a decal. One free with any order. Or one free with request accompanied by SASE. Or 3 for $1.00, 10 for $3.00, 20 for $5.00.

To order direct from III Publishing send cash, or check or money order for the listed price (postage & handling is free for orders of $7.00 or more in the US; otherwise add $2) made out to III Publishing, P.O. Box 1581 Gualala, CA 95445.